Squirrel & Swan Suspicious Things

S & S Investigations Book 6

M. D. ARCHER

SWARM Publishing

SWARM Publishing

First published in December 2022 by SWARM Publishing.

Auckland, New Zealand.

ISBN (kindle): 978-1-99-116702-6

ISBNN (epub): 978-1-99-116703-3

ISBN (paperback print on demand): 978-1-99-116704-0

Contents

The Series

1

Donald Perry Dash, known to his friends as Don (or more recently, The Donster), opened painfully gritty eyes. He became immediately aware of not only a throbbing headache, but a smell he suspected was coming from his own person. His stomach contracted unpleasantly but he forced away the sensation.

He blinked as his eyes came into focus, taking in his immediate surrounds: his Lexus. Why on earth had he woken up in his *car*? He inhaled a deep, rallying breath but immediately regretted sucking in so much of his own stale air. Squinting into the darkness beyond the car, a wave of relief rushed through his body. He was in his own garage. But what had happened last night?

He'd had dinner with Bruce, Stanley and Russell, after which they'd gone on for more drinks at the kind of place gentlemen of his ilk liked to go. But surely he'd taken a taxi home? He frowned. Yes, because he hadn't driven to work yesterday. So what was he doing sitting in his car now? He looked down as if there might be a clue on his body. In fact, there was. A dribble of something crusty on his shoulder. He aimed a sniff in its direction then recoiled. Yes, vomit. What this situation needed was some fresh air. He opened the car door and pushed it with his leg until it swung wide, then groaned. He ran a hand across his temple. He could summon a vague recollection of getting home but... then what? And he still couldn't fathom why he was in his car. He looked around. The keys were in the ignition. God, he hadn't been planning to drive somewhere had he? He shook his head, immediately wincing at the motion.

He fumbled in his pocket. Another ping of relief at the smooth metal oblong of his phone. He pulled it out to stare at the display for a moment—did he want to know what happened last night? Maybe it was better to leave sleeping dogs lie, so to speak. But then he sighed and scrolled down to Bruce's name. Better to play it safe. Forewarned is forearmed.

"How's the head?" Bruce answered the call. "Feeling a bit dusty myself."

"Ha-ha, yeah. End of the night's a bit fuzzy?" He hoped Bruce would take the hint and he did.

"Don't worry. No dramas."

"I guess I got into a cab?"

"Yeah?" Bruce's confusion at the question was audible.

"Like I said, a bit fuzzy."

Don frowned and massaged his right temple. He had to dial back these big sessions. Sixty was too old to be waking up with no memory of the end of the night. But that hadn't happened in years. Decades. Was Bruce somehow messing with him? It certainly was within the realm of possibility. Bruce had a nasty streak, for sure.

"I guess when you gotta go, you gotta go," Don added breezily.

Speaking of which, his bladder was beginning to complain.

"Talk to you later," he added before disconnecting.

Feeling like he was full of poison and a million years old, Don heaved himself out of the car. He staggered a little, then hit the garage door opener. He blinked a couple of times, his eyes adjusting to the harsh morning light. There was a space where Natasha's car usually sat. She'd already left. A flicker of hope ignited. Maybe his wife had no clue he'd had a stinker of a night and then passed out in his car. He'd on occasion slept in the spare room downstairs after coming home late. So as not to disturb her. Because he was a thoughtful husband. Yes, it was entirely possible. And with that, Don securely and irreversibly latched onto this kernel of unfounded optimism and went about addressing his hangover and getting on with his day.

• • • ●• ● ● • ∙

DS Roman Leconte took a seat in front of his home computer. After a rallying breath he opened his email account to check for the message he'd been waiting for. Immediately his shoulders dropped. Five new emails but not the one he wanted. The results had not yet come in. Was he relieved or frustrated? Both. This limbo was a kind of torture, but what if he got an answer that made life even more complicated?

He picked up his phone, trying to ignore the panicky buzz in his ears. He wanted to message Sophie. He *should* message her. Leo had told him they were back from their holiday. So why not? With another surge of nerves, he opened the messaging app and typed out, then deleted, then retyped a brief message.

Hi. Welcome back. Hope you had a good trip.

He eyed the message. Was the tone right? Was it enough? Was it too much?

"Damn," he growled. He felt like a teenager, reaching out to the girl he liked, riding that agonising wave of hope and uncertainty. He set his shoulders, clenched his jaw, and pressed send. There. It had gone through. He watched the display for a moment. It had been delivered but Sophie didn't appear to be online. He turned his phone face down as if this might shield him from whatever came next. Or dampen any future emotional blows. After ten minutes he checked again. It was still 'unread'. Was she in the middle of something or had she seen his name pop up and decided not to open the message. Had she had enough of him and his definite-ly-over-the-weight-limit baggage?

He dropped his phone to the desk and leaned back in his chair. He reached both hands up, pressing the heels of his palms against his eyes. They couldn't be finished before they'd even started, could they? But he couldn't blame her. She'd been through the ringer over the past few months. She'd taken the painful step of telling him about Anya's affair, and he'd said he needed to think and then walked away. It had been the right thing to do, given Anya's pregnancy, but it can't have been fun for Sophie. It wasn't at all fun for him. None of the past few weeks had been.

And was he even ready for Sophie? Part of him pulsed yes with a raw urgency, worried he might miss out. But another part was still reeling, recoiling in pain. He and Anya had been drifting apart for years, but the dissolution of a marriage was no small thing. And to find out Anya had not only been unfaithful but she was pregnant with another man's child. Maybe. Just as he'd started to get used to the idea of being a father.

In front of him his computer pinged with an email notification. His eyes immediately latched onto the message, his brain jumping to the unlikely scenario of Sophie deciding to email him using his work address instead of replying to his message. Of course she hadn't. But, he sat up straighter, this email *was* related to Sophie, if only indirectly. It was about Terry Garnet's death.

He and Sophie had first connected while looking into the possibly suspicious circumstances surrounding the death of Paige's father. It was a closed, cold case—ruled accidental—but Roman had questions and Sophie had agreed to help. But then life had gotten complicated. Still, he'd kept his off-the-books investigation ticking away, following up minor leads and double-checking reports here and there.

Now, someone from the Te Awamutu Police Station had finally replied to his question. Yes, retired Detective Sergeant Connolly lived in the area. He wasn't online but could be found at the pub at five o'clock every day, rain or shine, regular as clockwork.

Roman smiled and wrote down the name of the pub and the contact details of the officer who'd provided this information. He sent back a quick thank you and then closed his email. DS Connolly had led the (brief) investigation into Terry Garnet's death. If anyone could provide insight into the case, it was him.

And Roman also had Terry's colleague to talk to. They'd been playing phone tag—both obviously busy with more pressing (active) cases—but

Roman would continue to try to set something up. Speaking of which, he picked up his phone, scrolled to the number and listened to it ring.

"Laurie Jefferies," the man answered.

"Yes, DS Leconte, here. I contacted you a while back about the Terry Garnet cold case."

"Yes, I remember. What's up?"

"Can we meet?"

"About Terry?"

"Listen, I know it's a cold case but, uh, his daughter needs some closure."

"His daughter. Paige, right?"

"You know the family?"

"Spent one Christmas with them when I was going through my divorce."

At this, something unpleasant lurched in Roman's stomach but he pushed it away.

"Why is she looking now? Why wait five years?" Laurie continued.

"Not sure." Roman felt a little bad he was using Paige's name like this but he didn't want to give the impression the case had been reopened officially by the police. All sorts of trouble could come with that. Reopening cases unnecessarily was generally frowned upon.

"I guess she's curious," he said. "She's interested in the cases he was working on around the time of his death."

"Because...?"

"Because," Roman took a breath, "maybe he didn't drown accidentally."

"Shit, really?"

"Look, I think she just needs to run through her own pseudo-investigation, if you know what I mean. Just so she can move on."

"Right."

Laurie sounded unconvinced but Roman pressed on. "Can we meet in the next couple of days?"

"Sure. I can spare half an hour tomorrow if you can stand to watch me eat lunch at my desk."

Roman chuckled. "I understand. I'll come to your office at say, one?"

"See you then."

Roman disconnected and checked his messages again.

No reply from Sophie. He sighed.

2

Inside the meeting-slash-conference room at S & S Investigations, Paige, Sophie, and Leo took their coffees to their seats, ready to commence the *Current Clients Catchup* meeting Paige had scheduled. After a two-week holiday, Paige and Sophie were back on deck and Leo, who'd been holding the fort while they were away, had been asked to give them an update.

"Care to explain yourself?" Paige said, pointing to Leo's face.

She'd only managed to hold her tongue and reserve comment until now because she felt the situation on Leo's face was worthy of being properly addressed once they were seated. It almost needed its own item on the meeting agenda.

"Huh?" Leo paused with his coffee cup halfway to his mouth.

"The thing on your face," Paige said.

"Your moustache," Sophie added, for clarity.

In the time that Paige and Sophie had been away, Leo had, rather inexplicably, grown a moustache.

"Oh." He returned his cup to the table and lifted his hand to stroke the edge of his newly acquired facial hair. A hint of colour climbed his cheeks. "What do you think?"

Sophie and Paige exchanged a look.

"Um—" Sophie began.

"You look like a weirdo," Paige interrupted. "Why did you do it?"

"Ah. Just because. Why not?" Leo made a face. "You don't like it? You think I look weird?"

"Yes." Paige nodded firmly. "And I'm not sure I want you facing clients with that thing."

"Come on, Paige," Sophie said. "It doesn't look that bad."

"Is this some sort of cry for help?" Paige continued.

"Paige, stop it. You're going to give him a complex."

Leo turned stricken eyes from Paige to Sophie. "If we're deciding between it making me look like a weirdo and being not-that bad, I think I have my answer."

"If you like it, you should keep it," Sophie said kindly.

Leo raised an uncertain hand to his face.

"Okay, whatever. Let's move onto the update," Paige said.

While Paige and Sophie were away, S & S Investigations had had two walk-in clients. Both of which Leo and Zelda had dealt with.

"You used the client engagement and invoice templates I sent you?" Paige asked.

Leo nodded.

"And they paid the fee?"

"It's all in the file." He gave them a pleased smile as he pushed it over. Paige, who'd come in during the weekend and had already been through it (thus rendering these questions a touch pointless), redirected the file towards Sophie.

"But you know all this," Leo added to Paige. "We spoke on the phone most days you were gone."

"I know," Paige replied. "Just recapping."

Sophie shot a look at Paige, who looked away.

During their holiday, while Sophie had enjoyed relaxed mornings and—where possible—afternoons with her book, Paige had kept one eye pretty much constantly on what was happening at S & S Investigations. For Paige, it hadn't been so much a vacation as a stint of working shorter hours from a different location. But Paige was not naturally inclined towards any sort of relaxation, so this had been her version of a holiday.

"Zelda seems to be working out well?" Sophie said to Leo.

A smile immediately appeared on his face. "Yeah, great. She's great." He went to say something else but then seemed to catch himself and instead looked down to play with his pen.

"I've just asked her to do a few background check requests that came through from a client this morning," Paige said.

Zelda Ko, after quite successfully inserting herself into the S & S Investigations team with a casual work contract, had ended up being a very useful associate. And while Paige couldn't help but acknowledge that Zelda was a very promising young investigator, she felt her to be rather irksome as a person. She refused to accept that the reason for this was their similarities in personality—as Sophie had explained more than once—and preferred to just grizzle about it when given the chance.

"And in terms of the financials, all our clients are up to date with their invoices, so we don't need to put the hard word on anyone," Paige said.

"Yeah, I checked the account and our finances are looking very good. But has anything happened with that SOS Agency recently?" Sophie asked.

Paige shook her head. "They still haven't replied to any of my messages."

"I mean, I'm not surprised, they're our competitors after all. They're probably not interested in engaging in discussions with us."

It was a few months ago now that Paige and Sophie had first been made aware of the presence of the *SOS Agency*, a rival investigations outfit in Auckland. After Paige and Sophie had solved the murder of Scott Radsworth during the Murder At The Reunion case, the SOS Agency had somehow been given credit for their work. The reporter who'd (erroneously) written the credit-shifting story, one Andrew Finch, would not reply to their request to explain himself. And despite repeated emails and phone calls, neither would the agency itself.

And that they had such a catchy name and tagline—*SOS Agency: We Sort Out Solutions*—bothered Paige no end.

"But maybe there's more to it," Paige mused.

"Do we even care? We're doing well with our client list, and thanks to Zelda's article and regular tweeting and posting, our exposure is pretty good now," Sophie said.

"I've got an idea," Leo said. "What if we use Zelda as a spy to get the inside info on the SOS Agency."

"Ooh." Paige sat up. "We could send her to them pretending to be a potential client, and then she can report back."

Sophie nodded. "Not a bad idea, really."

"Because even if we're doing well, there's something underhand about their whole operation." Paige screwed up her nose. "I can just smell it."

· · · · ● · ● · · ·

Professor Richard Thinton eyed the two men sitting in front of him. One was classically handsome—anyone could see—tall, with rather piercing eyes, a well-defined jawline, and a dash of the debonair about him. He looked like he could be a spy. A James Bond type, but old-school—Sean Connery. And it was this man's good looks and air of mastery and intrigue that had given Richard the idea to set up a rival detective agency in the first place.

Richard's gaze shifted to the man's colleague, who hadn't been graced with the same genetic brush. He had somewhat bulbous eyes that seemed to both stare and skitter at the same time and he wore an ill-fitting, rumpled shirt that possibly had an egg stain on the collar. Richard had the sneaking suspicion he'd let off not one but two rather noxious farts during the fairly brief time they'd been in his office.

"Now, Michael," Richard began.

"Yes?" they both replied.

Richard took a controlled breath. He'd forgotten how annoying this was—that they were both named Michael. He hadn't seen either of them for months and now that he had them in front of him, he could remember, rather vividly, why he'd kept their previous interactions brief and by phone. Gastric emissions aside, there was something rather irritating about the two of them.

"One of you needs a nickname."

The two Michaels turned to look at each other.

"I suppose I can be Mike," the gassy one said. He thumbed in the direction of his friend and colleague. "He doesn't really look like a Mike, does he."

The not-Mike in question, Michael Lindell, shifted in his chair, seeming uncomfortable. "Well," he cleared his throat. "I suppose—"

"Fine. You're Mike and you're Michael," Richard pointed at each of them in turn.

"So what's the sitch, Rich?" Mike chuckled to himself.

Richard took another moment, pushing a weighty pause into the room to indicate his displeasure at this not very clever play on words, then continued.

"I'm still sorting out an investor for the SOS Agency, but in the meantime there's no reason the two of you can't rustle up some clients yourselves. Cold calling or networking or what have you. Whatever it takes."

"Righto. Yes, I suppose we—" Michael began.

"But you said you would take care of all that," Mike interrupted, his voice whiny. "That's the whole reason we agreed to it."

"I hardly think I promised I would find all your clients, but either way things change, don't they." Richard glared at Mike. Didn't this man realise he was talking to a *Professor*? It was rather frustrating interacting with people outside the world of academia. People who didn't really understand his ranking and standing in this, his scholastic kingdom.

"But—"

"Look, there simply isn't any alternative. The world is in a shambles and if you want to do this you're going to have to pull your finger out and do a bit of work. At least in the short term. We're all in this together, aren't we? Yes, the SOS Agency was my idea, but you two are the face of the operation.

At least...." He let the rest of the comment drift away. He perhaps didn't need to point out that if anyone was going to be the face of anything it should be Michael.

As Michael shifted in his chair, seeming uncomfortable with the general tone of the conversation, Mike leaned forwards. "But who's going to pay us?"

Richard slowly picked up his cup and took a sip of coffee, stalling for time.

He hadn't expected these men to be quite this entitled. Nor this lazy. When he first met Michael at a social gathering he'd been a bit blindsided by his handsomeness—Richard was comfortable enough in his own masculinity to admit this. He'd made the classic mistake of attributing positive personality traits and qualities to someone who was good-looking. He knew this phenomenon all too well—it even had a psychological term: The Halo Effect. And when he'd met the second Michael—Mike—he had taken Mike's blunt manner and somewhat relaxed approach to personal hygiene to be an indicator of a gifted mind. This, Richard felt he could blame on the academic environment. Often it was the smelliest and most rumpled people who displayed the greatest brilliance. But, alas, no. Over the last six months, he'd come to the slow and somewhat annoying realisation that neither of these two Michaels were particularly clever, nor inclined towards hard work.

But here they were and he would make the best of it.

"Erm, Richard," handsome Michael said into the silence. "How do we go about getting clients?"

"What did you two do for jobs before this?" Richard frowned. "I thought you worked in marketing."

"Sales," Mike replied, his eyes shifting away from Richard's.

"My father's car dealership. We were both on the sales team," Michael said.

"This is a form of sales, isn't it?"

Neither of them replied.

"And before that?" Richard said, moving his gaze from one to the other.

Michael cleared his throat. "Consultants. Investments." He dipped his chin and flashed Richard a reassuring smile.

"Both of you?" Richard asked.

They nodded.

"One of your father's companies?" he clarified.

"Yes," Mike said. "We've been working together forever. Best mates since uni," he added, completely missing the subtext of Richard's questions.

Richard nodded slowly. Things were clicking into place. Both of them had only ever worked for Michael's wealthy and well-connected father, it seemed. Now that he understood the situation a little better, he could picture precisely what their 'working day' entailed and what skills they had accumulated (or hadn't, as the case may be) over the years.

What on earth had they talked about when he first met them at that party? They must have said something to make him think they could run a detective agency. That's right, Michael had been talking about one of his favourite movies—*Kiss Kiss Bang Bang*—and then after a painfully lengthy description of one of the Batman movies (of its relevance Richard was still unclear), Mike had said he'd always wanted to be a private eye. Richard had latched onto this nugget, this seedling, and nurtured it into the establishment of SOS Agency. It now seemed a little ridiculous, but he'd started down this road and he would continue. Because he still believed he could use the SOS Agency to ruin that little upstart Paige Garnet's own investigations agency. At the very least he could make things difficult for them.

"Look, I'm sure you're both capable of figuring out how to get clients." Richard thought for a moment. "But I'd recommend going to the Viaduct on Friday afternoon with all the other businesspeople in Auckland. Have a few drinks, chat to a few people, network, you know, and hand out your business cards. You'd be surprised how effective that can be." Richard nodded at Michael, hoping he understood the assignment. After a Friday night stint handing out his phone number at the Viaduct, Michael would inevitably end up fielding a slew of calls from women who didn't need his investigative services but perhaps wanted a different kind of service. But maybe some of them would hire the SOS Agency anyway.

"We can do that," Michael said with a smile.

When Mike opened his mouth to say something, Richard quickly stood and reached out to shake their hands.

"Catch up in a couple of weeks, eh?" He shepherded them out the door. "You can find your way to the elevator bay?" he called out, not particularly interested in whether they could or not.

He stepped back into his office, about to close the door, then decided to leave it open. Mike had left one lingering fart as a parting gift.

3

K ate Dash, halfway through chopping onions for the spaghetti bolognaise she'd been tasked with preparing, paused at the sight of her new stepmother Natasha. She was clad only in a micro-bikini and gracefully stepping out of the spa pool as if she was in a photo shoot. Kate watched as Natasha hesitated, seeming to consider her options. It was amazing her teeth weren't chattering by now—it was the middle of winter. Then again, Natasha did hail from one of the colder parts of the world. The New Zealand winter had to be positively balmy compared to a Russian one.

Natasha disappeared into the pool house for a moment then reappeared with a towel in her hand and sashayed her way into the main house. Natasha had been the one to coax Kate's father into buying this sprawling residence in Mission Bay, Kate knew. Just like she knew her father was supposed to be edging towards retirement, cutting back on work and debt and acquisitions, finally handing over the reins to his kingdom. To her brother, of course, not the eldest heir which was Kate herself. But that was what the Dash family was like. Always had been, always would be. Father knows best, even when he didn't. Probably the reason their mother was currently sunning herself in Spain as far away from her ex-husband as she could.

"Have a nice spa?" Kate asked as Natasha entered the kitchen. This brand-spanking-new house boasted a pool as well as a spa. The pool would remain covered throughout winter, but the spa was getting used regularly, as far as Kate could tell. Every time she called her father he and Natasha seemed to be about to get in for a 'soak'. And the way her father said the word—soak—made her wonder what else happened in that spa. Kate would not be doing any 'soaking' in there, that was for sure. Soaking up germs and human detritus, most likely. She shuddered.

Instead of answering Kate's question, Natasha languidly inspected her nails. Kate felt irritation swirl around her shoulders. But she'd promised her father, and herself, that she'd make an effort, and she would. Because what else could she do? This woman was part of the family now.

"Natasha?"

Her new stepmother shrugged in response then waved her hand at Kate's preparations. "Dinner?" she inquired coolly, her Russian accent making her sound vaguely disappointed. Or maybe it was nothing to do with the accent. Kate had only known Natasha for three months and they hadn't yet warmed to each other despite being of the same generation.

Kate pushed away the scowl that was threatening to take over her face. "Yes. This is dinner."

Natasha stepped closer to inspect the food in front of Kate. She took this moment to open her towel under the guise of adjusting it but actually to show off her very flat stomach, Kate knew. Did Natasha think she was making her jealous? Her own stomach had never been that flat and never would be. Perhaps Natasha thought she was tempting Kate. As if her washboard stomach made her irresistible. *You aren't!* Kate wanted to (childishly) shout. Although she'd caught her brother Jack eyeing up Natasha more than once. Natasha had caught this too, no doubt.

Kate had noticed Natasha always wore something revealing whenever she and her brother visited. When they came for Sunday brunch she'd often be clothed in only a t-shirt and a pair of skimpy panties. "Sunday is day of rest," Natasha had announced in response to Kate's request that she put on some clothes. As if resting could only be achieved in not-quite-big-enough t-shirts and no bottoms. As if Natasha did anything remotely resembling work the rest of the week. Natasha also seemed to be constantly reaching up into kitchen cupboards during these get-togethers. Looking for seemingly non-existent tableware items (she always came back empty handed) for the sole purpose of showing off her pert derriere to whomever was trying to eat their breakfast in peace.

"You make pasta? Again?" Natasha said, gesturing towards the pot and raising one eyebrow.

Kate clenched her jaw, forced herself to release it again, then took a breath. "Dad, your *husband*, specifically asked for it."

Natasha pursed her lips. "Salad."

"What?"

"Salad. For me. You too, I think. Is best." Natasha nodded encouragingly then turned to amble away in the direction of the bathroom.

Kate suppressed the urge to throw the knife at the back of Natasha's caramel-blond-highlighted head. Or maybe the front. The pointy end. Instead, she gritted her teeth. "This isn't the eighties," she muttered. She didn't even know what she meant, exactly, but it felt appropriate. Natasha was so, *eighties*, somehow. Maybe because being Russian had an eighties vibe? But also because she was always going on about diets and saying dated things like how important it was to *look good for your man*. It made Kate want to scream.

But her father loved this woman. Apparently. He'd met her on a business trip to London in January and brought her back to New Zealand at the start of March. He'd then married her very quickly in a secret ceremony. At least, he'd hidden it from his children, only his awful friend Bruce had been there to bear witness. Kate suspected her father had done it in secret because he thought they'd try to talk him out of it. Maybe so but she and her brother would have known, even as they tried, that it was futile. Because her father generally did whatever he wanted. Why should this be any different?

Don Dash knew what was what and liked to tell people this all the time. God help anyone who disagreed with him. He could be very generous with the people he loved, those in his inner circle. but if you didn't share his beliefs... And if he hadn't been her father, her flesh and blood, Kate suspected she might have hated him. But she'd grown up with his world view. It had been imprinted upon her, etched into her psyche for so many years, it was hard to detach oneself completely. And despite his conservative views, he'd accepted her marriage to Tina, and that was the main thing.

"Is she getting you rarked up again?" Tina appeared behind her, whispering in her ear.

"She told me I should eat salad for dinner." Kate rolled her eyes.

"What a cow. You're not going—"

"Of course not. If she's so desperate for a salad she can make it herself."

And so, she did. When the food was ready and Kate started setting the dishes on the table, Natasha, casting an unimpressed eye over the array in front of her, sauntered over to the fridge.

As everyone else—Don, Jack, Jack's wife Madison and Kate and her wife Tina—took their seats, Natasha proudly deposited the bowl of lettuce, sliced tomato and diced capsicum in front of Don.

"What's this rabbit food," he bellowed predictably.

Natasha tittered. "Is good. For heart. Stay strong like ox." She leaned over to squeeze Jack's shoulder. "Stay young like son."

Jack grinned. Madison gave him a *look*. Kate flicked her eyes to her father. He didn't seem to notice or care that he was being compared, somewhat unfavourably, to a man nearly thirty years his junior. His own son, no less.

Instead, Don gave his new bride an indulgent smile. "I am. Healthy as an ox." He pounded his chest. Kate threw her eyes upward. What a cliché.

"You try some," Natasha said. "For me?"

"Fine, fine. Happy wife, happy life," he said, winking at his children as if they were co-conspirators. Kate met Jack's gaze and they shared an eye roll. This attitude was an almost comically opposite approach to his first marriage.

And so, dinner began, with everyone helping themselves to wine and spaghetti and to a lesser extent, Natasha's green salad.

Just as Kate was wondering what conversation topic to broach, which would yield the fewest arguments, her father suddenly began spluttering and choking.

"Darling?" Natasha said, placing one hand on his forearm. "You want water?"

"What's in this?" he gasped, pointing at the salad.

"Normal."

His eyes were watering. He coughed. "Sesame seeds?" he choked out.

"Oh." Natasha frowned. "Yes. Pumpkin, chia, and sesame seeds."

"Allergic," he spluttered.

Kate and Jack lurched up from their seats.

"You know that," Kate hissed, casting an angry look in Natasha's direction as she tried to loosen the buttons at the neck of his polo shirt.

"No, no," Natasha said calmly. "I not know."

"You did so! Dad told you. I was there," Kate said, glaring at Natasha.

"Dad?" Jack said, grabbing his father's shoulders.

In the next moment, Don slid off his chair and landed heavily on the floor.

"Call an ambulance," Kate screeched.

Natasha picked up her phone from the table. "Is 9-9-9?"

"I'll do it." Kate pulled out her own phone and called the emergency services number in New Zealand, 1-1-1, then handed the phone to Tina, hovering nervously nearby. "Tell them it's an allergic reaction."

"Christ, he's heavy. Help me get him into a recovery position," Jack said, pulling at Don's arm.

"Oh. His EpiPen," Kate yelled. "There should be one in the kitchen drawer." She leapt up and started yanking open drawer after drawer. "Where the hell is it?" She slammed shut the last drawer. "There's another one in the bathroom," she yelled at Natasha. Her wide eyes darted around the room.

"Go!" Kate yelled.

Natasha hurried away.

Kate ran back to kneel by her father. "See?" she hissed as they got him onto his side. "Do you believe me now?"

4

Sophie clutched at the edge of her skirt. Why was she so nervous? It wasn't as if she was about to give a presentation or go on a date—the two things that usually inspired her most gut-wrenching nervousness.

She looked around the empty, white-walled room. She'd been buzzed up about five minutes ago and told that the hypnotherapist would be ready to see her in ten minutes. There wasn't a receptionist, but there was a reception desk. Sophie wondered if this was one of those small practices that didn't have an actual person working the front desk and the clinician had to do the administration and reception duties themselves. Was that a good or a bad thing? Big slick operations with all the bells and whistles didn't necessarily mean better services or more quality products. And Sophie had done her due diligence on the hypnotherapy approach. Doctor Meadows had a PhD in psychology, was a Senior Professional Member of Hypnosis New Zealand, and had a number of good reviews. Sophie had even read a meta-analysis on the clinical benefits of hypnotherapy and all up it was like the placebo effect. If you believed in it, it could provide benefit. Plus, Doctor Meadows also used cognitive-behavioural and other psychological methods as needed, so Sophie felt reassured by the array of psychological tools at Doctor Meadows' disposal.

Sophie was distracting herself with mindless chatter, she knew, because of her nerves. She lifted her arms away from her body, trying to get some fresh air circulating near her damp armpits. Really, her nervousness should be no surprise because she'd never done this before, and this happened any time she did something new. For a moment she wondered, like she had before, what it would be like to be the kind of person who entered new situations with optimism. The promise of something positive: something new and exciting. Like a golden retriever expecting to make friends with everyone they met during their morning walk. What would that be like? To not worry about all the awkward or negative things that could happen but to be excited to experience the unknown. To be excited about the possibility of having a fun time or meeting some cool new people. Wow, how different life would be.

Her phone buzzed and she grabbed at it eagerly. Another good distraction. She could have been playing on TikTok this whole time, of course, having been indoctrinated to the app during lockdown and as yet unable to wean herself off, but that wasn't the right kind of anxiety interference, she knew. Because she wouldn't concentrate on the videos, no matter how funny or cute they were. Her mind would drift back to the thing she was worrying about.

But someone messaging her to ask a question would work. So who was her saviour? She checked the display. Something unidentifiable rushed through her chest and shoulders, settling in her stomach.

Roman.

It was a message from Roman. Well, she'd asked for a distraction and the universe had provided. He'd messaged a couple of days ago saying welcome back and asking how she was, but all she'd sent was a noncommittal "Good thanks" in response. She knew it wasn't enough but she didn't have anything else in her. It was too hard to pretend things were normal when they had this huge thing hanging over their heads. Couldn't he just tell her what the situation was so she didn't have to think or worry about it incessantly?

This new message said. **Everything okay?**

Great question. She let out a breath and looked at the ceiling. She'd been riding the Roman rollercoaster virtually from the moment she met him. Was she ready to get off? On one hand she yearned to talk to him. She ached with it. While on holiday, for two whole weeks, she'd successfully (mostly) put him out of her mind, even relinquishing her phone to Paige to make sure she didn't do anything she'd later regret. Paige had loved having this control, handing the phone back to Sophie for supervised usage or when Sophie's mother or someone else on the 'permitted people' list contacted her.

But now they were back and she was in complete charge of her phone and her life; she had to act like a grown-up. But what did that mean? What should she do? More than talk to him, she was desperate to see him. To be near him. To have him put his arms around her and say everything was going to work out. But what if he was messaging to tell her, just FYI, that he and Anya had worked everything out and she wasn't having an affair with that horrible Eric guy and the baby was Roman's and they were going off into the sunset with their newly perfect family. That message-slash-conversation she could do without, thanks very much.

"Sophie?"

She looked up with a start. From out of nowhere, it seemed, a young woman had appeared and now stood in the doorway with an expectant smile. She's too young to be a clinical practitioner, Sophie immediately thought. And too... *colourful*, with her crimson shirt and mustard trousers.

"Doctor Meadows?" She rose to stand, banishing her ungenerous thoughts. She knew what it was like to be on the receiving end of such assumptions and she would not inflict that kind of old-fashioned judgement on a fellow young female professional.

"You can call me Cassie. Would you like to come through?"

Sophie took one step and upended the chair next to her, having somehow managed to hook the strap of her bag around the chair leg. "Whoops," she said, before the momentum of this motion propelled her forwards, causing her to stagger and crash into Cassie.

"Oof," she cried, letting out a little squeal at the impact.

"Oh my god, I am so sorry." Sophie felt heat rising in her cheeks. Her ever-present klutziness tended to get worse the more nervous she was. Far too often she felt she was something akin to an octopus, but one without any control of its numerous appendages.

"No problem," Cassie said, managing a tight smile. "Let's go through and get started."

· · · • · • · · ·

Paige and Tim stood at opposite ends of the living room glaring at each other.

"Paige, we agreed to talk about this."

"Yeah, but not today, not right this second."

"Weren't you supposed to be thinking about things and clearing your head while you were away?"

"No. I just needed to get away. A holiday. I haven't had one in years."

Tim let out a heavy breath. "What are we supposed to do? How are we going to get past this?"

Paige shrugged.

"Maybe we need to go to counselling."

Paige narrowed her eyes. "Are you kidding?"

"Are you? You have a PhD in psychology."

"So?"

"You don't believe in talking to a trained counsellor about the stuff going on in your head and heart?"

"I'm a cognitive neuroscientist. What does that have to do with counselling?"

"I mean, don't you believe in the benefit of consulting mental health professionals?"

"Mental health?"

"You know what I mean."

Paige shrugged again.

Tim stared at her for a moment. "I cannot believe how immature you are being about this. All of this. Maybe you're right. Maybe you're not cut out to be anyone's mother."

He stalked away.

· · · · ●· ● · · ·

The Two Michaels picked up their drinks and hurried over to lay claim to the two-seater table in the corner that had just become available. This Viaduct bar had gotten steadily louder since they'd arrived an hour ago and was now an environment in which it was almost impossible to hear a single thing. But having finally secured a table it felt foolish to leave. And so, they sat down and huddled together so they could shout in each other's ears.

"But if we don't do this," Mike roared at Michael, "then what else are we going to do? Your father has all but retired. He said there's nothing for us at the moment, right?"

"Right," Michael shouted back.

"At least this investigations business is already set up," Mike screamed.

"True," Michael thundered in agreement.

Mike's phone buzzed. Rather than try to tell Michael this—his throat was already a bit raw—he held up the display. "Unknown number," he said, more to himself, then answered the call. He held one finger to the other ear in an attempt to block out the surrounding din and squinted with concentration. "Pardon?" he yelled. "Yeah, yeah. SOS Agency." He slid forwards then squatted down so he was crouched on the floor, as if being almost under the table might enable him to hear what his caller was saying.

"Say that again?" he yelled. "Listen, this is pointless," he bellowed into the phone. "I can't hear a bloody thing you're saying. Can you email or text me? What? TEXT ME."

With that, he disconnected and took his seat. Michael gave him an uncertain look. Mike gestured at his ears.

"Maybe we should go. This is ridiculous," Michael hollered.

"What?" Mike dropped his gaze to check his phone. He had a new email. He grabbed Michael's arm and pointed at the message. Michael leaned over to read it in the dim light.

Have something I need help with. A case. Can I meet you on Monday?

A possible client, Mike thought with excitement. Quickly, he typed out a reply.

Doing field work on Monday. City central. Can meet you for coffee at 10:00 a.m.

OK, the potential new client replied. **Rude Boy Deli? Sale Street. Sure.**

Mike smiled as he picked up his drink. "There you have it. A client already. Without doing anything. Easy as pie, this is going to be."

"What?" Michael shouted.

"New client," Mike shrieked.

"But what's the case?" Michael yelled directly into Mike's ear.

Mike shrugged happily and downed his drink, searching the room for a waiter. They would find out on Monday. Clearly, this investigative lark wouldn't be so hard after all.

5

Saturday night, after a day of golfing followed by a delicious steak dinner, Don and Bruce took their drinks out to the poolside patio. "A close call but no drama," Don said as they took seats. "That bloody allergy." He laughed. "Bit of excitement, ay?"

"The Donster lives life on the edge," Bruce replied.

"Always." Don raised his glass as a toast.

"Hey, turn the heater on would you?" Bruce pointed to the two outdoor gas heaters nearby. "It's bloody frosty out here."

"I thought those jeans would keep you warm."

"Huh?"

Don cast a wicked smile at Bruce. "You'll start a fire any second," he added, referring to the snugness of fit and the way the inside seams rubbed together when Bruce walked.

Bruce made a face and tugged at the crotch of his jeans. "Yeah, well. Maybe a few extra pounds have gone on recently. They're actually bloody uncomfortable. I thought they'd loosen up after a bit."

"Too tight," Natasha said as she appeared at the French doors. "No more children for you."

"You promise?" Bruce laughed.

"You need to be doing the business to have kids," Don said.

"Who says I'm not?"

"Your wife." Don threw back his head to laugh.

Natasha forced a smile.

"How were drinks with the girlies?" Don asked once he'd recovered from his own hilarity, lifting his chin and pursing his lips at Natasha.

She dutifully walked over to give him a kiss. "No jeans for you," Natasha said, waggling her finger at Don. "Need sperm to be working."

"You're going for another round of sprogs at your age?" Bruce said, widening his eyes. "Jeez, mate, you're a sucker for punishment."

Don shrugged noncommittally. "If the boys still swim, they'll get their shot."

"Ha!" Bruce barked. "Time for another one, ay?" He indicated the now empty bottle of shiraz sitting on the table between them.

Natasha's eyes slid from Don to Bruce. "I get."

She glided away, the two men appreciating both her exit as well as her return. She deposited an opened bottle on the table. "Where's wife?" Natasha asked Bruce.

"Who cares?" Bruce guffawed.

Natasha narrowed her eyes at Bruce.

"Hey, weren't Stan and Russ going to join us for a drink?" Bruce added, unscrewing the cap of the wine and pouring himself a generous glass.

Don shrugged then grinned. "Maybe Russell is still hurting from the thrashing he took at golf today. Didn't seem very happy at dinner, did he."

Bruce snickered. "Or maybe he's still pissed about what you said at the meeting on Friday."

"If you can't take the heat, get out of the kitchen."

Natasha yawned loudly then leaned down to kiss Don. "I go to bed."

"Night, love."

"You're not going to get all soft on me, are you?" Bruce said once she'd gone.

"What do you mean?"

Bruce lifted one hand and made a crack-the-whip motion. "Now that you've got a new piece. You're not going to be under her thumb, are you? Not allowed out to play like you used to?"

"Hardly." Don chortled. "I wear the pants around here. She knows her place. These eastern European birds, they're good like that. They're feisty and they look after themselves but when it comes down to it, they know their place." His eyes gleamed.

"Glad to hear it," Bruce said, raising his glass to clink against Don's.

· · • • • • • • · ·

The next morning, Kate and Tina joined Jack and Madison at their house for the 'impromptu breakfast' that Kate had engineered. She wanted to talk to her brother about their father, but so far it wasn't going very well.

Kate finished her mouthful of eggs and eyed Jack, currently delaying answering her question by taking a sip of coffee. When Jack set down the cup a little louder than necessary, Madison looked up. As Madison shifted her gaze to Tina, Kate caught the look and wondered what it was about. Madison's botoxed expression was virtually unreadable.

Madison and Jack had married two years ago after only six months of dating and she'd immediately abandoned her degree in information technology. They were 'head-over-heels', apparently, and didn't see the point in waiting. Why you couldn't continue your university studies while you got married, Kate didn't know. And Kate didn't think she'd ever met a couple who seemed less like they were in love. And that was including her own mother's marriage to her philandering father. At least their passion had been evident. But Madison had that twenty-something facial blankness common nowadays, the reason both chemical and cultural. Flawless but expressionless faces, heavy makeup and dead eyes. Doing everything they could to avoid expressive faces because that's what causes wrinkles and, gross, who wanted wrinkles? Jack had always gone for women like Madison and he didn't seem to mind the way she was, so maybe it was a marriage made in heaven. A disinterested wife and a workaholic husband. Love didn't have to be the same for everyone.

Maybe Kate could ask her own wife Tina about Jack and Madison's relationship, she mused. Tina had become good friends with Madison over the past couple of years. Maybe because they both had to deal with the Dash family and god knows they probably needed to offload sometimes. Or maybe because both of the Dash children had gone for younger women—they had their father's genes after all—and while their spouses' personalities weren't particularly similar, Tina and Madison still enjoyed getting dressed up for cocktail evenings and hitting the town once in a while. Kate was happy Tina was still getting her bar-hopping fix with someone inside the family. More so, she was grateful she didn't have to be involved. She felt as if she was done with all that. She now preferred a nice meal with friends at someone's house and to be tucked up in bed by eleven p.m. at the absolute latest. A somewhat nana-ish approach at only thirty-four but she'd always been a sensible sort. Not sensible enough to be included in her father's business of course. She was missing one key anatomical feature for that. She rolled her eyes. No matter, she had her own successful advertising company and she was perfectly happy with that. And Jack seemed so stressed all the time and had significantly less control over his work schedule than she did. No, it was much better this way.

"Jack?" Kate said into the silence.

He still hadn't answered her question.

"You're overreacting," Jack said, sounding irritated. "Dad's fine. Nothing gets to him."

"Not even a deadly allergic reaction?"

"No. Case in point."

"But he nearly died."

"He did not. He just gasped and choked for a bit. A shot of the EpiPen and he was fine."

"Speaking of which, it was weird we couldn't find the one he keeps in the kitchen drawer."

"Sorry to break it to you sis, but you are not exactly Sherlock Holmes when it comes to looking for things."

"Hey."

"And you were kind of panicked. It's probably sitting there right now."

"It wasn't there."

"Well, Natasha found one and it all worked out."

After Natasha had returned with the EpiPen and they'd used it on Don, his symptoms had calmed down. By the time the paramedics arrived he was almost normal again. They'd checked him over and declared him to be fine.

"He's supposed to have four in the house. Bedroom, bathroom, kitchen and in the pool house."

Jack arched one eyebrow and focused his gaze on her. Kate could also feel the weight of both Tina and Madison's attention. All three of them staring at her like this made her feel a little hysterical, but she felt sure she wasn't overreacting.

"Maybe someone moved it to make it harder to—"

"Kate." Jack made an annoyed sound.

"How can you not see it?" Kate said, exasperated. "Since they got married they've nearly had a car accident, Dad got mildly electrocuted, and now this? Natasha *knew* he's allergic to sesame. She said she didn't but she did. I was there when he told her."

"That kind of thing is easily forgotten." Jack's eyes shifted away.

"Babe?" Tina said to her. "Mads and I are going for a walk, okay? Back in about half an hour."

"Sure."

Kate and Jack each received a kiss on the cheek from their spouses then watched them amble down the hall, already huddled in conversation, to exit out the front door of Jack and Madison's Epsom home.

"Have you got the hots for her?" Kate said, once she was sure they were gone.

"For Natasha?" Jack laughed. "She's hot, yeah, but so what?"

"God, isn't Madison enough for you? You've only been married for two years and her body is insane."

"Already seen every inch of her body." He laughed again.

"Ugh, Jack. Don't turn into Dad, will you? Promise."

He grinned. Kate scowled.

"Listen, if Natasha was being dodgy, Dad would know. He has eyes everywhere." Jack waggled his eyebrows. "He likes to watch."

Kate frowned. "What?" She clenched her fists. God, her brother was annoying. "I wish you'd take this seriously."

"And I wish you'd drop it. You're being ridiculous."

"You're wrong. I'm right."

"Sure, whatever," Jack mumbled.

Kate stood up, heat rushing through her cheeks. His dismissiveness was infuriating. "I'm going to go see him right now. Have it out. Warn him properly."

"You're leaving? Tina will be back in half an hour."

"I'll text her. Mads can give her a lift home." Kate paused by the table. "I'm serious, Jack. He needs to watch his back."

"Kate, seriously, leave me out of it."

· · · ● ● ● ● · · ·

As Kate walked up to her father's front door she became aware that her jaw was still clenched and her shoulders were tight with tension. She'd taken a circuitous route from Jack's place to her father's house in Mission Bay to give herself a chance to cool down, trying as she drove to let her anger float off into the ether. But instead it had festered and bubbled even closer to boiling. Oh well, she was here now and she would say what she came to say. She'd need a bit of ire to confront her father.

She unlocked the front door and let herself inside.

"Dad?" she called as she stepped into the house.

Natasha appeared suddenly, barring her route down the hall. She folded her arms across her chest and dropped her gaze to take in the set of keys Kate held in her hand. Instinctively, Kate dropped her hand to her side.

Natasha sighed. "You have key?"

Kate lifted her chin. "Yes. So what?"

Natasha held out her hand. "No. Please give back."

Kate stared at her. "Dad gave it to me for emergencies."

This wasn't entirely true. She'd 'borrowed' his key and made a copy without him even being aware, but the reason was the same. Emergencies. Just in case.

"No emergency. I'm here."

"So?" Kate gestured to Natasha's *I'm off to Yoga* outfit. "You're always out."

"I need privacy."

"I bet you do."

"What you mean?" Natasha narrowed her gaze, making Kate think she knew exactly what she'd meant.

When Kate didn't reply, Natasha held out her hand. "Is illegal. Please."

Kate stared at her for a moment then rolled her eyes. "Fine." She wrested the key off her keychain and slapped it into Natasha's outstretched palm then stalked down the hall. It didn't matter anyway, she had another one at home.

"Come in," she heard Natasha mutter sarcastically behind her.

Now close to fuming, Kate carried on straight through the dining room and onto the back deck. "Dad?" she yelled, to get things rolling. It generally took a few minutes for him to first even register someone was calling his name and then another minute or so to disengage from whatever he was doing. But that was fine because she needed some air and some space to pace, to think before she commenced this confrontation. How could she find the words to warn her father that his new wife had impure intentions. No, impure wasn't the right word. It was Natasha's impurity that got her dad hooked in the first place, Kate would bet. Nefarious. Yes, that was the word. The Nefarious Natasha. Stepmother from hell. Probably.

Kate paced the back deck for nearly a minute, chewing the inside of her lip as she formulated her speech, when something in the spa pool caught her eye. A large and weirdly lumpy shape. Frowning, she stepped up to get a closer look. That looked like her father's t-shirt. Why was it in the pool?

When her brain finally registered what she was looking at she gasped and stumbled backwards.

Not a t-shirt, a body.

Lying face down in the water was her father.

6

Mike raced through the door and frantically scanned the inside of the café. He and Michael had planned to meet the potential new client here at ten o'clock, and it was now past eleven.

"There you are," he called cheerfully once he'd spotted Michael in the corner. Michael made a show of looking at his wristwatch, clearly unimpressed.

"Sorry, sorry. Time got away from me." Mike dropped into the chair opposite and let out a loud exhalation of breath.

"Time got away? You're an hour late and it was a proper meeting. With a potential *client*," Michael said, his mouth in a line.

Mike eyed him with worry. Michael was generally an easy-going sort and this was possibly as annoyed as Mike had ever seen him. He'd have to do some damage control, that much was clear. But Michael would come around. He always did.

"So where were you?" Michael asked when Mike didn't offer this information.

"You're so much better at the initial meet-and-greet. You know what I'm like, rough around the edges, saying the wrong thing. I can put people off. We both know that's true."

Michael continued to eye him. "Where were you?" he repeated.

Mike cleared his throat. "Ah...." He'd been at the casino but he didn't want to say this. Michael didn't really get the thrill of gambling and he certainly didn't understand that when you're on a winning streak you simply cannot leave your post.

"If you must know, I had a dodgy stomach, okay? I grabbed a mince and cheese pie from a service station for breakfast and it gave me the runs." Mike gave his best, *Hey, what can you do?* expression.

Michael did not look convinced.

"And I'm starving now. Guess I got rid of everything, ha-ha. Let's get an early lunch. On me, okay?" Mike beamed.

He had nearly a thousand dollars in his pocket and he felt like a million bucks.

"You're paying? You aren't going to mysteriously lose your wallet when we get the bill?"

"Nope. On me," Mike repeated. "How about the new fancy food court downtown. What's it called? Commercial Bay. Got a range of options and it's only a five-minute walk from here."

"Fine."

And after they ate they could go shopping, Mike thought, but didn't say. He needed a couple of new shirts and a pair of trousers and over the years he'd come to realise that he himself shouldn't be trusted in such matters. He'd come to rely on Michael's opinion.

As they walked down Albert Street towards the entrance to the brand-new mall, Michael said, "Aren't you going to ask me about the meeting?"

"Right, right. How'd it go?"

"I'm not sure. She wants to track down her birth mother."

"Oh. How would we do that?"

"Yes, well that's the issue. How *do* we do that? We're not trained investigators."

They both fell silent.

"We're smart chaps," Mike said. "We'll figure it out."

"I said I'd send her an estimate for the work and she'll let me know."

"Right." Mike frowned. "And how much *do* we charge?"

"Another very good question."

"We'll figure it out," Mike repeated.

• • • •• • •• • •

Kate went over to the large balcony window in the living room, the one she liked to stare out of when she needed to think, and leaned against the glass. After her horrible discovery on Saturday she'd had too much to drink that night and had woken up yesterday feeling terrible. She'd then tossed and turned and sweated through all of last night, eventually getting up at four a.m. to start her day because this at least was better than lying in bed catastrophising.

In the end, she'd let her team know she wasn't feeling well and would work from home today. She'd done her best to focus but her mind wouldn't stop both drifting and racing. She should really write this off as a workday and do something productive like clean the house. Or something else physical like one of those unappealing 'pump' classes at the gym to which she belonged but almost never attended. Maybe now was the time to get serious about exercise. Life was short, she was now aware, because even dying aged sixty-three seemed like a far too brief time to be alive. What was less obvious to Kate was how this knowledge should direct her behaviour. Should she get into shape, become the best version of herself? Be one of those people who is out running at six a.m. every day? Or go rock-climbing every weekend or whatever? Or should she not waste time on things she didn't enjoy? Huffing and puffing and ultimately going nowhere?

Kate took a deep breath.

And all this, this existential crisis, was over the death not of her father but his best friend Bruce.

Kate hadn't been the one to identify him, Natasha had had that honour. Kate, upon realising it was a dead body floating in the spa pool, had first shrieked then been shocked into immobility. Unable to do anything useful at all. Natasha, having heard her cry of distress, had calmly leaned over the side to flip the body to face upward. And that's when they both saw Bruce's mottled face. Natasha had then announced, unnecessarily, "Is not Don. Don's clothes, not him. Bruce."

Kate had always wondered how she would respond to a true crisis and now she had an inkling. Uselessly. Natasha, on the other hand, would be the type of person you'd want to stick close to in the event of a zombie apocalypse. Or similar. She'd definitely increase her chances of survival. Unless of course they were competing for resources. Then you'd have to watch your back.

Don himself had then appeared from somewhere in the depths of the house and the police had been called. Bruce had been drinking there the night before and had stayed over because he refused to pay Uber surge rates. This was a relatively common occurrence, apparently, with Bruce usually slinking home early in the morning. And neither Don nor Natasha had gone anywhere near the pool or the pool house that day. Nor had they seen his car still parked a little ways down the street.

Now chewing energetically at the skin at the edge of her thumb, Kate paced the relatively short length of the living room, tension rattling through her body, bunching her shoulders. She stopped abruptly, inhaled deeply, then let out a long, heavy sigh. There was nothing else for it, she was going to call her mother. It would be past midnight for her, but her mother had always been something of a night-owl.

She retrieved her phone from the dining room table and went back to the balcony door. There, she listened to the call go unanswered for nearly eight rings. As a surge of irrational tears rose up, and just before she was about to disconnect, her mother picked up.

"Kate, darling?"

Kate blinked, bit her lip and forced a smile. "Hi Mum."

"Everything okay?"

"Just had a bit of a scare, that's all."

"Oh?"

"Everything's fine, it's just...."

Kate's mother listened patiently as Kate told her what had happened in stilted broken words, sounding very much like a six-year-old recounting a dull and possibly made-up (at the very least, exaggerated) story.

"Gosh how shocking," her mother said, not sounding remotely shocked. "I never did like Bruce," she added, almost absentmindedly.

"*Mum.* He's dead."

"He can't hear me."

Kate rolled her eyes.

"You seem bothered."

Oh, you caught that did you? Kate thought uncharitably.

"It's just... I found his body and I thought it was Dad at first."

"Hmm," her mother murmured. "I can see how that would be distressing. How is your father?" she added, her voice hardening a little.

"Oh, the same, you know."

"How's the new tart working out?"

"That tart is his wife, Mum."

For a few seconds there was silence.

"Mum? I thought you knew?" Kate frowned. Jack had been tasked with telling her months ago when they'd found out about the nuptials (they had literally drawn straws to decide). He'd said they'd had a long conversation about it and their mother hadn't seem bothered.

"Mum?"

"Oh, I did know." Her mother made a lip-smacking noise followed by audible crunching.

"What are you doing?"

"Oh, just a bit of sangria with corn chips."

"You're drinking sangria? Now?"

"Everything happens so much later here. When in Rome, darling. Or I guess, Majorca. Ha-ha. And it's summer, remember."

Kate gritted her teeth at her mother's inappropriately jolly tone. But what had she expected in making this call? Her mother to be heartbroken? Hardly.

"I know it's a cliché, darling, but I say embrace the cliché. They exist for a reason. They're fun." She trilled gaily.

Was her mother a little drunk? She was completely retired and living the good life on the Spanish coast, so perhaps. And she'd earned it, after all. After putting up with her father for so many years. And Kate and Jack must have been a handful as well. Looking back, and after talking to her own friends about the trials of being a parent, Kate could see that it must have been difficult for her mother. Her father had almost never been at home to help with childrearing and two rambunctious children barely two years apart in age. And they'd always fought, she and Jack. Vicious physical fights. Once, she'd kicked him in the shin while wearing her roller skates (gosh, that had been satisfying even though she'd broken his tibia). He retaliated by spraying their mother's expensive perfume directly up her nose which remained, to this day, the most painful thing she'd ever experienced.

"Listen, darling, I'm sorry you had a fright, but I really don't want to talk about your father."

"Fine. How are you, anyway?"

For ten or so minutes Kate listened to her mother recount some mildly amusing story about people Kate had never heard of before while she looked out the window. After they'd each exchanged their news, they made some vague comments about visits and trips overseas when everything was a bit more settled, then said goodbye. Kate remained where she was. Despite the relative resolution of the weekend and her father's apparent lack of distress about his friend's death—did men of his age and generation simply not experience the same emotions or had society forced them to quash anything that resembled a feeling? —Kate felt very troubled by the whole thing.

Because the bit Kate kept coming back to was how Bruce had been wearing her father's clothes. He'd borrowed them because his own clothes had been too uncomfortable and with Don and Bruce being similar builds, this was an easy-enough fix. When Kate thought about it, the two men looked quite a lot alike in general. She herself had in the past mistaken the two from behind. Which meant someone else could have done the same.

Had somebody tried to drown her father and instead drowned Bruce? She couldn't stand this horrible gnawing unease, this dread. She was going to have to find out for sure.

7

Zelda took a moment to shake out her umbrella before entering the café, then paused just inside the door to pump out two globs of hand sanitiser and to scan the room. Myra Chadha, Zelda's coffee date, must have had her eyes trained on the entrance because as soon as Zelda's eyes caught hers she smiled and waved. Zelda waved back then nodded at the counter to communicate that she'd grab her beverage before joining her.

It was ten-thirty and while there were a number of people waiting for takeaway orders, only about a third of the tables inside were unoccupied, typical for a Monday morning. Semester two had just begun and neither Myra nor Zelda had classes on Monday but a meeting on campus had suited them both.

"Hey, it's been ages," Zelda said as she set down her coffee and took the chair opposite. "Obviously," she added, rolling her eyes. "How was lockdown? You were staying at the flat with Victoria while Sophie was down south, right?"

Myra and Zelda both attended University of Auckland, but it was Myra's living situation that had been the real reason they'd connected. Zelda, eager for an 'in' with the detective duo Paige and Sophie, had made friendly overtures once Myra had mentioned in passing that her flatmate was something of a private investigator. Zelda had then used her new friendship with Myra to shoehorn herself into a barbecue at Paige's house, and eventually, into a casual work arrangement at S & S Investigations.

But over time, Zelda and Myra, who shared a couple of classes, had gotten together to study and brainstorm assignments, and a bona fide friendship had developed.

Now, with Zelda entering her final semester of her undergrad programme, she had to decide what her next move would be. And while she loved working on S & S cases, she still felt decidedly 'outer circle'. Would she ever break through Paige's defences and was it worth even trying? She'd started to wonder whether she should maybe give another avenue a go. She'd arranged this catchup with Myra because they hadn't seen each other in ages, but also because when Zelda was in research mode she liked to gather information from a variety of sources. And when it came to Paige and Sophie, Myra was a source.

After a brief conversation about how they'd coped with lockdown and how university was going, Zelda launched into the subject she wanted to discuss.

"Do you hang out with Paige very much?"

Myra's eyes went wide, almost wonderous. "No. Why?"

Zelda frowned. "Sorry, was that a weird question? She's your flatmate's best friend."

"Oh I know. It's just—" Myra broke off to give the question some thought. "I just can't imagine it. Like, what situation would she invite me to hang out with them, you know?"

"I do."

"How's it going working with her?"

"Good. She's just quite standoffish. I can't tell whether she likes me. Or like, whether the job is going somewhere."

Myra nodded sympathetically. "Can you talk to Sophie about it?"

Zelda tilted her head. "Yeah, I suppose I can."

"She's easier to talk to than she looks."

"What about Leo?" Zelda blurted, surprising herself. She hadn't even planned to ask about him.

"Yeah. I'm sure you could talk to him as well." Myra frowned. "Is that what you mean?"

"Um...." Zelda thought for a moment. Was this part of the reason she'd had this burning urge to catchup with Myra right now? Because she wanted to find out more about Leo's situation?

"Zelda? What's up?"

"I think I got the impression you might have been into Leo at one point. Was I right?"

Myra blushed and looked down. "Maybe, yeah. But I've actually just started seeing someone." She gave Zelda a nervous smile.

"Oh, cool."

Zelda felt tension ease from her shoulders and mentally rolled her eyes at herself. It was now obvious that part of the reason she'd chosen Myra to 'gather intel' was because deep down she wanted to make sure Myra wasn't hoping to date Leo. An interesting development, Zelda acknowledged to herself, of which she hadn't been consciously aware until now.

· · · · ·· · ·· ·

A few minutes after midday, Roman took a seat across from Laurie Jefferies, the lawyer who'd worked with Terry Garnet in the months leading up to Terry's death. Laurie was in his late forties and had a head of brownish blond hair but a definitely-ginger beard, and the large-but-soft physique of an ex-rugby player (probably).

"Sorry I had to reschedule last week. Stuff comes up, you know how it is."

"Sure do."

"Don't mind me," Laurie added as he unwrapped his lunch: a foot-long subway sandwich. "Starving. What about you?"

"Late breakfast," Roman replied, patting his stomach as he marvelled at the huge hunk of bread Laurie was now cramming into his mouth. It was hard to interview people and eat at the same time, Roman knew, especially if you wanted to take notes. But not if you ate this quickly, Roman noted, watching Laurie devour his meal, making loud and appreciative noises as he chewed.

"Did you notice any changes in Terry's behaviour in the months leading up to his death?"

Laurie's munching slowed as he looked off into the distance. "Not sure I can answer that one. It was a while ago and we weren't that close. We went for a beer here and there, but I didn't see much of him socially."

"You mentioned you spent Christmas with his family?"

"Ah, right, yeah. Went through a bad patch with the wife. Ex-wife, now. All a bit of a blur, really. But Terry was the type to notice a mate struggling and reach out. He thought I shouldn't be alone."

Roman nodded.

"You want to speak to Daniel. Best friends for years, those two."

"Daniel Crane? The same Daniel who went on the fishing trip with him?"

"That's the one."

Roman made a note. He'd tried to reach Daniel but the listed phone number and address were both out of date. He hadn't been able to find any other trace of him. Daniel had retired and at the same time, it seemed, had taken the opportunity to go off the grid. He was probably living in a bach up north or something, Roman mused. But really, he could be anywhere. He could have moved overseas for all Roman knew.

"What about his cases? Anything jump out?"

Paige's father Terry Garnet had been a defence lawyer who had worked both civil and criminal cases, not being so concerned with the area of complaint so much as making sure maligned individuals (or in some cases small businesses) got fair and quality representation. This had sometimes involved acting as a liaison to connect clients with other lawyers more experienced in their particular issue. In considering the possibility that someone killed Terry, Roman needed to look at Terry's full range of clients.

Laurie wiped some mayonnaise from his chin and swallowed his mouthful before replying. For this, Roman was grateful. He'd already seen enough of Laurie's partially digested sandwich.

"I've been thinking about that. Terry always had a pile of cases on the go, things ticking over. Some just peripherally involved, others taking the lead, you know how it is. But I remember him coming out of a busy patch and saying he needed a break. That's why he went away that weekend."

"Right."

"But when I think about it maybe he was a bit stressed because of something that had happened recently."

"Yeah?"

"It was this old case. It might be worth looking into." Laurie paused to eye him. "Because you think there's something off about his death, right?"

Roman made a noncommittal noise. "Like I said on the phone, I think Paige just needs some closure, to satisfy her inquisitive mind. She started her own investigations agency so I guess it's been on her mind recently."

God, when did he get so good at lying?

"Anything she can get her teeth stuck into would help with that, ah, closure process, I think," Roman continued.

Laurie nodded thoughtfully. "Terry mentioned this one guy who I think gave him a bit of grief."

Roman leaned forwards. "Who?"

"Gang affiliated but swore his innocence. Terry took on his case, determined to make sure justice was done, to see he wasn't railroaded by, uh, you lot." Laurie nodded. "Not everyone gets a fair go by the police, you know." He gave him a guarded look, to which Roman nodded.

"I know. You won't hear me trying to convince you that we don't have any issues on the force."

"Anyway. Terry wasn't successful and the guy got put away. When he was released a few years later, he contacted Terry and threatened him."

"Physically?"

"Over the phone, but yeah."

"Got his details?"

Laurie picked up a napkin to wipe the fingers of one hand and pressed a button on his office phone. "Jenny?"

"Yes?" came the reply through his speakerphone.

"Can you pull the Coates-Smith file?"

"No problem."

Laurie disconnected. "I'll email you a summary."

"That would be great."

As Laurie wiped his hands and deposited the empty wrapper in the rubbish bin next to his desk, Roman stood up.

"If you think of anything else, don't hesitate to contact me."

"Will do."

Roman turned back. "You don't have Daniel's contact details, do you?"

"Sorry, mate. Can't reach him?"

Roman shook his head. "What about Phillip Zuckerman?"

"Is that the other guy that was on the boat?" he asked. Roman nodded. "No idea."

"Okay. Thanks anyway."

"Wait," Laurie said.

"Yeah?" Roman paused at the door.

"Might be worth talking to Jenny. She used to work for Terry too."

"Thanks." He let himself out of the office and stopped at the desk that sat only a few feet away. "Jenny?"

The fifty-something brunette woman who'd shown him into Laurie's office looked up at her name. "Yes, Detective Leconte?"

"Call me Roman. Do you have a minute?"

Her phone rang. "I do, but just give me...."

As Jenny dealt with her caller, Roman made a mental To Do list. He would have a look at that old case Laurie had mentioned, that was a good lead. But he also needed to find Terry's friend Daniel. Could he ask Alice Garnet without her relaying their interaction to Paige?

· · · ● · · ● · · ·

After one go-around of the food court and restaurant section of Commercial Bay, Mike and Michael decided on a Mexican-themed restaurant that was the right kind of full to suggest the food was okay without it being uncomfortably crowded.

"How's it going with what's-her-face?" Mike asked once they were settled into their seats.

Michael wasn't often without some sort of lady friend but they tended not to last very long—Michael's decision—and Mike had stopped trying to remember all of their names.

"Olivia."

"Yeah, how's that going?"

"It's gone."

"What happened?"

Michael looked away. "Nothing, I just couldn't see a future for us."

"Can you see a future with any of them?"

Michael's face turned a little morose for a moment. "No, not really."

Mike thought his friend was probably now thinking about his *one true love*, the one who'd gotten away. His university sweetheart (whom he'd dumped in search of more fun and freedom), had gotten married a couple of years ago, and Michael still hadn't recovered. Michael had as much admitted he'd assumed the two of them would find each other again after they'd done their 'playing around', as he said. A hard lesson to learn, but that was life.

Mike himself wasn't so fussed about the romantic situation. He knew he was at risk of becoming the weird single uncle (his mother had said these very words to his very face), but he was going to try to pull off the debonair bachelor instead—the George Clooney—for as long as possible. He was in his thirties so he had a while yet. Maybe society wouldn't care so much about single people in a few years—he couldn't fathom why they cared so much about singlehood now. But more and more people were eschewing marriage and kids, apparently. His older sister had two daughters, eleven and fourteen, and they had confidently assured him that this was the case. Marriage was "so retro", according to them, which gave him hope.

"Clare is available." Mike winked at Michael.

Michael gave him a look. "You can't seriously want me to date your sister."

"Just joking."

But he wasn't, not really. He couldn't think of anything better than having Michael get married to his sweet but slightly unusual younger sister and being part of the family. Plus it would mean he wouldn't have to worry about her anymore. Not that he actively worried about her in a losing sleep kind of way, but sometimes he did wonder where her life was going. Would she work as a clerk at Hammer Hardware for the rest of her life? She was only twenty-nine but he couldn't imagine her doing anything else.

After their meal and a spot of shopping, Michael flagged down a taxi to take them home. Michael could be weirdly old-fashioned sometimes.

They quickly reached their destination—St Mary's Bay was only a ten-minute drive from the central city unless you attempted it during rush-hour and then you could expect to spend forty-five minutes in traffic—and Michael paid the driver. Mike didn't offer any cash because he'd paid for lunch.

Michael lived in a large villa on a bigger-than-necessary chunk of land, and Mike lived in the granny flat at the back of the property. This arrangement had worked very well for nearly five years now. It had started as a temporary measure after Mike was somewhat abruptly ejected from his flat when the owners decided to sell, but Mike had quickly taken to the situation. Having his best friend only twenty metres away was rather nice, so instead of looking for a 'proper flat' he'd simply set up residence. He paid rent, of course, he was no free-loader, but it made life simpler when your landlord wasn't one of those money-hungry bastards who raised the rent every five minutes to 'keep up with the rising costs of property ownership' which everyone knew was code for 'I can get away with it, so I do'.

As they walked up to the door of the main house—they'd agreed to spend a couple of hours brainstorming the issue of how one might find a long-lost mother and how much money one should charge for this service—Desiree, the woman who lived next door, rushed out of her house.

"Michael, Michael, coo-eee," she called as she hurried over.

Mike exchanged an eyeroll with Michael as they both turned to face her. Michael's next-door neighbour was obviously, almost comically, in love with Michael but didn't seem to have the sort of self-awareness that would stop most people from making it so obvious. Or perhaps it was a sense of embarrassment she lacked. The presence of either one of these would have prevented her from making such a fool of herself on such a regular basis.

"Did you find out if you have to work tonight?" she gushed, patting her hair. "The new episode of Outlander will be streaming at eight."

"Desiree, don't you look nice," Michael said, smiling. "Been to the hairdressers?"

Mike eyed Desiree's made-up face and her bouffier-than-normal hair and surmised that she'd had something of a makeover.

"You noticed." She beamed, patting her hair again. "Thank you."

Mike sighed inwardly. He was too nice to her. That's why she kept coming over like this. It was like feeding a stray cat, she'd forever be mewling at the door wanting more. Michael would never be free of her.

"Sorry, I do have to work," Michael said to Desiree, indicating Mike.

Mike nodded to confirm this, hoping she'd immediately go away without a fuss. Desiree had been making up excuses to run into Michael for years, but more recently, after learning that Michael also watched the TV show Outlander, these efforts had intensified. She now invited him over to watch the TV show every single week. Michael had politely given her excuse after excuse but she didn't seem to get the message.

"Maybe next week?" he offered.

Desiree's face lit up. "Oh, lovely." She clapped her hands. "Perfect."

"I'd better get to work now," Michael said, still smiling. "See you later." He unlocked the door.

"Byeeee," Mike said, failing to conceal his facetious tone.

As he closed the door behind him he caught one final glimpse of Desiree watching them go inside. He frowned. Her expression offered a strange combination of determination, thrall and... something else.

Something he couldn't quite put his finger on.

8

Tuesday morning, Sophie was reclining in the hypnotist's chair trying to force her mind to stop racing.

"Now that you're at the bottom of the stairs, you feel completely calm," Cassie continued, her voice low and breathy. "Very, very calm, and very, very relaxed. You see a door and you open it and walk through into the room. Inside, you feel even more relaxed. You feel as if nothing can bother you here. Everything is going to be fine. You aren't anxious anymore, you feel completely fine," she whispered.

But her voice was more than just a whisper, Sophie noted. It was breathier, almost to the point of sounding... seductive?

She hadn't spoken like this at their first session, had she? Surely Sophie would have noticed. Right now, she couldn't seem to notice anything else. In the first appointment they'd had a chat about why Sophie was there and what she wanted to achieve and she'd done a questionnaire which was easily identifiable as a measure of whether she was hypnotisable or not (not everyone is). They'd then gone through this same 'induction' process and Sophie had felt herself go into something of a trance. But now they were doing it again Sophie had the sneaking suspicion that the first time she might have just nodded off. She'd had a stint of badly broken sleep in the days leading up to the session and once she'd relaxed a little, what with the questionnaires and chatting about her anxiety and then lying down, it was definitely possible she'd fallen asleep.

"Just relax, everything is fine," Cassie breathed.

But every time Cassie said "just relax" Sophie felt a little less relaxed. She was beginning to feel downright irritated. At herself, for resisting this treatment, or for Cassie and her stupid breathy voice? She forced her face to remain neutral. She felt as if she was becoming irrationally irritated and part of the problem was the awareness that it couldn't be working if she was feeling so irritated. If she was 'under' then wouldn't her conscious brain be idle? Wouldn't it feel like she was dreaming? She took a slow breath, trying to stay calm. Should she say something? Should she interrupt this ridiculous breathy monologue to tell Cassie that she didn't feel remotely hypnotised? No, she couldn't. Paige would have no trouble doing such a thing. She could easily imagine Paige blinking open her eyes, fixing Cassie with a quizzical glare and very clearly telling her what was wrong. But Paige never felt awkward, she simply didn't experience any sort of cringe. Sophie, on the other hand, sometimes felt as if avoiding awkward situations was the single most important factor directing her behaviour.

"In the corner of the room, you see a man," Cassie continued. "He's tall, with blond hair and blue eyes, and you immediately notice how kind and attractive he is and how safe you feel with him there."

At this, Sophie couldn't help but frown. What did tall blond men have to do with anything? A tall dark-haired man was more than a little responsible for the panic attacks she'd experienced of late. Wasn't it a bit risky to be bringing up men in general? Especially tall ones. Sophie had told Cassie all about the Josh situation in their first session so maybe she was trying to replace the image of a scary tall brown-haired man—Josh Spencer—with this apparently not-scary blond one? It made sense, in a way, Sophie could see. She couldn't walk around being scared of tall men for the rest of her life, after all.

But Roman wouldn't be described as 'tall', she found herself noting.

"You go over to him," Cassie intoned in her whispery voice. "You're inexplicably drawn to his kind warm aura. You start talking, and you realise that you feel a special connection."

Sophie frowned again. She was really starting to think she should say something. She clearly wasn't hypnotised and these sessions weren't cheap. For whatever reason she'd fallen out of the spell, so shouldn't she say something so they could start again? But that would be so awkward.

And so, she let Cassie drone on for another ten minutes until she said, "And then I'll count backwards from ten and click my fingers. When I do, you'll wake up totally refreshed, feeling good, totally relaxed."

Sophie mentally counted along with her and then promptly opened her eyes as soon as she heard the click of fingers. She fixed her gaze on Cassie.

"Oh." Cassie blinked at her, seeming surprised at how quickly she'd awoken.

"How do you feel?"

"Ah, good I think." Sophie managed a smile. "Great. Really great." She forced another smile. "That's us then is it?" she said, trying to sound cheerful and, above all, completely relaxed.

· · · ● · ● · · · ·

In the main office of S & S Investigations, Paige hung up the landline and took her laptop into the conference room where Sophie was waiting.

"That was our potential new client, Kate Dash. Guess where she heard about S and S Investigations?"

Sophie shrugged. "No idea."

"Okay, guess who her accountant is? I'll give you a hint. She was also the accountant to another client. Sort of."

Sophie thought for a moment, then turned wide eyes to Paige. "Not Estelle Royce?"

Paige grinned. "Yep."

One of their more recent cases, the death of Estelle Royce, had involved Paige making several calls to Estelle's accountant. Paige, being Paige, had not let societal conventions and pleasantries get the way of acquiring the information they needed. And this was the reason for Sophie's surprise at her referral.

"She seemed so annoyed at us," Sophie said, generously using 'us' instead of 'you'.

"Yeah, but we got results, didn't we."

"True. And I guess ultimately it was Estelle's children who bothered her, not us. We probably gave her closure in a way."

"Kate wants us to meet her at her house after work, six o'clock."

"You already said yes?"

"I did."

"Where does she live?"

"Newmarket. Nice and close. And she'll provide dinner if we want."

Sophie made a face. "Isn't it a bit awkward to have a meal with a brand-new client? Potential client."

"Yeah, doesn't seem professional, does it? But you and I can still go for dinner. We'll have the meeting then get food."

"Sounds good."

As silence fell, Paige fixed her gaze on Sophie. "Are you not going to tell me about your appointment this morning?"

Sophie pursed her lips. "How did you—"

"Your calendar was blocked out."

Sophie sighed. She hadn't told Paige she was going to hypnotherapy because she hadn't wanted Paige's take on the situation before she had a chance to decide for herself. Or perhaps it was that she didn't want Paige observing it; being an audience. Seeing things through Paige's eyes was sometimes helpful and other times not so much. But now, after two sessions and a growing uncertainty about the utility of it all, she thought it was probably time to let Paige in on the situation.

"I had a hypnotherapy session." Sophie waited for Paige's reaction. It could go either way.

"For the panic attacks."

"And generalised anxiety, yeah."

Paige nodded, looking thoughtful. "And? Is it working?"

"Not really. Maybe? I feel less jumpy than I did before, but maybe that's just the passage of time." Sophie shrugged. "I'm not sure whether to give it another couple of sessions."

"Why wouldn't you?"

"Well, it's not cheap. But also…." Sophie hesitated. Did she want to let Paige in on her doubts? If Paige ruined hypnotherapy for her, then she'd have one less therapeutic option.

"But?"

"She was kind of annoying. Like, she used this weird breathy voice, almost like she was trying to be sexy?"

"Sexy?"

"And I don't think I was hypnotised."

"Neither time?"

Sophie shook her head. "I think I fell asleep the first time and thought it worked, but the second I just got more and more annoyed."

Paige chuckled.

"Don't dump on it though, okay?"

"I won't. Hypnotherapy is a valid form of therapy for the right person."

"Not you, though, right?"

"Nope. Will you go back?"

"Not sure."

"Maybe try out ACT?" Paige said. "Acceptance and commitment therapy?" she added.

"I know what you meant." Sophie smiled. "I didn't think you were telling me to join up to a right-wing political party."

Paige laughed. "Fair enough."

"I'm going to give myself a bit of time to mull it over. I'm kind of bummed the hypnotherapy wasn't more effective, to be honest."

"Hey, how about some retail therapy," Paige said. "If we're going to Newmarket, I wouldn't mind a go around the shops."

Sophie perked up. "I was thinking the same thing. As soon as you said where she lived."

"Should we go now?"

"Let's do it. But—"

"Let me guess, we're not allowed to take my car?" Paige rolled her eyes.

"It's four o'clock. School plus rush-hour traffic? It will be ridiculous."

"Fine, fine."

"It's not raining. We can walk down to the K' Road intersection and get the bus from there."

"I said, fine. But you're giving me the scoop on Roman as we walk."

"Sure. And you can tell me what's happening with you and Tim."

Paige made a face.

· · · · ● · ● · · ·

At a quarter to six, after a decent stint of (mostly) window shopping, Paige and Sophie walked the five-minutes from Broadway, the main street of Newmarket, to the apartment building in which Kate lived with her wife Tina.

After identifying them through the intercom, Kate buzzed them up and moments later they were seated in Kate's living room, introductions already made, and with glasses of water in front of them should they get thirsty.

"Thanks for doing a home visit. I had a zoom call that finished ten minutes ago and back-to-back meetings tomorrow and I felt this couldn't wait."

Paige leaned forwards, excitement in her eyes, her little black *I'm a detective* notepad at the ready. "What seems to be the problem," she began.

"My dad recently got remarried."

"Your mother was his first wife?"

"Yes, they divorced about six years ago. She lives in Spain. Dad cheated throughout the marriage. He's a total cliché. His new wife is virtually the same age as me and he 'met her overseas'," Kate said, air quoting.

Paige and Sophie exchanged glances.

"What do you mean by that?" Sophie asked.

Kate sighed. "He met her in London. Love at first sight apparently." She rolled her eyes. "As if you could fall in love with my dad at first sight. Fell in love with his Rolex, more likely. And with the way he was probably throwing money around at whatever bar they were at. My dad has the kind of ego that bats away any nagging questions about why a woman like Natasha would want to spend her life with a man like him."

"Ah," Paige said. "You think she's a gold digger."

"He outright refuses to talk about it. He's banished any conversation on the subject of his marriage to Natasha."

"And you don't trust her?"

"About a week after they were married, they went for a drive up north to Matakana. Made a day of it, you know. Went to the markets, bought wine and cheese and went for a swim, etc. On the drive home, Natasha was behind the wheel, and they had an accident. She swerved to avoid an animal and drove into a tree. But only the passenger side in which Dad was sitting got hit."

"Was he hurt?"

"No, they were both fine, but it was weird. And then another couple of weeks after that we all went to visit this farm owned by a family friend. Dad wanted Natasha to experience 'Kiwi stuff', you know? And we're just looking around, showing her the sheep and the cows, and there's this fence and Dad started droning on about electric fences in rural New Zealand and how you have to check for a sign or be watchful and then Natasha said she'd already touched it without realising and this one wasn't electric so Dad grabbed it and he got a big shock. And then it turned out Natasha was standing right next to a sign that said *Do Not Touch: Electric Fence*. Dad was fine and everyone laughed it off, but I thought it was a bit off. I got the distinct impression that Natasha had known exactly what she was doing. And then we had the sesame seed salad and the allergic reaction I already told you about and now his best friend Bruce is dead."

Kate looked from Paige to Sophie.

"I'm pretty sure that Dad's new wife is trying to kill him."

9

Paige and Sophie emerged from Kate's building and walked back to Broadway, the main street running through Newmarket.

"We can have a working dinner and go over the case," Paige said.

"Sounds good."

"Wild about Kate's theory, ay? That her new stepmother is some sort of Femme Fatale. Ooh, like a Black Widow."

"Doesn't there have to be a pattern of killing before you get that title?" Sophie said. "More than one husband, I mean."

"Maybe we're about to uncover a string of murders across the globe!" Paige's eyes flashed with excitement.

"So you think Kate is right."

"We're going to find out." Paige's phone rang. She checked the display. "Crap," she said before answering. "Hi Mum. Yeah, I'll be there in twenty minutes." She disconnected and grimaced.

"You forgot you're supposed to be having dinner with your mother?"

"And Tim, yeah. Sorry. I probably shouldn't flake on that."

Sophie waved her off. "It's fine. Oh, but your car is still parked near the office."

"I'll get an Uber to Mum's. Tim is already there and he has his car. He can drop me off at my car after dinner. You're okay to jump on the bus from here, eh?"

"Yeah, the Outer Link takes me almost right to my street."

"Hey!" someone yelled. Paige and Sophie turned at the same time to see Leo jogging over to where they stood.

"Leo, what a nice surprise," Sophie said, smiling. "What are you up to?"

"Uh," Leo glanced behind him. "Getting dinner," he said, looking a little uncertain. At this, Sophie frowned.

"Perfect," Paige said. "Sophie you can eat with Leo. I have to go."

"Oh," Leo suddenly looked panicked.

Sophie's frown deepened—why was he looking so stressed at the idea of eating dinner with her—but in the next moment, she understood. Roman appeared, coming to stand next to Leo.

"Roman and I are, uh...." Leo trailed off but the answer was obvious. They were hanging out.

Sophie eyed the two of them, standing next to each other with obvious familiarity. They of course had met each other before, but when had they become friendly enough to eat meals together? It must have happened while she and Paige were away. Had Roman shown up at the S & S offices to talk to *her* and found Leo instead? Had they ended up chatting (Leo was very easy to talk to), and had Roman confided in Leo? Sophie's stomach contracted at the idea of this but she didn't even know why.

"How long have you two been walking around like that?" Paige said, gesturing first at Roman's face then at Leo's.

Roman frowned. "Like what?"

"With matching moustaches."

Roman turned to inspect Leo's face, as if only properly noticing now that both he and Leo sported moustaches.

"You look like you're in costume," Paige continued. "On your way to a Magnum P.I. party or something."

Roman grinned. "I'll take that as a compliment. Tom Selleck has a legendary moustache. And he's a heartthrob." His eyes flicked to Sophie. She gave him a half-smile, still a little stunned by his unexpected appearance. The moustache was almost too much to deal with right now.

"Whatever." Paige waved her hand to dismiss the topic. "Gotta go. See you."

Sophie almost reached out to grab Paige's arm, to stop her from leaving. Because with her gone, suddenly everything felt even more loaded. But all she did was say, "Bye," then turned back to face Roman. God, she felt weird. Roman gave her a small smile and pushed his hands into his pockets as he looked down. Sophie looked at the ground too.

"Uh," Leo said into the silence. "Roman and I are going to get dinner. Do you want to come?"

Sophie swallowed. She wasn't prepared for this. What should she do? On one hand, having Leo there for her first interaction with Roman since, everything, might help. But on the other, Leo's presence would mean they couldn't have any sort of real conversation.

"Sure," she found herself saying.

Well, that was that. Her subconscious had spoken.

"We were just going to the pizza place around the corner," Roman said, "if that's okay with you."

"Of course."

At least one mystery had been cleared up, Sophie thought as they walked over. The reason for Leo's moustache was now obvious: he was copying Roman. Roman was about ten years older and Leo obviously looked up to him. But why had Roman grown one? And how could she find out the answers to such questions without Paige no-filter Garnet around to be blunt and tactless on her behalf?

As soon as they were seated, Leo excused himself to use the loo and Roman and Sophie were left awkwardly looking at each other, the restaurant, then each other again. Sophie felt as if she almost couldn't control where her attention went. And her gaze kept coming back to him, just as his returned to her.

"So…." they both said at the same time.

God, where to begin, Sophie thought. Should she just outright ask him what's happening with Anya's pregnancy? Did he know whether the baby was even his? No, she wouldn't. She couldn't. He would have to bring it up first.

"Before Leo gets back," Roman said. "I might have a lead on Terry Garnet's death."

"Oh. You carried on without...." she trailed off, unable to say, *without me*, because obviously, he had. For some reason Sophie hadn't expected this, but why not? They'd never talked about dropping the investigation.

Roman rested his elbows on top of the table, his fingers laced together in front of him. "If it pans out, do you want to help me chase it down?"

Sophie's eyes looked down at his hands, then up to his eyes.

"Yes," she said simply.

Roman was no longer wearing his wedding ring.

· · · ●·● · · ·

Paige took a seat at the dinner table, noticing that, somewhat unusually, the table had been set so that she was alone on one side of the table. Tim and her mother were sitting side-by-side facing her and it didn't feel at all natural or comfortable.

"Are you two interviewing me or something?" she joked, her gaze moving from her mother to Tim. "What's the job?"

Tim glanced nervously at Alice.

"Ha-ha," Alice trilled. "No, it's just the way the table ended up." She shrugged.

Paige narrowed suspicious eyes but let the comment go. "Can you pass the bread rolls?" she asked Tim.

"Sure." He smiled widely.

"Thanks." She helped herself to the steaming pot of ravioli then added a bit of green salad to her plate. "Did you two cook dinner together?"

Tim cleared his throat. "No, your mum made this."

"But Tim helped. He's so handy in the kitchen, Paige. Do you know how rare that is?"

"Maybe for your generation."

"I think that even nowadays women generally do more cooking than their partners."

"Even when two women form the partnership? How does it work then?"

Alice took a breath then pressed her lips together. "You're being unnecessarily antagonistic."

"Am I? Or am I helping you step into the twenty-first century with the rest of us?"

"Paige," Tim started. "She's not trying to—"

"How do you know what she's trying to do? Are you two sharing a brain now?"

Silence fell.

"I don't know why a simple dinner has to be like this," Alice said.

Paige put down her fork. "Because it's not a simple dinner is it?"

Alice fluttered one hand to her throat. "What do you mean?"

"This whole thing is... weird. It almost feels like an intervention."

Tim exchanged yet another look with her mother.

"Oh my god. Can you stop exchanging looks like you two are co-conspirators or something?" She stood. "Actually, I'm starting to think that's exactly what you are. So maybe it's totally appropriate."

"This is a rather large overreaction, darling," Alice said.

"Is it?"

Paige glared at them. They'd brought her here to force a discussion about the baby situation. She knew it. She just *knew it*.

And it was outrageous.

"What do you think is happening here?" Alice asked, raising her eyes to meet Paige's.

But Paige couldn't say it. She couldn't throw the accusation at them, even though she could tell by her mother's expression she was right. Because to say the words out loud would somehow give them more power. It would make her acknowledge the issue. And she couldn't do that. Not yet.

· · · · ●·● · · ·

As soon as Roman got home from dinner, he shut himself in his office. He was the only one who lived there now but closing the door somehow helped him focus. He started up his computer and pulled out the growing file on Terry Garnet.

Seeing Sophie tonight had been thrilling, and as much as he wanted to dwell on the memory of the evening, he wouldn't. He couldn't let himself go down that road until he had an answer about the baby. He couldn't do that to himself. He couldn't bear it.

So he would focus on this instead. In addition to the coast guard reports and the additional weather information he himself had found, he had the box of evidence from the brief police investigation into Terry's death and the case file summary Laurie had emailed through as promised.

First, Roman looked up Vinny Coates-Smith, the gang-affiliated person Laurie had mentioned. The one who had threatened Terry. Roman made a few notes as he went through his police record. It wasn't great, but who knew how much of this was exaggerated or bad luck, acquired simply by existing in proximity to the wrong crowd? Some people didn't have much of a choice in that matter, he knew. Had Vinny turned on Terry? Had he blamed him for his incarceration? And if so, was it the type of bitter resentment that eats away at people until they're consumed by it, or had it been just a passing attempt to shift the unpleasantness of guilt. Blaming other people is easier than dealing with negative feelings you hold about yourself, Roman knew.

Since his release Vinny had kept a relatively low profile, apart from one public disorderly event which could mean anything, really. And his name had come up in association with an aggravated robbery. Roman made a few more notes and wondered whether he could speak to him in person. That way he could at least get a read on Vinny's reaction to questions about Terry. Maybe he should take Sophie with him. If anyone should be reading behavioural responses it was her. But what if Vinny was dangerous? He couldn't expose Sophie unnecessarily. He put the idea to one side and went back to the evidence he'd copied from the police investigation.

The two men who'd been on the fishing trip with Terry, Daniel Crane and Phillip Zuckerman, had both been interviewed by DS Connolly, according to the summary report. But Roman couldn't find the transcripts of these interviews. He frowned. And not only were the transcripts missing, but there was a reference to video recordings. According to this note, there should be two video interviews on file. But Roman could find nothing. No tapes, no USBs, no reference information.

Had someone removed them or had they never existed?

What had been revealed in those interviews?

He turned to his computer and opened a new search. Ten minutes later, he sat back and let out a low whistle. For each step he took, things became clearer. Something was off with this investigation. DS Connolly was now retired and the other two officers named on the investigation had moved overseas. And of the three men who had been on that boat, Terry Garnet, Daniel Crane and Phillip Zuckerman, two were dead and the third had seemingly disappeared.

10

Paige and Sophie took their coffees and laptops to the conference room. Once they were seated, Paige eyed Sophie expectantly. "Well? How did it go with Roman? You never messaged me back last night."

"Honestly, I didn't know what to say. I couldn't find any words." Sophie's mouth twisted. "And it was a little weird, but kind of nice. Having Leo there as a buffer was both good and bad. It was a nice way to ease into seeing Roman, but at the same time, we couldn't talk about anything important or personal, you know?"

Paige nodded. "So you still don't know about the paternity situation?"

The rather shocking discovery of Anya Leconte's pregnancy had been followed by an even more shocking discovery that she'd been cheating on Roman for some time, which led to some obvious paternity questions. None of which had been resolved, as far as Paige and Sophie knew.

"I thought Roman might give me a lift home so we could talk, but Leo kind of insisted on driving me back."

"He can be so clueless."

Sophie tilted her head, looking thoughtful. "Maybe it was for the best. I'm not completely sure I'm ready to hear it. Because if Roman had news and it was good, he would have told me already, right?" She wrinkled her nose. "Ugh, I feel sick just thinking about it."

"Ooh," Paige said suddenly. "Maybe Leo knows. They're obviously hanging out now."

"Yeah. Maybe Roman is confiding in him. He's a good listener, so it's possible."

"I could ask?"

Sophie chewed her lip. "No. Roman will tell me when he's ready, I'm sure he will."

"He probably doesn't have the paternity tests results back yet."

"No, probably not."

"Because that's going to affect things, right?"

"It sure will." Sophie made a face. "Hey, can we change the subject? Thinking about it stresses me out and there's no point in worrying until we know the situation."

"Sure." Paige left her coffee on the table and went over to bring out the whiteboard. They generally didn't use it for the more bread-and-butter cases, like running background checks and the P.I. staple: adulterous spouses. No, getting out the whiteboard was still something of a special occasion.

"What about you?" Sophie asked, as Paige located the whiteboard markers and eraser. "How was dinner with Tim and your mum? Was it a baby ambush again?"

Paige pushed away an unpleasant stomach contraction and shrugged. "I didn't give them a chance to talk about it. It's so not fair for them to gang up on me."

"I don't think they're—"

"Soph, I don't want to talk about it, okay?" She uncapped a marker. "We'll figure it out," she said under her breath. Just then her phone, sitting on the table next to her coffee mug, rang. "Ooh." She hurried over to pick it up. "Hi, Kate," she answered, putting it on speaker and setting it down so that Sophie could also listen. "We've just started working on your case."

"Great, but that's not why I called," Kate replied through Paige's phone. "Our whole family is going away this weekend. It's kind of last minute but Dad, Natasha, Tina and I, as well as Jack and Madison, are all off to Waiheke. Something of a mid-winter Christmas."

Because most of New Zealand celebrated the Northern Hemisphere holiday of Christmas but did so in a Southern Hemisphere climate (i.e., summer), many also put on a midwinter Christmas festivity, in which one could enjoy cooking and eating a heavy roast meal in somewhat more appropriate temperatures.

"Lucky you?" Paige replied, catching Sophie's eyes and lifting her shoulders into a shrug. Had Kate called to brag about going away on a fancy minibreak to Waiheke Island? (The Napa Valley of Auckland).

"Everyone will be away so I thought you could search Dad and Natasha's house."

"Oh." Paige perked up. "I see."

"Kate?" Sophie said quickly. "Hi, it's Sophie here." She leaned over the phone. "We can't do anything illegal."

After a brief pause, Kate said, "It won't be illegal, I'll give you the key. Don't worry." Kate cleared her throat. "Dad is okay with it and it's a good chance to search for clues that Natasha is, uh...."

"Trying to murder your father?" Paige finished cheerfully.

Sophie shot Paige a look.

"So you'll do it?" Kate continued.

"Yes. With permission from the homeowner, we can do it," Paige said.

"You're leaving Friday?" Sophie asked.

"And back Sunday afternoon. Dad wants us to spend some quality time together in order to accelerate the process of getting to know our new stepmother," Kate added, sounding glum.

"Righto," Paige said. "Let us know when we can get the key and if there's an alarm code or anything else we should know about."

"I'll drop the keys and code to you on Friday at around lunchtime, okay?"

"Sure."

Kate rang off.

"Um, Paige," Sophie said. "I'm not entirely sure Kate has her father's permission for us to snoop around his house."

"All we can do is take our client's word on things. Kate said it's cool, so as far as we know it's cool."

"I guess."

Paige turned back to the whiteboard. "Okay, so Kate thinks someone is trying to kill her father, and that someone is Natasha, the new wife." Paige wrote *Natasha X* on the board next to the photo she'd printed off, then turned to Sophie. "We don't even know her maiden name so that's obviously a place to start. Because a big chunk of this case is essentially an extensive background check on Natasha, right?"

Sophie nodded. "We're going to need Leo on this one. You included him in the quote for services, right?"

"Of course. He's coming in this afternoon."

"Kate didn't say it explicitly, but she clearly wants to know more about where Natasha came from."

"Whether she could be some sort of Black Widow." Page nodded. "Because figuring out if she's actually trying to kill him might be tricky. Unless you catch someone in the act, how do you prove something that hasn't happened yet. But if we can find out whether she's done it before.... Oh." Paige snapped her fingers as an idea struck. "We should ask Roman about the coroner's report on that guy Bruce's death."

Kate had told them all about finding Bruce in the spa pool wearing Don's clothes, including that they didn't yet know whether he'd drowned during the night or the next day.

"Yes, because if Kate is right and Natasha, or someone else I suppose, was actually trying to kill Don instead of Bruce, then we need to know more about Bruce's death," Sophie said.

"And if he actually drowned. It's possible he was poisoned or something. Or even that he had a heart attack and fell into the pool."

"He fell from his bed to the pool?"

"Well, obviously something else happened first to get him out of bed."

Sophie bit her lip. "But Roman wouldn't be able to tell us that kind of thing, would he? That must be confidential to the investigation. And who says he even has access to it?"

Paige eyed her for a moment. "I can call Roman if it's weird for you."

"But will it be weird if I *don't* call him?'

"Does he know about your phone phobia?"

"I do not have a phone phobia."

"But you kind of do."

"Fine. You call him." Sophie folded her arms.

"Great." Paige picked up her phone. A moment later, she was leaving a voice message. "Hi Roman, Paige and Sophie here. Any chance you could give us a little intel on a recent death?" She recounted the details of Bruce's spa pool death. "Coroner report probably won't be in yet, but any preliminaries? We need time of death and cause of death. Or any information, really. We'll, uh, owe you one," she finished, winking at Sophie before hanging up.

"Why did you wink at me? You made that sound really dodgy."

"Roman couldn't see the wink."

Sophie didn't reply.

"Okay, back to the case." Paige pressed her lips together as she thought. "Kate said Natasha only arrived in New Zealand earlier this year and Kate doesn't know her maiden name. Hopefully Leo will be able to work his magic, but in the meantime, I think the only thing we can do is to follow her. See where she goes, who she talks to, etcetera. If she is trying to kill Don, it's possible someone is helping her. Or she's already taken a lover. That would be motive and we can tell Kate that, at least."

"We'll have to do that tomorrow because they're leaving Friday and Leo is coming in this afternoon to go over the case with us."

"Good point."

"And I'll drive," Sophie added quickly.

Paige frowned. "Whatever, sure."

As Paige turned back to the whiteboard to start writing up the key names in the Dash Case, her mind returned to what Kate said about their family going away to accelerate the process of getting to know her father's new wife, their new stepmother. She quite liked the sound of that: *accelerating the process*. Because she sure was sick of the arguments and the tension with Tim at the moment and something had to change. She'd never felt so distant, so unattached to Tim in all the time they'd known each other, and that was including when they had first met and hardly knew each other. Whatever was going to happen next, Paige wanted it to be sooner rather than later.

· · · · ● · ● · · ·

Mike finished typing his scathing rebuttal of the loser known as *NoACjust-theDC's* idiotic take on the latest Batman movie and hit enter. He only had to wait a few minutes before reply comments started to appear. All agreeing with him, of course. He grinned. *NoAC* always lost their jousts; why did he even bother?

He clicked over to his other active tab and wondered whether he should start another game of online chess—he'd gotten hooked over lockdown and now it was the first thing he did in the morning. A cup of coffee and a game or two. Or ten. Mike's stomach let out a loud rumble, reminding him he hadn't eaten breakfast and it was nearly time for lunch. He stood up to look through his window to the main house. What was Michael up to? Was he even home? Mike hadn't seen him at all this morning. Either way, if he wandered up to the main house he'd probably find something tasty in the kitchen. Michael had an actual housemaid—perhaps house manager was a better description because she also did things like make sure the fridge and pantry were well-stocked, including the presence of frozen meals in the freezer. Michael really had a Prince-like existence, which wasn't at all fair, Mike grumbled mentally, as he had done many, many times before. To have wealth on top of good looks and a charming personality? Mike was no oil painting, he was well aware, and he'd seen first-hand from watching how people treated Michael (second-hand, really), that it did make a difference.

His stomach rumbled again, more insistently this time. "Okay, okay," he muttered, exiting the cottage and walking up the path to the back door. He gave the door a quick rap to announce his presence, then used his key to open it as he always did, calling out as soon as he stepped inside. "Michael? You about?"

No reply. The kitchen was completely devoid of any signs of life, such as coffee remains or breakfast dishes, so he walked into the hall. The house was oddly still. From the hall he went to the front living room where he knew Michael liked to read the paper, but this too was empty.

Empty, but not undisturbed.

He stared at the mess in front of him. A lamp had been knocked over, there was dirt ground into the carpet, and right next to that, a spilt cup of coffee.

"Michael?" he called, louder this time. He lurched into a jog as he ran to the stairs and quickly ascended. On the way to Michael's bedroom he checked the two spare rooms and the adjoining bathroom, just in case. Each was vacant.

His stomach now churning with worry, he came to a stop at Michael's door. It was closed. He knocked. "Michael?" he called, an audible tremble in his voice. "Michael, mate, are you there?" he said again. Slowly, cautiously, he pushed open the door.

It was almost ghostly still, as if no one had ever occupied this room. He rushed to the window to check the driveway. Michael's car was gone which meant he could have popped out already, running an errand or what have you, but this didn't feel right. Not at all.

He hurried back downstairs, his eyes darting from side to side as if to pick up any stray clues. In the hallway he froze, noticing something he hadn't seen before, his eyes finally latching onto something significant.

Blood.

There was blood on the hardwood floor of the hall.

His stomach contracted and he let out a squeaky fart of distress. What happened to Michael?

11

Thursday morning, Paige and Sophie were seated in Sophie's car outside Don and Natasha's house in Mission Bay waiting for Natasha to emerge. They'd received intel from Kate that their target started off each day, fairly reliably, with a ten o'clock exercise class at the Newmarket Les Mills. After that Kate had no idea how Natasha spent her time but it was probably wafting around with other ladies of leisure, lunching and shopping (in Kate's words). When pressed about who these ladies might be, Kate couldn't say.

It was now nine thirty a.m., and Natasha's zippy silver Audi was still in the driveway. "I guess we'll find out if Kate's right about the morning gym session," Paige said as she munched on an Egg McMuffin. "And if so, we'll wait while she works out and tail her for the rest of the day."

"Yes, I figured as much. I skipped breakfast and coffee and dehydrated myself so I don't have to go to the toilet while we're staking her out." Sophie turned to look pointedly at the large coffee that Paige currently held in her left hand and the McMuffin in her right.

"Oh." Paige cast guilty eyes at Sophie. "If worst comes to worst, you can drop me at the loo and pick me up later."

"Paige—"

"Look, here she comes." Paige nodded as Natasha bounced out of the house in workout gear and into her car. "Someone's in a good mood."

They followed her to the gym, parked in a loading zone across the road, and proceeded to wait. After about half an hour, Paige started wriggling in her seat.

"What's up with you getting McDonald's for breakfast, by the way?" Sophie said. "You don't normally do that do you?"

"Easy and yummy."

"Is it tasty, though? And the coffee? Is it good?"

"Hey, I could look up the Les Mills timetable online and see what class she's at, see what time it finishes," Paige said, still wriggling.

"There are probably multiple classes on right now, but they're generally an hour aren't they? Or possibly ninety minutes? So eleven or eleven-thirty."

"Hmm. It would be good to know which one."

"But she might do two classes in a row," Sophie said. "Or hit the weights after a class. Or have a shower." Sophie eyed her for a moment. "Let me guess—"

"Yeah, yeah, you were right, I need to use the loo. But I have an idea."

Sophie raised one eyebrow.

"I'll slip in and use their facilities, and on the way out I can talk to the gym receptionist."

"About what?"

"Whether they know Natasha?"

"And whether she's tried to kill anyone so far?" Sophie added wryly.

"Okay fine, but either way, I'm going in to use the loo."

"You'll need a membership, won't you?"

"Have you forgotten about my superpower?"

Sophie smiled. "Your ability to fly under the radar."

"I'll get in no problem, you'll see."

Paige hopped out of the car and hurried across the road. Sure enough, Paige was not immediately ejected. A full ten minutes passed before the door to Les Mills opened and Paige was shooed out by a very fit and very annoyed-looking guy in bright yellow bike shorts.

Sophie chuckled to herself.

"How'd you get in?" she asked once Paige was back in the car.

"I hung around reception for a minute then tailgated someone inside."

"Don't they have turnstiles in there?"

Paige grinned. "I got in didn't I? I looked around as much as I could but didn't see her."

"Did you ask the receptionist?"

"I showed her a picture on my phone and asked whether she knew her."

"She wouldn't talk?"

"Actually, she was very chatty, but Natasha types are a dime-a-dozen in Les Mills. She didn't seem to recognise her. And then Mr Spandex showed up and asked what I was doing and told me to leave." Paige looked at her phone. "Oh, I have a missed call. My phone is on silent." Her eyes slid to Sophie's. "Guess who."

Sophie took in Paige's excited expression. "Roman?"

"Nailed it." Paige hit the call button and waited for him to answer. "Hey, Roman, I missed your call. I was in.... indisposed." As Paige chatted to him, Sophie tried to eavesdrop. As it turned out, being able to hear Roman's voice but not what he was actually saying wasn't at all fun. Instead, she watched Paige's face for clues.

"Well, thanks for telling me what the coroner said," Paige said after a while. "I know you're probably not supposed to share that information." She turned to Sophie to say, "No official report yet but likely to be an accidental drowning probably around midnight or the early hours of Sunday morning."

Sophie nodded.

Paige listened for another moment. "Yeah, she's here with me right now." Paige glanced at Sophie. "She's good."

Sophie bit her lip.

"Okay." Paige turned to Sophie. "Roman says hi."

"Oh." Sophie felt herself smile. "Hi back. How is he?"

"How are you?" Paige relayed the question then turned to Sophie. "He's okay. What?" She brought her phone to her mouth again. "Oh," she leaned away to say to Sophie, "he's waiting for some important news. Results."

Sophie's eyes went wide.

"Oh, okay, bye." Paige disconnected and turned her now also wide eyes to Sophie. "Important results. That must be—"

"Yeah." Sophie nodded, thoughtful.

"I wonder why he didn't just message you that directly."

"Actually, he did message first thing this morning but I didn't reply."

"Why not?"

Because Roman's message had been mostly about Terry Garnet with just a "we should catch up" tacked onto the end. But Sophie couldn't tell Paige this.

"Uh, it's just too hard to be all casual and like, "hey, how are you?", when there's this massive elephant in the room," she said to Paige.

That much was true, at least.

"Well, now you know. He's still waiting for paternity test results."

· · · ● ●● ● ● · ·

After the gym, Natasha's next stop was, as Kate predicted, the mall. They followed her into the parking lot and were able to get a carpark near enough to her car to tail her inside and continue to do so as she moved from one clothes or makeup outlet to the next. After an hour, both Sophie and Paige were thoroughly sick of walking around the mall but not shopping (neither window nor actual) and were also both rather hungry. Luckily for them, Natasha then headed to the food court where she took a seat and consulted her phone. While Paige watched Natasha, Sophie went over to the Japanese place (somewhat oddly named St Pierre's) and procured them both takeaway sushi trays.

When Sophie returned, Paige got her to sit opposite so that Sophie had her back to Natasha.

"But I can't see," Sophie said.

"That's the point. She won't look twice at me, but if she sees you staring at her not only will she notice but she'll pay attention."

"That's not—"

"Yes, she will. She's obviously very focused on beauty and appearance which means she will look at you. She'll eye up your hair and wonder if it's dyed and whether it's the best colour for your skin. She'll inspect your face, probably trying to find flaws or figure out whether you've had work done. And she'll look at your clothes and judge you for your outfit."

Sophie looked down at her jeans, boots and hooded jacket. "What's wrong with—"

"They're boring."

"Hey—"

"I mean they're not designer. But that's not the point, the point is she'll notice you and we don't want that."

Sophie was quiet.

"I'm right and you know it."

"So, the coroner said the death was likely accidental," Sophie said to change the subject. "Which means the reason Bruce died wasn't because someone is trying to kill Don, as Kate believes."

"Yes, but just because someone didn't drown Bruce, it doesn't mean someone isn't trying to kill Don," Paige said.

"Well, no, but—"

"Ooh, two women are joining Natasha."

"I have an idea," Sophie said, getting out her phone. She turned on the camera and positioned it so she could see behind her. "I can see them." She continued to watch through her camera. "They all look kind of the same, don't they?"

"Like models from the same catalogue."

All three women had slim builds, oval-shaped faces, unnaturally pouty lips, dyed hair (in a range of colours), false eyelashes and enhanced bosoms.

"We need to listen to their conversation," Sophie said. "Can we get any closer?"

Paige looked around the food court. "The people at the table on the other side of them are leaving." She turned back to Sophie. "Put the hood of your jacket up." Sophie did so. "Okay now you're almost more eye-catching. You look like a celebrity who sort of doesn't want people to notice her but also sort of does." Paige waved her hand. "But it will have to do."

Once they were seated at the new table, now less than ten feet away, they could indeed hear the three women. They appeared to be speaking in Russian.

"Well, fat lot of good that did us," Paige said quietly.

"But it's interesting she's meeting friends and following the expected schedule."

"You mean instead of shagging some other dude and plotting Don's death?"

"Exactly."

"Oh, they're leaving. Let's follow."

They stood at the same time as the three women and waited while they said their goodbyes with a flurry of air kisses. Just as Paige and Sophie moved to follow Natasha towards the exit, one of the three ladies turned back. "Oi, babe, I got your scarf. Dontcha want it back?"

Natasha whirled around. "Shush, your voice," she hissed, running over to her friend and yanking the scarf from her before stalking away.

For a moment, neither Paige nor Sophie moved, both surprised, then Paige grabbed Sophie's arm and they lurched into motion.

"I didn't imagine that did I?" Paige said as they followed Natasha out of the food court. "That was not a Russian accent."

"Nope, that was a full-on British one. If I had to guess, I'd say Manchester."

"How'd you know?"

Sophie grimaced. "Love Island."

Just then, Paige's phone rang. "S and S Investigations," she answered. She listened. "Who? Yes, I've heard of the SOS Agency, but who are you?" She turned to mouth a quick "*oh my god*" to Sophie.

"Who is it?" Sophie whispered.

"I see. Yes. We can meet you tomorrow. That's fine. Send me the address."

She disconnected and turned to Sophie who was waiting expectantly.

"Well, well, well," Paige said, a smile spreading across her face.

12

The next morning, Paige and Sophie were on their way to meet with Mike Warren at his residence in St Mary's Bay. The rest of the previous day had been spent tailing Natasha through the entirety of her rather indulgent lifestyle, from which they'd gathered no further clues. After a bit more window shopping, she'd gotten her nails done, had a massage, and then returned home at around six o'clock. Less than ten minutes later Don's car had pulled into the driveway. At this point, they'd clocked off, planning to go over what they'd learned and decide on the next steps the following day. They'd also relayed to Leo the revelation that Natasha's friend had been speaking Russian one moment, then English with a strong Manchester accent the next. Given Natasha's reaction, they both suspected a British accent might also be lurking under Natasha's Russian drawl, and this was a good avenue to pursue. While it wasn't the clue of the century, it was a lead and one they could follow. And Leo was rather pleased to receive this news because figuring out who 'Natasha from Russia' really was had so far proved to be rather challenging.

As they pulled up at Mike's address, Sophie, in the passenger seat this time, glanced at Paige, still grinning ear-to-ear.

"You're loving this, aren't you?"

"Are you not?" Paige cackled. "It's so perfect."

"Karma," Sophie agreed.

"Ooh, I wonder if Richard knows," Paige said excitedly. "I hope I get to tell him. We should go see him after this."

"If you want to confront Richard, you can leave me out of it," Sophie said.

Unlike Paige, Sophie did not enjoy a 'good confrontation'. Generally, she avoided them like the plague.

Yesterday afternoon, Paige had called back Mike to get more information and Mike had ended up confessing the whole sordid background of how SOS Agency got started after meeting Richard Thinton. Richard had been trying to find them financial backers but had been stymied somewhat by Covid. Now, in some sort of karmic twist of fate, Mike's best friend and business partner was missing, and since Mike was not a real investigator he had no clue how to find him. And so he'd reached out to the real detectives, S & S Investigations, for help.

Paige cackled again. "It's so good, I can't even stand it."

"Aren't you mad that Richard was behind the SOS Agency?"

"Honestly? I think on some level I'd already figured it out. I knew something was up with that whole thing. It was fishy from the get-go."

They got out of the car and walked up the path to a large and rather impressive-looking villa.

"This is Mike's house?" Sophie said.

Paige consulted her phone. "No, his is the cottage at the back. We're supposed to go down the side of the house."

And so they did, walking down the narrow path towards the rather cute cottage in behind. As the pathway took them past the neighbour's house, Sophie saw a woman's face pop up in the front window and then in a second one farther back, clearly following their progress by running from one room to the next. She didn't wave or offer any other greeting, she just kept staring, apparently without awareness that the see-through nature of windows worked both ways—the object of her attention could see in just as clearly as she could see out.

"Come on, Soph," Paige called as she went to knock on Mike's door.

When it opened, Paige eyed Mike up and down with blatant suspicion. "So you're the culprit."

Mike looked taken aback. "Pardon? No, I want you to find Michael."

"The culprit behind SOS Agency," Sophie clarified.

"Really, Richard is the one," Mike started, then changed tack. "But, yes, I'm sorry. I feel bad about all that."

Sophie suspected his apology wasn't entirely genuine. At least, he didn't actually *feel bad*, because there wasn't any real emotion in his eyes or his voice.

"Come in."

They followed him into a cosy living room. "Cup of tea?" he asked.

"Peppermint, if you've got it," Sophie said.

"Not for me," Paige replied.

"Back in a tick."

As Mike bustled away and the sounds of a kettle boiling and other tea preparations floated out of the kitchen, Sophie looked around the room. The whole thing was rather charming, she concluded. It was small, but not at all claustrophobic.

"Kind of like Leo's setup, eh?" Paige said. "A unit at the back of the main house."

"I suppose. This is bigger, though. Leo's is a proper granny flat."

Neither Mike nor Leo were grannies, obviously, but this term had originated because small self-contained units were often built at the back of properties for elderly relatives. Perhaps because women generally outlived men, it was more likely to be the granny in the flat.

As soon as Mike returned with two cups of tea, Paige pulled out her small black notepad.

"We'll listen to your situation and then provide you with an estimate for the work. You'll then need to pay a retainer before we start the case."

"Fine, fine," Mike said, taking a seat on the armchair opposite. "I last saw Michael on Tuesday afternoon. On Wednesday lunchtime I discovered evidence of a struggle and that he'd disappeared."

"We'll need to see this evidence."

"Of course."

"Did you go to the police?" Sophie asked.

"Yes, but they won't tell me anything. Because I'm not the owner of the house and Michael's car and wallet and phone are also gone, they're not interested."

"Who is the owner of the house?"

"Michael's father."

"You've tried calling Michael, obviously," Paige said.

"Phone is switched off."

"Have you checked with Michael's other friends?"

"No one knows where he is."

"We'll still need a list of their names."

Mike looked pained. "I suppose you want their contact details as well?"

"Ideally, but if not, first and last name will have to do."

"All of them?" His voice took on a whiny quality.

"Do you want us to find him or not?"

"How long have you known Michael?" Sophie asked.

"About fifteen years. Since university."

"Do you know his family?"

"Yes, and I even tried his father who's currently in Singapore. His secretary said she'd relay the message."

"And he hasn't called you back?"

"No." Mike looked away, a splash of red appearing on his cheeks.

"Is there an issue with him?" Sophie asked. "Michael's father?"

"He thinks I have "a predilection for drama"," Mike said, using air quotes. "He's said that more than once. He's not my biggest fan, but he's not overtly hostile or anything."

"What about Michael's own relationship with his father?" Sophie asked.

Mike thought for a moment. "A bit distant in that kind of posh way, but fine. No issues."

"We'll have to call him as well," Paige said.

"If you must."

"Anyone Michael has had trouble with recently?"

Mike shook his head quickly. "The only person I can think of is his latest girlfriend. Ex, I should say."

"He broke it off?" Sophie asked.

"He always does, a bit of a commitment-phobe our Michael, a heart-breaker. I don't think she was particularly thrilled with it ending the way it did."

"Do you have her name and contact information?"

"I only have her first name. Olivia."

"How recently did they break up?" Sophie asked.

"Oh, very. Last week, maybe? Or a couple of weeks ago?"

"Okay, let's see the scene of the crime," Paige said, flipping shut her notepad and standing up.

Paige and Sophie followed Mike up to the main house. He unlocked the back door and led them through the kitchen to the hall.

"The back door is always locked?"

"Yes."

"And it was on the day Michael went missing?" Sophie added.

"I always, *always* lock it," Mike said vehemently. "I'm very security conscious."

Sophie made a quick note in her own notepad. His overly eager assertion suggested he perhaps hadn't been so vigilant in the past. Or that he possibly doubted whether he had in fact locked it on the day Michael disappeared.

"What about other security. Alarms, etc."

"Normal locks on the doors, and there is an alarm, but Michael doesn't use it very often. He's quite trusting, you know. And he knows that even if he's not there, the housekeeper will be, or I go into the house sometimes."

"Because?" Paige said.

"Because?" Mike repeated.

"Why do you go into his house sometimes?"

"Oh, to use the kitchen or just hang out next to the fire. Whatever. He doesn't mind. It's such a big place."

"And you have the alarm code?"

"Yeah, it's in my phone but like I said, I've never had to use it, the alarm is only ever set when the both of us are away."

In the hall, they stopped next to a few brownish marks on the runner.

"Blood," Mike said.

Paige took a photo. "Not a lot of blood, though."

"You're sure it appeared around the same time Michael went missing?" Sophie asked. "It's not an old stain?"

"The housekeeper would have cleaned it up by now."

Paige turned to Mike. "There's a housekeeper?"

"Yes." Mike stared dumbly at her.

Silence fell.

When it became obvious Mike wasn't going to say anything else, Paige let out an exasperated sigh. "Maybe she's a good person to ask about Michael?"

"Why?"

"If she's here regularly, she might have seen him," Sophie interjected before Paige could say something tactless. "He might have had a guest or something."

"Right. Uh, I'll ask her tomorrow."

"Give her our information and tell her to call us." Paige handed him another of their business cards.

"Okay." Mike took it then gestured for them to continue. "There's more," he said as he led them to the front-facing room in which a lamp had been knocked over and a plant had spilled some of its soil. "I haven't touched anything. I found it like this."

"So your theory is that someone struggled with Michael in here, the struggle moved out to the hall and maybe they knocked him over the head or one of them suffered a superficial wound—"

"He could have been—"

"It's not enough blood to be a deadly injury," Paige interrupted. "And then they took him away in his own car?"

"I was thinking Michael probably let them in since the locks on both doors are intact and there aren't any broken windows or anything."

Sophie made a note.

"The person knocked on the door and Michael either knew them or trusted them enough to let them inside," he continued.

"Possible," Paige conceded. "But you can't think of anyone, apart from Olivia, who might be responsible? He had no enemies?"

Mike shook his head. "People tend to like him. I'm the one they object to." Suddenly, he looked sad.

"Okay. If you think of anything, let us know, but otherwise we'll write up a quote for the work and send it through later today."

"Thanks." Mike seemed relieved. "I'll show you out the front."

As they emerged from the house and started towards the car, the woman from next door who Sophie had seen following their progress down the side of the house came tearing out but then suddenly stopped as if she didn't quite know what she was doing. She quickly turned around and ran back inside.

"Weird," Paige said as she and Sophie got into the car.

As she started the engine, the woman appeared in the front window of her home, staring at them with a pair of binoculars.

"Well," Paige said. "I'm no expert in human behaviour but that doesn't seem particularly normal."

"No," Sophie agreed. "No it does not."

13

Late Friday afternoon, Leo and Zelda were settled at a corner table in a campus café, both drinking hot chocolate. Leo, who'd attended only one year of university before deciding his time was better spent teaching himself how to be a hacker, was quite enjoying being on campus this time around. It helped that he was only there to meet Zelda and didn't have any exams to study for, coursework to read, or early lectures to get up at an ungodly hour for, of course.

"So what's new? I haven't spoken to Paige and Sophie in ages," Zelda said. "We should really have a team meeting or something. We should have one every month."

Leo didn't want to tell her they'd recently had one of these catchup meetings without Zelda, nor that they did in fact meet quite regularly. But she had a point about a scheduled monthly catchup with all four of them.

"Good idea. I'll suggest it to Sophie."

It wasn't lost on either of them that Paige was a little standoffish, terse, sometimes almost rude to Zelda, but Leo had assured her she was generally a little prickly with everyone. Which was true. He hoped Paige would soften towards Zelda at some point. But he also thought it maybe wasn't a huge problem because it didn't really bother Zelda so much.

"I know what Paige has me working on, but what about you?" Zelda asked.

Leo grinned. "A possible Black Widow Situation, as Paige puts it."

"A woman who marries then kills her husbands?" Zelda leaned forwards, eyes wide. "Tell me everything." Suddenly, she scowled. "Why don't I get put on cases like that?"

"I guess because you're still new?"

Zelda made an annoyed sound and looked out the window. Leo made a mental note to talk to Paige about Zelda's work. The last thing he wanted was for her to leave their little team.

"I still want to hear about the case," she said eventually, turning back.

"Sure." Leo gave her a rundown. As they chatted and theorised and sipped their drinks, Leo tried not to think about all the sugar and calories in hot chocolate. The fainting spell from a month or so ago had been a bit of a wakeup call, and while he wasn't quite able to give up the whole calorie-counting and exercise thing completely, he had taken on board what Sophie had said about overdoing it. And after reading the two articles she'd sent him about orthorexia (being unhealthily obsessed with being 'healthy' was an actual thing!) as well the disordered gym-obsession culture, Leo could recognise that some of the guys he'd been following online were a little extreme in their approach. And that spending hours staring at yourself in the mirror, being obsessed with body fat percentage and muscle mass, and counting the protein percentage of every molecule you put in your body was problematic (if not a full-blown eating disorder), plain and simple.

"Hey, what do you know about Richard Thinton?" Zelda said.

"Paige's ex-supervisor? Why?"

"He comes up when I look at postgrad psychology programmes."

"He's a total dick. He keeps trying to sabotage S and S Investigations."

"He does?" Zelda raised her eyebrows with interest.

"Both Paige and Sophie turned down working with him." Leo scratched his head. "I think that's the only reason. He's bitter and used to getting his own way. According to Paige, anyway."

Zelda nodded, thoughtful. "I know the type."

Leo's phone buzzed. "Oh, it's Roman." He smiled. "DS Leconte," he added. "You haven't met him yet, but he's cool. He and Sophie have this kind of epic will-they-won't-they situation."

"Epic?" Zelda said with a smile, but Leo's attention was on his phone.

Free for a beer and food? Roman's message read.

Sure, Leo replied immediately. **Where?**

How about somewhere in Kingsland?

Sounds good.

"Hey, I have to get going soon."

Zelda lifted her gaze to meet his. "You do?"

"Yeah, Roman needs me."

"Oh." Zelda frowned and looked down.

Leo took in her bummed-out expression and then frowned himself. "What's wrong?"

"Nothing." Zelda shrugged. "I just thought we might get dinner."

"You did?" Leo felt confused. "But we didn't—"

"I know...." She waved her hand, then tucked her hair behind her ear. "I guess I thought we might both be hungry and could go down to one of the High Street places for food or something."

"Oh."

Leo stared at her for a moment, conflicted. "You can join us if you like?"

"It sounds like I'd be interrupting Bro-Time."

"Huh?"

"Don't worry. It's no big deal," she said, abruptly dropping her attention to her lap and fiddling with her phone.

"Okay, cool."

Leo nodded to himself. No big deal. Because he and Zelda hadn't made plans which meant he was free for dinner. As he slid his phone into his bag and located his bus pass, he felt pleased with himself. The old Leo would probably have already fallen in love and had his heart broken by Zelda by now. No, he would no longer be making assumptions about anything.

Zelda was his friend and colleague and they hung out sometimes. End of story.

"Okay, see you later," he said. "I'll mention that meeting thing to Sophie."

"Sure," Zelda mumbled, offering up a half wave before looking down again.

As Leo walked out of the café, he felt a tiny twinge of uncertainty, but pushed it away. They were friends, that was all.

· · • • • • • • · ·

At nearly six o'clock, Sophie and Paige pulled up outside Don and Natasha's home for their definitely-not-breaking-and-entering snooping session.

The street was quiet. It wasn't a throughway and there weren't even many cars parked on the street. Most of these houses had two-door garages and then extra space on their driveway for all their automobiles. Sophie wondered, not for the first time, whether her old and slightly junky Volkswagen Jetta might get noticed by some meddlesome neighbour and reported as being out-of-place. But they weren't doing anything wrong. They were following their client's wishes.

"Okay, let's do this." Paige hopped out of the car.

"I'm going to record with my phone," Sophie said once she'd also exited. "So we can go over the footage later."

"Good thinking."

Paige used the spare key Kate had dropped off to unlock the door then entered the alarm code in the pad to the left. Once this beeped green, Sophie let out a breath of relief.

Paige smiled. "Told you it would be fine."

They walked through the living room. Sophie gestured at the pool area. "Shall we check out the pool and pool house first?"

"Sure."

With Sophie recording on her phone, they walked slowly around the pool and spa pool area. The pool was covered up, clearly not used much in winter. The spa pool was also covered, possibly because of recent events. Apart from pool cleaning equipment stacked neatly to one side and the patio furniture set, there wasn't anything else to see.

"Nothing," Paige said, sounding disappointed.

When they entered the pool house, where Bruce had stayed, they found it similarly sparse. It was a basic room clearly meant for overnight guests or perhaps a place designed for parents to banish teens once they became too messy, unruly or smelly. It had an ensuite bathroom, a double bed, a small coffee table and two chairs, and a minifridge. Paige went over and opened the door. Inside were a few bottles of beer and an unopened bottle of tonic water. The room had clearly been cleaned since Bruce slept there.

"I guess any evidence is gone," Paige said.

"There possibly wasn't any evidence to start with."

"Okay, let's go back to the house and snoop through Natasha's stuff. We still know almost nothing about her."

They returned to the house and after a quick check of the downstairs rooms, headed up the stairs to locate the master bedroom.

"How are we going to figure out if she's actually British?" Paige said. "Oh, we could confront her and you could do your lie-detecting thing?"

Sophie made an uncertain face. "I think Leo is our best bet."

"But he hasn't had any luck, right?"

"With no maiden name and a possibly fake first name, it can't be easy."

"We need to find out where Natasha came from and what she was up to before she met Don. Whether there's a pattern of dodgy behaviour."

They stepped inside the master bedroom. "Urgh, going through a couple's private space is kind of gross," Sophie said.

"Does Natasha potentially being English instead of Russian make her more or less likely to be a Black Widow, do you think?" Paige said, clearly not feeling as creeped-out as Sophie.

"I don't know but it would certainly confirm that she's not who she claims to be, which is something we can take back to Kate."

Inside the huge built-in wardrobe that spanned the entire wall of the bedroom, they found a rack of what were clearly Don's clothes, and large rack of Natasha's garments.

"Where does she keep her personal papers and things?" Paige mused. "You know, all that crap that you accumulate and have to keep because it's important but you also don't need handy. Ooh, like your passport."

"Good question." Sophie nodded. "Mine is all in my desk drawer in my room. What about you?"

Paige was thoughtful. "Some of it is in the hall table, and the rest is in the spare room. It's all merged with Tim's." A funny expression suddenly flitted across Paige's face but she shook it off. "We have a cupboard filled with stuff."

Sophie, noticing the expression, waited a beat in case Paige wanted to say something else, then continued. "One of those rooms downstairs was clearly Don's home office-slash-mancave," she said. "And the other two were obviously spare rooms, but maybe Natasha has her own space up here somewhere?"

"Let's go look."

Sophie was pleased to leave the master bedroom without having to inspect the contents of the bedside table (not just yet anyway).

And so they went in search of Natasha's 'woman cave'. In the room on the other side of yet another bathroom, at the end of the hall, they found it. Inside was a yoga mat with some small weights piled neatly nearby, and then in the other corner, right by the window, a sewing station.

"She sews," Sophie said. "Huh."

They both walked over to the desk on which the sewing machine sat and while Sophie opened the cupboard behind it to find a rather impressive array of threads and fabric and buttons and zippers, Paige started going through the drawers of the desk.

"Anything?" Sophie asked, turning to look at Paige who was now rather aggressively flinging papers about. "Are you going to be able to put that back in the same place again? So she won't know?"

Paige immediately stopped. "Erm...." She continued to shuffle through the contents of the two desk drawers in a much more orderly manner for another minute but then closed the drawers and straightened. "Nothing that looks relevant." She nodded at the sewing cupboard. "Anything in there?"

"Lots of sewing stuff."

"What about that?" Paige pointed at the very bottom of the cupboard where two plastic storage containers sat. Unlike the rest of the cupboard, nothing glittery or cloth-like was visible through the clear plastic.

They both kneeled down and pulled out a box each.

"Okay this is more like it," Sophie said, starting through an assortment of old Christmas cards and a bunch of photos of Natasha looking glamorous with an array of other equally glamorous women.

"Aha!" Paige cried.

"Her passport?" Sophie said hopefully.

"No." She held up an envelope.

"What's that?"

"It's addressed to Stacey Morris."

"That could be Natasha's real name."

The two grinned at each other until a loud clatter rang through the house.

"Crap. Did they come home early?" Paige said.

They returned the containers to the cupboard then crept as quietly as they could downstairs. Tiptoeing through the living room, they scanned the area to locate the source of the sound but found nothing.

"Maybe it came from next door?" Sophie whispered.

They both straightened. "Yeah, maybe," Paige replied.

But in the next moment, with a shriek of distress, a woman rushed in from the hall, her face red and her eyes wild. "You!" she screeched at Sophie.

"I think I forgot to lock the door behind us," said Paige.

"Natasha," the woman hissed, lunging again at Sophie. "How dare you."

"N-no." As Sophie took a step back, Paige stepped in between the red-faced woman and her friend.

"Who are you?" Paige demanded pushing on the woman's shoulders to keep her back. "You can't just show up and attack people."

The woman jerked back, seeming confused.

"And this is Sophie, not Natasha. Who are you?" Paige waited for a moment but the woman didn't reply. "What. Is. Your. Name?" Paige clapped her hands near the woman's face.

She drew back even farther, looking bewildered, but seemed to snap out of her cloud of anger. "Patricia."

"Patricia who?"

"Bruce's wife." Suddenly her face crumpled and she started sobbing. Loud snuffling noises and shuddering shoulders immediately followed.

Sophie, mostly recovered from the shock of nearly being attacked, ushered Patricia into a nearby seat and then hurried over to the kitchen to get her a glass of water.

"Bruce the guy who was found in the pool?" Paige asked excitedly.

Patricia nodded, her chin still hunched into her chest.

Sophie handed her the glass of water. "Drink some of this."

"Why are you after Natasha?" Paige asked once Patricia had loudly slurped back some liquid.

"Because they had an affair."

14

Saturday morning, Paige and Sophie arrived at S & S Investigations ready to put in a full day of work. They'd agreed to work this weekend because they had only a limited timeframe to access Don and Natasha's house. Today, they would go over the recording Sophie had taken and discuss what Patricia had told them as well as everything they'd learned so far. If they needed to go back and have another look they had Saturday night and Sunday morning to do so.

"Since we're working this weekend," Paige said, her voice sounding weird, "I'm going away for a couple of nights. I mean, Tim and I are going away. We'll leave Tuesday night, be away Wednesday, back on deck Thursday morning. You should do the same. Take Wednesday off. We could leave Leo and Zelda in charge again, just in case."

"They seemed to enjoy that, didn't they?" Sophie said, smiling. Paige didn't reply. Sophie took in Paige's uncertain expression and her hunched posture and added, "Hey, is everything okay?"

"Tim booked a few days off work and said that since I seem to be working weekends at the moment, I should take some time midweek for us to get away. He kind of insisted."

"Where are you going?"

Paige shrugged. "Tim is sorting it out. Not far. Maybe Omaha? He promised me a fireplace." Paige gave Sophie a small, tense smile.

"If you want to talk about anything, just let me know, okay?" Sophie said, squeezing Paige's arm.

"Thanks. We'll see." Paige pushed back her shoulders and lifted her chin. "Right. Let's go over the case."

Last night, they'd established that Patricia didn't have any proof of Bruce and Natasha's affair, she'd just made a grief-stricken assumption after finding a blurry photo of Natasha on Bruce's phone. After reviewing said photo, Paige and Sophie had agreed that this grainy, candid photo to which Natasha appeared oblivious (she was in her bikini and standing by the pool but looking away), was probably an opportunistic snap Bruce had taken so he could ogle it later at his leisure.

To Patricia, however, they'd said they would look into it. And then Paige had given her a business card and added, "For a fee, of course".

As Paige poured them both coffee, Sophie transferred the video she'd recorded on her phone last night to her laptop.

"What if we got a big screen?" Paige said, setting down their coffees. "It could go across the far wall. We could use it to look at clues and footage but also have movies nights here at the office."

Sophie threw a sceptical look her way. "Tell you what. If we end up doing this, reviewing footage for a case, *four more times*, we can get a projector or a big screen."

"Agreed." Paige nodded happily. At the whiteboard, she added Patricia's name to the suspect list.

"Do you think?" Sophie said, wrinkling her nose.

"Not really, but I think at this point we should be more inclusive and not rule people out. And she didn't have an alibi for the night Bruce died."

"Asleep at home." Sophie nodded. "With her husband at Don and Natasha's house."

"She'd have known where he was, and if she thought he was having an affair she could have driven over there and confronted him. They could have gone out to the pool area to talk and she could have pushed him in and held him under. Even if the coroner rules accidental drowning, if he didn't struggle that must be hard to prove."

"It's definitely possible," Sophie conceded.

Paige returned to the table to hold up the envelope she'd swiped from the house. "Do you think Stacey Morris is Natasha?"

After a quick internet search on the way home last night, it had been immediately obvious that they would not have their answer quickly. There were far too many people named Stacey Morris in the world. But they'd sent the name to Leo, along with an explanation, and he was on the case.

"I think Leo will figure it out. He has Natasha's photo from her current Facebook page, so it might be a bit of a painful trawl through the internet, but he'll get there."

"Okay, let's start the footage you took and make sure we didn't miss anything."

For a few minutes they watched Sophie's rather shaky recording as they walked through the house.

"I'm going to do this job next time," Paige said with a loud tsk. "I'm starting to get motion sickness."

"It's harder than it looks, okay?"

"Stop," Paige cried. "What's that?" she pointed at a dark blob in the corner of the frame.

Sophie sucked in a breath. "That's a security camera."

"Rewind the footage. Is there a camera covering the spa pool?"

Less than a minute later they had their answer. Not one but two cameras were located on the outside of the house, looking down over the pool area.

"Well, well, well," Paige said.

"We're going to need to see that footage," Sophie said.

"We sure are."

Sophie frowned. "Hang on. Why is this the first we're learning of possible footage. Why didn't Don immediately review the cameras to see what happened."

"Maybe he did."

"But when you asked Roman about the case it's not as if he said oh there's no case, we know what happened from the camera footage."

"He did not."

They looked at each other.

"How strange," Sophie said after a while.

· · · · ● · ● · · ·

Kate inched the car forwards, making sure she kept close behind her father's SUV as she followed him off the Waiheke Island car ferry. Don and Natasha had taken Don's larger than necessary jeep but Kate had convinced a reluctant Jack and an indifferent Madison to travel with her and Tina. Kate wanted one last chance to talk to them about Natasha but all three of them had been obstinately refusing to do so in a way that made Kate wonder if it was pre-planned. As if they had had a meeting to discuss 'the Kate situation' and decided on their own plan of attack. Namely, to ignore her insistence on discussing Natasha as a possible murderer. Or attempted murderer.

The wine that had been consumed by Kate's three passengers during the 45-minute ferry ride from downtown Auckland hadn't helped matters. Jack, who'd arrived at the ferry terminal looking even more exhausted than usual, had been pressing drinks onto everyone. He seemed intent on spending the weekend getting drunk and making sure everyone else did too. Kate was now surrounded by people singing (badly) to Taylor Swift's Blank Space at top volume and she already had a headache. Hopefully she would have a chance to nap before dinner tonight. Or maybe she could beg off dinner this evening altogether. Based on the way the day was going so far, she suspected it might turn into one of those chaotic evenings in which further drinks were consumed and no one ended up sitting down for dinner at all.

And her father had already confessed that two of his buddies, Stanley and Russell, who together with Don and the late Bruce had made up a golf foursome, were also going to be on Waiheke this weekend. Kate, having known her father her whole life, understood quite clearly that this meant Don planned to spend the majority of the weekend golfing, leaving Natasha to 'get to know everyone better' without him. He'd already said he would be out most of the day tomorrow and they should all take advantage of the vineyards Waiheke was famous for. They would all convene for dinner at Mudbrick, a restaurant attached to one of these vineyards, which would no doubt be delicious and all paid for by her father, but Kate still felt resentful. Her father had always been self-serving though. Why did this behaviour continue to surprise her? God, how she had been stupid enough to expect anything else.

"What's up, Katiekins?" Tina leaned over to ask, using the nickname she only used when she was tipsy.

"Nothing."

"Please don't be grumpy," Tina said, her wine-breath reaching Kate and ratcheting up her annoyance.

"I know your dad might end up being AWOL but we can still have a good time. We should try to make friends with Natasha, don't you think?"

"Sure, whatever," Kate mumbled. Tina's dispositional optimism was both attractive and irritating.

Kate's prediction for Friday evening turned out to be correct. While her father connected with his friends, Jack, Madison, Tina and Natasha spent the rest of Friday drinking and snacking at the large villa Don had rented for their stay. Kate, however, had made herself a sensible sandwich from the groceries she picked up on the Island, then taken a single glass of wine up to her room to pretend to read her book while she actually let her bad mood fester into a stench.

The next day Kate, annoyed with herself and tired of being the wet blanket of the weekend, got up early and took a walk along the beach, determined to shake it off. She let herself appreciate the beautiful green rolling hills as she walked along the beach, an invigorating activity in winter, with the bracing wind playing with her hair and pleasantly numbing her cheeks.

By the time she got back and had stepped out of a long, hot, shower, she was ready to have a good time.

That afternoon, with everyone else's hangovers drifting away into vague memories, Don left for more golfing and the rest of them went wine tasting. By the time they all met up at the Mudbrick restaurant, everyone, including Kate, was feeling merry. Kate was not at all surprised to see Stanley and Russell show up to dinner with her father, but dismissed the small flicker of irritation immediately. All throughout her childhood he'd hijacked family dinners for the purpose of advancing business goals. Typical Don.

"Told you," her father bellowed as he playfully (but not entirely jokingly) punched Russell in the arm. "Last time was a fluke and you know it."

Russell said something under his breath that Kate couldn't hear but could still tell was not at all polite.

"Right then fellows. Piss off, would you? I've got the family here. I'll see you tomorrow." Don said, slapping both of them on the backs and giving them a little shove. Kate was as surprised at this turn of events as Russell and Stanley seemed to be, and thought her father had probably intimated that he'd buy them dinner. Classic Don power move. She watched as they exchanged glances and head shakes then walked over to see the maître D about another table.

Once they'd all taken seats and a waiter had appeared Don took it upon himself to order both wine and a range of food for the table.

"We don't get to choose our own dinners?" Madison said to Jack, fairly quietly but not timed particularly well, with Don pausing his instructions long enough to take a sip of water as well as to hear what she said.

"What's that?" Don said loudly. "Being ungrateful are we? I thought you liked free meals, Madison."

Madison cleared her throat. "I don't eat meat."

Don snorted and rolled his eyes.

"The grilled eggplant please," Madison said to the waiter. "And the broccolini as a side," she added.

"Listen—" Don began.

"You know what, Dad?" Kate said suddenly, unable to hold it in any longer. "You don't seem very upset about Bruce." She could hear the slight slur in her voice, but at this point she didn't really care. She was sick of his bullying.

"I should be crying all over the place like some little girl?" Don sneered.

"When's the funeral?" Jack asked, clearly trying stop this escalating into a fight.

Don eyeballed Kate until she looked down, then answered his son. "Friday. I expect you all there, by the way."

Natasha, who hadn't said much at all at this point, suddenly stood up and said, "Shut up. Please. I am hippo. A hungry, hungry hippo."

Everyone turned to look at her, the table quiet for a moment. Tina was the first to laugh, a bubble of mirth that erupted from her mouth. It caught quickly, like a flame applied to dry kindling, as Jack, Madison, Don and finally Kate also started chuckling. And so, the tone was set and by the end of the evening, spirits (and blood-alcohol levels) remained high and the group eventually returned to the villa without anything that resembled an argument.

Kate didn't know what it was that woke her later, but when she did she immediately knew she was going to be sick. She lurched to the toilet and threw up as discretely as possible. Once she was done, she cleaned her teeth and headed out to the kitchen. She wasn't cut out for all that rich food and wine. She didn't know how her father did it on such a regular basis.

As she filled a glass with water from the kitchen tap, something on the patio caught her eye. A shape, in the spa pool.

"Oh, god. Not again," she cried, rushing forwards.

15

The intriguing revelation about the cameras at the Dash residence would have to wait until Monday because Kate had not answered Paige's call and neither had Roman.

Today, Sunday, Paige and Sophie were focusing on the Missing Michael case and this afternoon were on their way to ambush Michael's most recent ex, Olivia, as she went about her day. Even though Sophie reminded Paige it was Sunday and they shouldn't expect Leo and Zelda to be checking emails or working, Paige had still sent them each a message with instructions. "I didn't tell them they had to complete their tasks today," Paige reasoned. "They can do them on Monday."

Leo was to work on a contact list for everyone in Michael's life, and she'd tasked Zelda with the job of contacting them all to see if they knew anything about his disappearance. If anyone acted suspiciously or was hard to get hold of, they'd be passed over to Paige and Sophie to look into. After updating the whiteboard, the delegation of investigative duties to their small team was perhaps one of Paige's favourite things to do.

If Olivia's Facebook feed was at all accurate, she could currently be found at the arts and craft market in Mt Eden. Olivia had been easy to locate online because she and Michael were still Facebook friends. Over lunch, Paige and Sophie had scoured social media to put together a timeline of their fairly brief relationship and this Sophie was studying as Paige drove them to their destination.

"It doesn't seem like theirs was the relationship of the century, does it?" Sophie said, finally looking up.

"Why?"

"Because if they were really hot and heavy and then they split, they would have unfriended each other and even deleted each other from their timeline."

"True."

"Based on this, they met around four months ago and their last public outing or posting, I guess, was nearly a month ago. But she could still tell us something about him and his life," Sophie mused.

"Depending on how this goes, we might have to dig deeper into Michael's dating past."

"Yeah, Mike made it sound like there were a few ex-girlfriends, didn't he," Sophie said. "But on the other hand, it's possible that's because of Mike's own relative inexperience."

"How'd you know he's inexperienced?"

Sophie thought for a moment. "I can just tell."

Paige suppressed a smile. "Fair enough. I trust your judgement."

"Let's ask Leo to create a subcategory in his list. Michael's Romantic Past."

"And Zelda is also working on getting us access to Michael's family," Paige said. "Just because his dad is in Singapore and his sister is in Tauranga doesn't mean they can't help." Paige glanced at Sophie. "It would also be helpful to know what the police are doing."

Sophie's eyes slid to Paige. "You think we should ask Roman?"

"I tried calling this morning and he didn't answer."

"I think we should limit our Roman favour requests to just the important ones, don't you?"

"It would be good to know if they're treating it as a suspicious disappearance. Just because Mike doesn't live in Michael's house doesn't mean he can't file a police report."

"But you're not going to tell him that." Sophie raised her eyebrows.

"Of course not, he's a grown-up. But we should be aware of what the police are doing." She looked over at Sophie again. "Haven't you and Roman broken the ice?"

"Um, sure." Sophie looked out the window and Paige returned her attention to the road. "I'll message him later."

"Okay, we're here."

The craft fair was taking place in a church on Mt Eden road. After more than ten minutes of driving in circles and getting clogged up in the relentless stream of Mt Eden Road traffic, they found a park and walked for nearly five minutes back to the church. Inside was a crowded but contained space so it only took one circuit of both Paige and Sophie scanning each face they passed before Paige spotted Olivia on the other side near the entrance/exit.

"Ooh, there she is, and it looks as if she's leaving." Paige hurried over to where Olivia was pulling on her coat. Olivia was taller than average, with dark hair and green eyes and a kind of preppy-yet-alternative clothing style.

"Olivia?" Paige said, coming to an abrupt stop in front of her.

"Yes?" She looked from Paige to Sophie who'd just caught up.

"Can we talk to you for a few minutes?"

She looked confused. "Do I know you?"

"No." Paige handed her a business card. "We're investigators and we're looking into the disappearance of Michael Lindell."

Olivia's eyes went wide. "What?"

"Tuesday night was the last time he was seen, we believe."

All the colour drained from her face. She pulled at her scarf and cast frantic eyes around the room. When they finally latched onto something over Paige's shoulder, both Paige and Sophie turned around. A hipsterish guy with a beard and a beanie was walking directly towards them. He tilted his head and adopted an uncertain half-smile as if he wasn't sure about something.

And when they turned back to Olivia, she'd gone.

· · • • · • • • · ·

Paige and Sophie took seats at Frasers restaurant on Mt Eden Road and ordered a flat white coffee (Paige), a peppermint tea (Sophie) and a beer for Leo who was on his way (and who definitely misunderstood Paige's intentions when she messaged him to say they were right around the corner and did he want to join them for a drink).

"Olivia got out of there fast," Paige said, pulling her notepad out of her bag.

"She sure did."

They'd both run out of the church after Olivia, but she'd evaporated into the ether. When they'd gone back inside to see if the hipster guy knew anything, he'd also disappeared.

"Her expression when you mentioned Michael's disappearance...." Sophie said.

"I know. Even I picked up on that reaction. The question is, why did she freak out?" Paige tapped her pen against the table.

As the server delivered their drinks, Leo appeared in the doorway.

"Leo," Paige called, waving him over.

"Hey." He pulled out the third chair of their small table and picked up his beer. "Cheers." He took a sip then set it down. "How's it going?"

"Where's your laptop?" Paige asked.

"Why would I bring... oh. Is this a work thing?" Leo made an unimpressed face.

Paige raised one eyebrow. "We need you to do a deep dive on Olivia Carson. We need her address pronto."

"But it's Sunday."

"I know but she might be the culprit and she could be destroying evidence right now."

Sophie glanced at Paige. "I'm not sure that's—"

"It's possible."

Leo sighed and stood up again. "Okay, I'll be back in a second. Don't drink my beer," he warned, mostly joking. Neither Sophie nor Paige were beer drinkers.

Paige picked up her phone. "I'll see if I can find that hipster dude in her friend list."

"Good idea," Sophie said, pulling out her own phone. But not to go on Facebook. Instead, she took this opportunity to message Roman. Since Paige had told her to take Wednesday off, a seed of an idea had sprouted. And now that Paige had essentially ordered her to ask Roman about the Michael case, she felt weirdly emboldened to put her idea into action. Because Roman had a lead on Chris Connolly, the ex-cop who worked on Terry Garnet's case. He was living in Te Awamutu. Only a few hours' drive from Auckland, and Roman thought it was worth a trip down to talk to him about Terry's case.

Sophie, forcing herself not to overthink the situation, typed out a quick message to Roman.

Hey, how are you? I have Wednesday off if you think a trip to Te Awamutu is worthwhile.

Sophie set down her phone, trying to keep calm, but it pinged almost immediately with a reply. She grabbed at it, nearly knocking it off the table. Paige glanced at her, frowning as Sophie scrabbled to pick it up again.

I can take a half day on Wednesday, he said. **Pick you up at around two?**

Sounds good.

Sophie was able to resist the urge to sign off with an X but found she couldn't do anything about the huge grin now threatening to split her face in two. Was her face aflame? It sure felt hot. She raised one hand to touch her check.

"Are you alright?" Paige said, putting her phone down. "You look weird."

Sophie swallowed, forcing herself to act normal. "I'm fine."

Once Leo had returned, they got to work trawling the internet for information about Michael's evasive ex-girlfriend, Olivia.

"Okay, what do we know about Olivia?" Paige said after a while.

"Instagram has told me she has a dog. Acquired fairly recently. Last month, I think. A whippet named JoJo," Sophie said.

"A whippet?" Leo frowned.

"Yeah, they're like little greyhounds." Sophie showed him a photo.

"Cute," Leo said. He was a cat person but he could appreciate dogs as well.

"She went to Westlake Girls High and she likes crocheting," Sophie continued. "But there isn't any evidence she has a new boyfriend."

"And I can't find that hipster guy," Paige said, putting down her phone. "Olivia has nearly four hundred friends and he could be one of the ones with a picture of the beach or whatever as the profile photo. Plus he might not even know Olivia. He might have just happened to be walking towards the exit at that moment."

"Leo?" Sophie said. "How are you getting on?"

"I've found a residential address for her."

"Nice one."

"What is it?" Paige said, picking up her notepad and pen.

"But get this," Leo added, looking up to lock eyes with Paige then Sophie. "She's just deleted her Facebook profile."

Paige nodded as if she'd been expecting this to happen. "Well, well, well."

16

Monday morning, Paige and Sophie met Kate at S & S Investigations for a hastily scheduled meeting. Kate had taken the day off work and needed to talk to them too, apparently. Urgently.

"What happened?" Sophie said, taking in the grey tinge to Kate's cheeks.

"You don't look so great," Paige added unnecessarily.

"I feel as if I haven't slept in a week," Kate admitted. "This whole thing is getting to me. Someone is definitely trying to kill my father."

Paige and Sophie exchanged wide-eyed looks. "Something happened at Waiheke?" Sophie asked.

Kate nodded. "Natasha tried to drown him in the spa."

"The spa," Paige said. "Again?"

Kate shrugged. "It worked the first time."

"You saw her?" Sophie asked.

"Well, no."

"But... he's okay?"

Kate nodded, looking exhausted. "I must have interrupted her. He was face down in the pool but he was completely alone. I got there just in the nick of time."

"But you didn't actually see Natasha?" Sophie repeated.

"No."

"If he was alone, how do you know someone tried to drown him?"

"He said so. At least, at first. He'd had a lot to drink, we all had. After everyone went to bed he decided he wanted a spa. Sweat out the booze or something. He was sitting there, relaxing, when...." Kate trailed off.

"When?" Paige prompted.

"This is where the story gets murky. Okay, so here's what I saw. I went to the kitchen to get a glass of water and I saw him face down in the pool. I rushed over, yanked him up and got him sitting upright. I checked his pulse, which I could feel, and then he spluttered and came to." Kate shook her head. "He immediately said, "someone pushed me, they pushed my face under", but then when the others came out and he'd had a chance to kind of collect himself, he changed his story and said he just passed out. Based on the way I found him, sitting in the pool but slumped forwards, someone could have easily come up behind him and held his face under the water. With the amount he'd had to drink and in that position it would have been hard for him to struggle. I think I must have made enough noise coming downstairs for that person to hear me and run away. I sounded the alarm and then everyone came running." She wrapped her arms around her body. "God, it was terrifying."

"No one else was awake at first?"

"Not as far as I could tell. I yelled and called out for the others as soon as I saw Dad but it took about a minute for Jack and Madison to come out, both clearly having just woken up. They helped me get him out of the pool. Then Natasha and Tina appeared."

"Did you call an ambulance?"

"No. As soon as the others appeared he said he'd just fallen asleep and that I was overreacting." She rolled her eyes. "He refuses to admit what he said when I first pulled him out. He said I must have misheard. He basically implied I was being hysterical. He said he was fine and that's the end of it. God he's so stubborn."

"But you're sure that someone tried to drown him?"

"I didn't actually see a person holding his head under, but he definitely said someone held him under. At first, anyway. Why else would he have said that?" Kate looked unsure for a moment.

"If you're right, it was likely to be someone staying with you at the villa."

Kate nodded. "But everyone looked as if they'd been asleep."

"That wouldn't be hard to fake," Sophie said.

"We're going to need to talk to your family," Paige said.

"I know, but they won't like it. Especially Dad. Or Natasha, for obvious reasons. You'll have to ambush them and you'll probably have to pretend you're not investigators."

"Don't worry, that's my favourite approach," Paige said with a smile.

"Kate, do you know someone called Stacey Morris?" Sophie asked.

Kate frowned. "No. Should I?"

Sophie exchanged a look with Paige. "No, just a lead we're following up."

"How did the, ah, assessment of the house go?" Kate asked.

"Were you aware your dad has security cameras in the house?" Paige replied.

Kate's eyes went wide. "I had no idea." She went quiet for a moment. "It's a new house and I haven't been there as much as I would have, what with lockdowns and everything."

Paige turned her laptop around to show her some stills in which the cameras were clearly visible. "There could be more but there's definitely one in the living room, one at the front of the house and two out the back. One covers the pool house and another the pool area."

"But that changes everything," Kate said. "It would have captured Bruce's death."

Paige nodded. "Your dad hasn't said anything? Surely he would have reviewed the footage straight away."

"Not a word." Kate seemed puzzled. "And wouldn't the police have looked for a camera system? Surely they would have asked Dad the same question."

"Yes, that's what we wondered," Sophie said.

Kate thought some more. "Oh, the cameras must not be switched on. They must have been there when Dad bought the house and he hasn't bothered to activate them. Or remove them, I guess. Natasha is probably planning a big renovation." Kate rolled her eyes. "No point in doing anything until that happens."

"So as far as you're aware, your father isn't responsible for the cameras, they aren't active, and no one knows about them," Paige confirmed.

Kate started to chew on her thumbnail. "Maybe I should talk to Dad." She looked off into the distance for a moment, then suddenly stood up and hoisted her bag onto her shoulder. "I'll get back to you."

"So you'll talk to your father about the cameras?" Sophie said to clarify.

"Yes." She gave them a wide, nervous smile as she hurried out. "Talk soon," she called back.

Sophie eyed Paige. "That was a bit of a rapid exit."

"Sure was."

· · · ● · ● · · ·

A little surge of unease pulsed through Kate's stomach as she let herself into her father's home and deactivated the alarm. This whole security camera thing was worrying her and she wasn't entirely sure why. "Hello?" she called out as she walked down the hall, just in case. Both her father and Natasha were supposed to be out for the day getting massages and a detox wrap at some spa in the central city but sometimes plans change.

As Kate walked through the living room she glanced up at the small black circle in the corner of the ceiling. She'd definitely never noticed it before. Shouldn't there be a red blinking light or something? She carried on through to her father's home office. If he did have cameras recording the goings-on in this house, then he would have an onsite security console. He wouldn't use an app or anything like that. Not Don Dash.

Against one wall in the office was a L-shaped desk with a laptop, a landline and a tray of papers on one end and just a screen on the other. Kate's eyes latched onto this, the monitor that sat on the desk seemingly without a keyboard. She took a seat in her father's chair and found the keyboard and mouse on a roll-away tray under the desk. When she jiggled the mouse the monitor came to life and a series of icons appeared at the bottom of the screen, including one for a file manager which she double-clicked to open.

Immediately she saw rows and rows of file folders, labelled by date, starting in March, right after he bought the house. She sucked in a breath as the meaning hit home. The system wasn't just a leftover from the previous owner. She clicked on a random date from about a month ago. It took a few moments to download and open, and then she had four files to choose from, one for each camera: living room, out front, pool house, and pool. She closed this folder and went back to the file manager to check the dates again.

There were files from months ago but nothing, *nothing*, for the past two weeks. Kate swallowed the hard lump in her throat. The cameras had been functional until a week before Bruce 'drowned'. Had someone deleted the recent files or had the whole system been turned off two weeks ago? Either way, it seemed like too much of a coincidence. Because if the cameras had been recording, they would have captured what happened to Bruce. Her father must have told the police the cameras weren't operational. But had he been telling the truth?

Kate leaned back in the office chair, trying to think. Suddenly, she sat up and opened the drawer immediately to her right. If she knew her father at all, and she did, there would be... *Aha*. She grabbed the A4 package with *Alpha Home Security System* written on the front. Her father never threw away instruction manuals. Ever. From this she pulled out the manual and warranty information and started flicking through it, noting the date of installation and handwriting on a few of the pages. Wait. This wasn't her father's scrawl. But it was familiar. Her brother's. She kept flicking through the pages. The system did come with an app you could download to your phone to access the footage remotely, but there was no way her father would have used this. It was her brother Jack who took charge of all the high-tech things in the Dash household. Alarms, sound systems, smart TVs... and probably this monitoring system.

Kate pushed away the roll of nausea in her stomach as a memory of something Jack had said appeared in her brain. It hadn't made sense until now. *"Dad has eyes everywhere".* It had been something like that. *"He likes to watch",* maybe. And then something about how Dad would know whether Natasha was dodgy. Did this mean her brother knew about the cameras? That he had access?

She felt sick as she turned off the monitor and pulled out her phone to make a call.

Paige answered immediately. "Kate? You have news?"

"You need to talk to my brother."

17

Leo arrived at the office at a little after five o'clock, just as Paige and Sophie were setting out the takeaway food Paige had picked up from Sri Penang. They would have an early working dinner before going over to Kate's apartment at about eight o'clock to talk to her brother Jack. Kate had assured them that she would get him to her house, whatever it took.

As Sophie opened the vege deluxe container and then the one with chicken roti curry, she tried to ignore the desire to take a photo of the food and send it to Roman. The two of them had once had an impromptu takeaway meal from Sri Penang very similar to this one. But would Roman wonder why on earth she was reminding him of this? To Sophie, all the time they'd spent together was emblazoned in her memory. Was it the same for him?

"We should have a monthly meeting with everyone," Leo said as he sat down. "Or a dinner, even."

Paige frowned. "But we have meetings all the time as needed. Who knows how cases are going to develop. Like this one, we needed you to come and do some unexpected work."

"Okay, but some people are getting left out," Leo pressed.

"He means Zelda," Sophie interpreted. "And he has a point."

"Start of the month, we all get together and talk about cases, etc," Leo said.

"Fine, fine." Paige suddenly brightened. "The Monthly Investigative Report Meeting."

"We can call it whatever you want," Leo said with a grin.

"Okay so we're here to talk about the Dash case. We'll get back to the case of the missing Michael tomorrow."

Leo nodded.

"The big news of the moment is that after going through Don and Natasha's home we found two things. One, a reference to someone called Stacey Morris, which you already know about," Paige said, nodding at Leo. "I'm assuming you have the promised update?"

Leo nodded. "I do."

"We told Kate earlier today and she'd never heard the name before," Sophie said. "We'll run it by her brother and his wife Madison this evening."

"And two," Paige continued, "the presence of a camera system at the Dash residence."

"Oh, wow, really?" Leo said. "Have you seen the footage? That must change everything."

"We're not sure there is footage." Paige relayed to Leo what Kate had told them. "If it was recording and it has been deleted, could you recover it?"

"Depends on the set up, but probably. I'd need to get onsite at least once to see the system."

"That might be tricky," Sophie said. "Kate said her father refuses to acknowledge even the slightest suggestion that Natasha is anything other than his adoring wife, and Natasha, if she's the culprit, is hardly likely to let us either."

"But that doesn't mean we can't do it," Paige said. "We'll just have to find a way to get back in when they're out."

"But we have to run that idea past Kate first, okay?" Sophie cautioned.

"Fine. We'll ask her tonight." She turned to Leo. "What did you find out about Stacey Morris?"

Leo made a drum-roll sound on the table, grinning as his eyes moved from Paige to Sophie.

"I forget what a dork you are sometimes," Paige said.

"Hey!"

"I mean that in the best possible way. Sophie and I are total nerds."

"Yeah, but nerds are different to dorks," Leo said grumpily.

Paige frowned. "They are?"

"Dorks are like, dorky," Sophie clarified. "Nerds know stuff. They're smart."

"Right, sorry." Paige grinned. "Okay, you're a nerd. But you can also be kind of dorky."

"Great, thanks for clearing that up."

"Anyway, what did you find?" Paige said.

He turned his laptop around to show Paige and Sophie a photo of Natasha with a similar-looking woman next to her, their arms slung around each other's shoulders.

"That is Stacey Morris," he said pointing to the unfamiliar woman, "and Mandy Morris." His finger moved to the image of Natasha.

"Ha!" Paige cried. "Natasha is a fake name."

"Stacey is her sister?" Sophie nodded.

"Older by two years."

"Is Mandy actually British?"

"She is, but get this. Her mother is Russian but she married an English guy and had two daughters with him. They lived in Lancashire, which is near Manchester. So you were close with that accent, Sophie."

"All that Love Island finally paid off." Sophie grinned. "Now I don't feel as guilty for watching it."

"And check this out."

Leo showed them an online news article in which two teenage girls stood on either side of a woman in front of a blackened shell of a house. "That's Mandy on the left."

This version of Mandy was from at least ten years ago and looked noticeably different.

"Her father died in a house fire."

They all exchanged looks.

"A suspicious fire?" Paige asked.

"Not according to this news article. But there was an insurance pay-out."

"She's had plastic surgery," Sophie said, examining the photo. "Since then, I mean. Her nose is smaller, her lips are bigger and her chin is a different shape."

"So Mum paid for her daughters to get plastic surgery with the pay-out then sent them off into the world to find rich husbands?" Paige said. "Yikes."

"We don't know that's what she did," Sophie said, not sounding very certain.

"From what I can piece together on social media," Leo said, "Mandy-slash-Natasha was living in London doing the semi-fake Russian thing for about two years before she moved here. She dated another old dude before she met Don and the rest is history."

"How did she meet Don, can you tell?"

"Hard to be sure, but probably at a charity gala or whatever you call them. There are a couple of photos of them together and she alludes to this being their first meeting, but maybe that's a coverup."

"Alludes to?"

"She posted something like, "When you meet the man of your dreams, you know"."

"Whether she's pretending to love Don or he really is her soulmate, she got married with a fake identity," Paige said. "I mean, she didn't legally change her name to Natasha, right?"

"I wouldn't even know how to access British records to find out," Leo said.

"Either way," Sophie said. "If someone has a fake identity it usually means they're covering something up."

"Something she's already done or something she's going to do?" Paige added, raising one eyebrow.

· · · · ●● · ● · · ·

Once they'd eaten and finished summarising the current situation, Sophie and Paige said goodnight to Leo and drove across to Kate's apartment. As soon as they walked into the living room and were introduced to Kate's brother Jack and his wife Madison, as well as Kate's wife Tina, it was obvious that their arrival was unexpected.

"Investigators?" Jack repeated looking from Paige to Sophie with obvious scepticism.

Clearly, Kate had also not told her family she'd hired them.

"Kate, honestly, when are you—"

"Mandy Morris," Paige blurted, her eyes moving quickly from Jack to Madison, then Tina's face.

"Pardon?" Tina said.

"Do you know Stacey or Mandy Morris?" she said, stepping farther into the living room where Tina was leaning against the kitchen counter and Jack and Madison had been talking near the balcony door.

All three shook their heads.

"Should we?" Jack asked.

"Did you know about your father's camera system?" Paige asked Jack as she moved across the room to get closer to him.

Jack sighed. "Yes. I helped Dad with the setup, but that was months ago." He cleared his throat. "I mostly forgot about it."

Sophie glanced at Paige who nodded and took another step closer to Jack.

"Did you delete the footage?"

"No."

"Ha!" Paige cried triumphantly. "How did you know what footage I was asking about?"

"Of Bruce's drowning, right? What other footage could you possibly mean," Jack said. "I'd forgotten about the system, yes, but when Bruce died I remembered and thought to check. But Dad must have turned it off because I couldn't find any recent footage."

Sophie glanced at Kate who was staring at her brother with an urgent expression. "Why didn't you say anything?" she said.

"About what? A non-operational camera system?"

"So Dad turned it off?" Kate said.

"I assume so," Jack said, shrugging. He turned back to Paige. "If you want to know more about it you'll have to talk to Dad and Natasha."

"Do you have an app for the system on your phone?" Kate asked.

Jack blinked then scratched his head. "I don't think so, no."

"Does Natasha know about the camera system?" Paige asked.

Jack thought for a moment. "She's smarter than she looks. If I had to guess I'd say she does."

Paige glanced at Sophie then turned back to Jack once more. "So you didn't delete the footage."

"I just told you there wasn't any to delete," Jack said, frowning as he followed the look Paige threw Sophie.

"The thing I don't get," Kate said, moving across the room to where Jack stood, "is why install a camera system and then switch it off?"

Jack shrugged, then grinned. "Maybe he realised he didn't want cameras rolling for everything he got up to in the privacy of his own home."

"What do you mean?" Kate said.

"Doing the nasty with Natasha in the pool every night."

"Ew, Jack—"

"Kate. Enough. Seriously. If you want to know what Dad was thinking, you're going to have to ask him."

Kate rolled her eyes and stalked over to where Tina had resumed doing the dishes. When Sophie turned to see whether Paige would keep questioning Jack, she found Madison standing less than a foot away from her.

"Oh." Sophie took a step back to create a bit more space. "Hi."

"Do we know each other?" Madison said, scrutinising Sophie's face.

Sophie took another step back. "I don't think so."

"You look so familiar."

"Oh." Something unpleasant just occurred to Sophie. "Do you know someone called Hannah?"

Madison looked exactly like the kind of person her half-sister Hannah would hang out with. They certainly had the same Instagram aesthetic.

"Maybe." Madison tilted her head. "Why?"

"Um...." Sophie decided she didn't want to get into the whole drama about her problematic half-sister so she waved it off. "Nothing, don't worry."

Madison shrugged and ambled over to the half-bottle of red wine on the kitchen counter. As she topped up her glass, Jack suddenly appeared next to Sophie. "Hi," he said.

"Oh, um, hello."

"Do you want a top up, Babe?" Madison said loudly.

"Uh." Jack dragged his eyes away from Sophie. "Sure."

As Madison poured wine, Paige came to stand next to Sophie.

"Take us through what happened during the weekend," Paige said to the room.

"I assume you mean the bit about Dad," Jack said. "You don't want to hear about next season's chardonnay crop?"

"You would be correct in that assumption," Paige said.

"Can I ask you something, Jack?" Sophie said, aware that Paige's confrontational style probably wouldn't get them anywhere with Jack.

"Sure." He smiled.

"You don't think someone is trying to get at your dad?"

"His mate drank too much and drowned and then Dad nearly met the same fate."

"Kate said—"

"She was likely still drunk and half asleep. I think Dad would know if someone tried to drown him or not. He says it didn't happen so it didn't happen."

"Show us your phone," Paige said, holding out her hand.

Jack jerked back. "Pardon?"

"If you don't have the camera system app and you've got nothing to hide, then show us your phone."

Jack stared at her for a long moment. "I don't have to prove anything to you."

"Last chance," Paige said, still holding out her hand.

Jack turned away. "Madison, come on, we're going. Thanks, Kate," he said sarcastically as he moved out to the hall. "What a fun night."

Madison gave Tina a hasty kiss on the cheek and squeezed Kate's arm before hurrying out the door after Jack.

"Kate," Tina hissed, clearly angry.

"What?"

"It's time to stop, okay? You're causing major issues in this family." She threw down the tea towel she was holding and stalked off. A moment later the sound of a door slamming reverberated through the apartment.

Sophie turned to check on Kate's reaction and saw her staring at the front door.

"I don't know about you two but Jack is definitely still on my suspect list," Paige said into the silence.

"Yeah," Kate said quietly. "He's just as stubborn as Dad."

18

On Tuesday, after a painfully early start followed by a long and boring morning, Paige and Sophie returned to the office with nothing to show for their efforts on the Missing Michael case.

When Olivia had declined to answer any of Paige's calls, they'd decided to stake out her home, hoping to catch her before she left for work. After sitting outside the cottage for several hours, Paige's impatience had won out and she'd gone and knocked on the door. A rumpled-looking person, Olivia's flatmate it soon transpired, had blearily informed her she hadn't seen Olivia in days, but that was normal. They kept very different schedules and didn't socialise together at all. Unsurprisingly, she hadn't known anything about Olivia's life, including the situation with Michael.

Paige and Sophie took their laptops and the case files to the conference table in the second office. "You all good?" Sophie asked Paige who'd been quieter than normal all day.

"Fine."

This evening, Paige would leave for her minibreak with Tim, and despite her best efforts to pretend otherwise, it was clearly bothering her. But as she still refused to discuss the situation in any detail, Sophie could do nothing. And since Sophie herself was still hiding her plans with Roman, she was glad Paige wasn't particularly interested in discussing personal matters in any depth.

"So we'll try Olivia at work later today," Paige said. Olivia worked downtown for a small consultancy firm. "We have to find out why she ran away from us. She's obviously hiding something, but what?"

"And Leo and Zelda are still working on those contact lists of other people who know Michael. Nothing so far."

At around three-thirty, they took a bus into central Auckland, then walked straight into the converted warehouse-style building where Olivia worked.

"Good start," Sophie said, pleased they wouldn't have to bluff their way past security.

They took the lift up to the fourth floor and found themselves in a poky reception area. After a few moments, the young man at reception tapped his keyboard, pressed a button on his headset, then looked up and smiled. "Can I help you?"

"Olivia Carson, please," Paige confidently.

"Oh, did you have an appointment? She's taken a few days off," he said. "My apologies, I thought I'd rescheduled everyone."

Paige and Sophie exchanged a look. "Was it a last-minute thing?" Paige said.

"Can someone else help you?" he said brightly.

"No. When will she be back?"

"Friday."

"She's definitely coming back on Friday?"

The man's smile started to thin. "What's this in reference to?"

"Thank you," Sophie said, pulling at Paige's arm.

They paused on the ground floor to confer.

"Was he lying about her being away?" Paige said.

"He didn't seem to be."

"It's pretty suspicious timing."

"Agreed. A possible coincidence that Olivia has gone away right when we started looking for her, but given she also deleted her Facebook, I'd say she's trying to hide something. So do we come back on Friday?"

Paige thought for a moment. "If you'd thought the guy was lying and Olivia was hiding in there, I would have suggested we do the you-distract-while-I-snoop thing."

"I don't think Olivia is hiding upstairs."

Paige pursed her lips. "But it would still help to talk to her colleagues. We could ask them about her and Michael."

Sophie nodded. "True."

They retraced their path back to the office. The man behind reception didn't look thrilled to see their return.

"What's going on?" he said at their approach.

"Do you know Michael Lindell?"

He frowned. "Who's that?"

"A guy Olivia was dating. He's missing."

He gasped, his eyes widening as he leaned forwards. "He is?" he breathed.

"We're Private Investigators," Sophie said, noticing his interest. His eyes went even wider.

"How dramatic," he whispered, then smiled conspiratorially. "So you're looking for a missing man?" he added, clearly thrilled by the idea.

"We are."

"Do you know anything about Olivia's life?" Paige said.

"Or whether Olivia is close with any of her colleagues?" Sophie added.

He thought for a moment. "Olivia doesn't talk about her love life at work. She's not exactly an open book."

"Anyone who might know?"

"Maybe, but I can't let you go back there. The boss is onsite and he's—" He broke off to make a face. "Let's just say he's not at all chill." He leaned forwards again. "But let me do some snooping. I'll find out who she confides in." His eyes flashed with excitement.

"Perfect," Paige said handing him a business card.

"I'm Aaron, by the way."

"Paige," she pointed to herself, "and Sophie." She nodded. "Let us know."

Aaron took the card, clearly exhilarated. "Will do."

They left the building and walked to the bus stop.

"It was a nice change to have someone so helpful," Sophie said.

"Yeah, but this way we don't get to snoop and ambush," Paige said, obviously a bit disappointed. "Whether he gets in touch or not, we'll come back on Friday."

"The timing works out well, really," Sophie said. "With you away tomorrow."

Paige's shoulders immediately bunched with tension.

Sophie noticed this. "Do you want to chat—"

"I'd better go home and get myself sorted. Pack and whatever."

"Sure. Hey, good luck."

Paige made a face. "What are you going to do tomorrow?"

Immediately, Sophie' stomach lurched. "Uh, not sure yet. Probably just sleep in and laze around."

Paige gave her a tight smile. "Sounds like fun."

Sophie nodded. Oh god, she'd just outright lied to Paige.

· · · · ● · ● · · ·

Zelda walked down the corridor towards the hum of conversation drifting out of the twelfth-floor meeting room. As she approached the location of the *Psychology Meet and Greet* session, she slowed, mentally preparing herself. She had some specific goals for this evening and she wanted to make sure she achieved them. All going well, by the end of the night she would be significantly closer to a decision.

"Welcome," an earnest looking guy said to Zelda as she stepped into the room. He gestured at the trestle table set up along the back. "Help yourself to some food," he chuckled, as if this was funny, "and don't forget to check out the information pamphlets over there." He pointed across the room where another trestle table was laden with stapled wads of paper and several glossy brochures. "Any questions, just sing out. We'll start the information session in about ten minutes."

"Thanks," Zelda said absentmindedly as she headed towards the snack table. An array of classic party fodder was laid out, but it was clear Zelda had arrived too late to get at any of the good stuff. Only a few worse-for-wear cocktail sausages, some sausage rolls, and the less desirable sushi pieces were left. Zelda hadn't wanted to spend too much time drifting around before the information session began—she was not interested in meeting new people or chit-chatting with strangers—but perhaps all that was worth enduring to get the good snacks.

When Zelda looked up, a hopeful looking woman about her own age started towards her, seeming to be gearing up to introduce herself. Zelda turned away, walking determinedly towards the brochure table. Small talk was the worst; an evil only to be endured when you had to extract information from someone.

This information-plus-meet-the-faculty session was for an Applied Psychology programme. The course helped students learn about the basics of advanced research as well as the range of areas and industries in which they could use psychology skills (first year), then a more specialised programme the student could select papers for in year two. Those wanting to pursue PhDs would at this point be able to launch themselves directly into the programme, assuming they could find a supervisor and were accepted, while those who had decided they'd had quite enough, thanks very much, or perhaps that graduate study wasn't for them in general (Zelda assumed; she didn't think one would get to this point only to realise that psychology itself wasn't their cup of tea), could instead opt to try out the 'real world' and get a job with the skills they had already acquired.

"So what area are you interested in?" someone directly to her left said. She looked up to see the man she already knew to be Professor Richard Thinton.

"I'm Professor Thinton," he added.

"Zelda Ko," she replied, ignoring his proffered hand and instead pointing at the programme of which she knew he headed up. "This looks good. Can you tell me what people usually get into once they graduate?"

""Well. The top students, the clever ones," he tapped his nose, "go on to do PhDs." He leaned down as if telling a secret. "No point otherwise. You can't get anywhere good without one of those." He nodded.

"In what kind of industries or specialities?"

Richard took a breath, but at the front of the room an officious looking woman clapped her hands loudly. To the right, a man who was both rumpled and self-assured, put his fingers in his mouth to produce a shrill whistle.

"That's me," Richard said, already moving away. "I'll cover your question up there anyway. Talk to me later if you want to know anything else." He winked.

Zelda watched him go. She'd known he'd be here, of course she had. That was the whole point of coming. Well, some of the point.

She moved forwards to take a seat at the front.

19

P aige and Tim arrived in Omaha, an idyllic beach-front town about an hour-and-a-half north of Auckland central, at about eight p.m. They left their luggage in the living room, both seemingly feeling unsure, and as Tim got the fire going, Paige opened a bottle of red wine. They would have this in front of the fire. If 'romantic' was a bit of a stretch for them at the moment, they could at least be cosy and relaxed.

The bach was a modern, square, single-level unit, common in the newer builds that had gone up over the last fifteen years. Omaha was very popular with wealthy Aucklanders, as a place to both visit during the summer as well as purchase second homes, and while some original baches remained, fiercely clinging onto their rustic, classic style, the overall vibe of Omaha was now of wealth and modern convenience.

They took the large pillows from the corner, clearly meant to be placed in front of the fire, and sat there sipping wine and not saying much because there was too much to be said and once they started they might not ever be able to go back to this serene moment.

"So," Tim said eventually.

Paige glanced at him. "So?"

"Are we going to talk?"

"Sure, we can talk. What about? World Affairs? Imminent climate disaster?"

"Why are you being like this?"

"Talking was your idea. I was happy to just sit here and mung out."

"I'm kind of sick of this, Paige."

"Yeah? I'm getting pretty sick of it too."

"I can't believe I have to say that to you, of all people, the most confrontational person I know, but avoiding the issue won't make it go away."

"Are you sure? Even if I set my mind to it?"

Tim sighed. "I want to have kids. I thought you did too. Was I wrong?"

Paige mumbled something in reply.

"What?"

"I don't know, Tim. The answer is I don't know."

"But why? What changed?"

"I just said I don't know."

"It doesn't have to be now, but in five years, I want to start a family."

"Just because you want something doesn't mean you get it."

Tim turned to face Paige square on. "Are you saying no? A hard no. Concrete. Done. No? Are you saying kids are out of the question?" Tim's face was now pale.

Paige sighed and stood up. "I'm taking a shower."

In the bathroom, Paige sat on the edge of the bathtub and stared out through the window to where she could see part of the beach. Her shoulders felt heavy and her stomach was a coil of knotted rope. Try as she might, she couldn't get those knots to untangle or that weight to lift.

After a while, she let out a sigh, pushed away the tears threatening behind her eyes, and started a bath.

· · · · ● · ● · · ·

Mike, sitting comfortably in the cosy den-like study of the main house made a rude gesture at his phone as Richard continued speaking.

"You did what?" Richard's voice raised an octave.

"Well what did you expect me to do? I needed help and you didn't return my calls."

"But... but... you're now their client? You're actually going to pay them? After everything I did for you?"

"And what would that be, exactly?" Mike said raising his voice to match Richard's. He was actually starting to enjoy this conversation. "As far as I can tell we went along with your scheme and have had nothing but one headache after the other. Broken promises, cancelled plans."

Richard hung up.

Mike stared at his phone for a moment longer, then set it down. Richard Thinton, the one who'd gotten him into this mess (he wasn't quite sure how this worked but it certainly felt that way) had avoided his calls for days, and then when he finally called Mike back, he had the audacity to get annoyed about Mike hiring S & S Investigations. It was clear Richard had no interest in the wellbeing of either Mike or Michael, and it was all a little outrageous, to be honest.

He stood up and marched to the kitchen. He felt restless and irritated. He needed a distraction and preferably a tasty one. As he let his gaze wander around the kitchen, he noticed his dishes from yesterday's lunch still sitting in the sink. He frowned, immediately even more irritated. The whole point of eating meals in the main house was so that he didn't have to do dishes (or even make the meals, if he was honest with himself). He let out an annoyed breath, then marched back to retrieve his phone from where he'd been sitting in the study. He'd order a pizza and find a loud distracting movie to help him forget about his problems for one night at least.

It was just then that he saw it. A flash of white in the window. Immediately, he froze. It had looked very much like a face moving past the window. Perhaps he had imagined it? He walked cautiously over to the window and peered outside, immediately recoiling when he saw it again. A flash of a white face under a dark hood. No question about it this time. And not just a hood, the person wore a *cloak*.

"Hey," Mike cried. He hurried out of the den into the kitchen, following the direction of the cloaked figure. He switched off the lights and cupped his hands against the glass to peer into the darkness.

Nothing.

But then, just as he leaned back, the motion-sensitive lights above the back door came on, illuminating the lawn behind the house, the door to his own little cottage, and finally, the cloaked figure running away and disappearing into the darkness at the back of the property.

20

Sophie looked over at Roman, his hands at ten and two on the wheel, his gaze fixed straight ahead. "Warm enough?" he asked, then glanced over at her. "Or too hot?"

"It's pretty toasty in here. Almost too toasty?" Sophie added tentatively.

Roman smiled and adjusted the temperature. "No problem. I'm not a fan of being overheated either."

Sophie cleared her throat. "Your, uh, moustache is gone."

"Oh." Roman raised his hand to touch his face. "Yeah." He chuckled. "Don't know what I was thinking. A mate of mine called it my 'stress moustache'." He turned to grin at Sophie and she let out a little chirrup of laughter.

"Did you prefer it?" he asked, suddenly seeming concerned. "I can grow it back."

She tilted her head and studied his face. "You made it work, but I think I like you this way better."

"Good to know," he said, almost more to himself.

Something gripped Sophie's stomach, a pulse of nervous excitement, and she turned away to look through the window at the rolling green hills and farmland zipping by. They'd been driving for nearly twenty minutes and Sophie's heartrate had finally calmed down but her stomach was still doing nervous flips every so often. She couldn't quite believe this was happening. She and Roman, on a trip together. Incredibly, for the two or so days since they'd made this plan, she'd even managed to stop overthinking the situation. She refused to get too far ahead of herself, again. Not about this. And not when she still had no clue what Roman's situation was.

"So apparently Chris Connolly, the retired detective who worked on Terry's case," Roman reminded Sophie, "appears at his local pub in Te Awamutu at five o'clock on the dot every day. People set their watches by him. We should get there about four-thirty, all going well."

"Does he know we're coming?"

Roman glanced at her. "No. I thought maybe it was better to just show up. I'm getting a sense that people aren't very eager to talk about this case. Are you comfortable with that?"

"I'm used to ambushes. Paige is a fan."

"I believe you." He grinned. "How is Paige? I assume you haven't told her about this trip. Or even our investigation?"

"Why?"

"Because if you had, I'm pretty sure Paige and I would have had a conversation by now. A loud one." He gave her a wry smile. "Or she'd be in the car with us?"

Sophie nodded. "I feel kind of bad about it, to be honest."

"Me too."

"But I think we're doing the right thing. Keeping it from her until we have a better handle on what actually happened."

"Agreed."

And so they drove the rest of the way chatting about the case and other things as they arose, the conversation ebbing and flowing in a way that felt, to Sophie, like the most natural thing in the world. By the time they arrived in Te Awamutu all Sophie's nerves had disappeared, replaced by a warm glow of ease, comfort and just a hint of tingling anticipation.

They were a little early, so they used up the remaining hour or so by taking a driving tour of the small Waikato town. At ten minutes to five, Roman pulled up at the pub that ex-DS Connolly frequented and they went inside. They each ordered a beer (Sophie wasn't really a beer drinker but it seemed the right thing to do in a place like this), and hovered at the bar, waiting for Chris to come in.

As they'd been promised, at precisely five o'clock a man easily identifiable as Chris from the photograph Roman had downloaded walked into the bar. He did one very quick round of the room, saying hello to four or five people, and then settled on a barstool at the end, facing the door.

Roman turned to Sophie and leaned in. "So, the plan." As the warmth from Roman's body reached hers, Sophie's pulse quickened.

"Uh-huh?"

At this proximity it was very hard to concentrate. She would have to stand a little farther away from him if she was going to be able to put any of her behavioural analysis clues to good use during their interview with Chris.

"Are you okay with me doing most of the talking? At least at first?" Roman said.

"Of course. You're the cop. He'll respond better to you. Plus that frees me up to observe."

"Great, and, uh," Roman looked away, seeming almost embarrassed. "And are you okay if I introduce you as my girlfriend?"

Sophie swallowed. "I, uh, I—"

"I think explaining that Terry was my friend and I want to understand what happened to him is maybe a better angle than you and Paige and S and S Investigations. It should make things easier, but if you don't feel—"

"No, of course. Yes. Good idea."

For a moment they smiled into each other's eyes.

"Okay, let's do this."

Roman took the lead, as discussed, and introduced himself as a detective sergeant in central Auckland and Sophie as his girlfriend. Even though Sophie knew this wasn't real, the way Roman had gently placed his hand on her back and smiled at her as he made this introduction had made her lightheaded with pleasure. She'd then taken a surreptitious step to one side so she was far away enough from Roman to properly concentrate.

After about five minutes of blokey "and do you know so-and-so" chat, Roman explained what he wanted to talk about. Chris seemed at first taken aback, then nodded knowingly. "Honestly? I'm not surprised evidence has gone missing. That case felt wrong from the beginning. But on the surface it was solved and that was good enough for the brass upstairs."

Roman and Sophie settled into seats next to him at the bar and while Roman asked questions, Sophie discreetly got out her notebook and wrote down anything important. Her first impression of Chris was that he was honest and genuinely wanted to help.

"Here's the thing," he said, nodding his thanks as Roman slid another beer over to him. "Both men who were on the boat with Terry...." He paused, clearly trying to recall their names, then snapped his fingers. "Phillip and Daniel, right?"

Roman smiled. "Good memory."

"Both said they saw a person on the dock talking to Terry before they set sail."

Roman widened his eyes. "They did?" He glanced at Sophie then turned back. "That's new."

"They both mentioned it when I interviewed them, but I never found out who it was. And then I got pressure from the higher ups to close the case and move on."

Roman nodded slowly. "That witness might be the key to all this. Whoever tampered with the file maybe wanted that piece of information erased."

"That was my initial thought."

"What did they say about him?"

"Not much. He wore a hat and sunglasses and the conversation was brief. I don't think either Phillip or Daniel knew the man, but Terry clearly did. Phillip, I think, said the conversation didn't seem entirely friendly."

"Interesting."

"He said something like, "It obviously wasn't a mate saying have a good trip", but it wasn't overtly hostile either. Just a sense of animosity, I suppose."

Roman frowned. "So this person makes a point of meeting Terry at the dock to tell him something before he goes on a fishing trip, and then Terry disappears. What could he have said?"

Chris eyed Roman. "I assume you haven't been able to find either Daniel or Phillip?"

"Phillip is dead and Daniel is off the grid somewhere. He's keeping a very low profile."

Chris nodded slowly. "Here's something else you might be interested to hear."

Roman nodded for him to continue.

"Phillip was a bit of a drinker and it sounds like he got stuck into the booze that night, so take this with a grain, but he said he thought he saw someone on the actual boat."

"He *thought* he saw?"

"Like I said, he'd been into the booze that night. I take it this wasn't in the file?"

Roman shook his head. "More tampering?"

"No, that one's on me."

"You left it out of the file?"

"He said it as an afterthought, as we were walking out. He wouldn't go back on the record so I didn't include it. It wasn't the most reliable piece of evidence I've ever gathered."

"Because he was drunk?"

"Very, apparently."

"When was this sighting?"

"Early the next morning. He woke up needing the toilet and thought he saw someone dressed in black go past the window. He couldn't find anyone when he looked, but they were moored in a cove so the interloper could have already slipped off the boat and swum to shore. It's also possible he was still drunk and saw a shadow."

"What do you think happened?"

"This wasn't some dinghy, it was a yacht. They'd borrowed it from a wealthy client. It slept up to twelve people so logistically, at least, it's possible. Phillip wasn't a great witness though. Hard to know."

"So there could have been someone hiding on board waiting patiently for his chance."

Chris nodded. "They sailed to the bay and moored there before nightfall, as planned. It was in the morning they discovered Terry wasn't on board."

"Did Daniel see the extra person on board?"

"He didn't admit to it." Chris took a sip and wiped his mouth with the back of his hand. "It's pretty telling that you can't find him now. With the other two dead and doctored evidence, Daniel going off the grid sounds like a motivated decision to me. A smart one."

"I can see that."

"You want to find Daniel, find out what he knows," Chris added.

"I agree."

After a bit more discussion, with Roman going over some of the details of the case, Chris finished his beer and said goodnight.

"Should we get a table and go over what Chris told us?" Roman said, pointing to a free two-seater by the front window.

"Sounds good. I'm not the biggest fan of barstools, to be honest," Sophie said. "I always feel as if there's a risk I'm going to topple off backwards."

Roman grinned. "Has that happened to you before?"

"No." Sophie smiled back. "It's completely irrational." She spread her hands as if to say, *what can you do.*

"Well, I can't have you being uncomfortable, Sophie Swanephol."

Sophie swallowed. When he said her full name like that....

Just as they started to move across to the table, Roman pulled his phone from his pocket, glanced at the display, then stopped. "Sorry. Just got to use the gents. You're okay to grab that table?"

"Sure."

"Back in a sec."

With this Roman hurried across the bar to the men's toilets. Sophie watched him go, wondering why he suddenly seemed so tense. But when he came back five minutes later, he seemed completely fine. Better than fine, even.

As he sat down opposite Sophie, he gave her a warm smile and patted his stomach. "I'm starving. How about you?"

"Yeah. I read the menu and it all sounds pretty amazing."

As they both perused the hearty pub meals on offer, the rain that had been pattering all afternoon started to really drum against the glass. And even though both the carpet and the walls were an unsightly combination of brown and red, the overall atmosphere was both welcoming and cosy. Sophie shivered with pleasure.

"Cold?" Roman said, frowning.

"Not at all. One of those good shivers, you know? Like, I'm all snuggled up inside while it's yucky out. You get those?"

Roman smiled. "Yeah, I do. Love them." For a moment their eyes clung to each other, Sophie enjoying the weight of his attention, the intimacy of his gaze, as she took in the warmth of his hazel eyes and the way they crinkled at the edges.

But the sound of a plate smashing in the kitchen broke the spell. He glanced towards the sound, then turned back to hold up the menu. "What do you think?"

"I might stick with the classics. Like, a mince and cheese pie with chips or something," Sophie said, grinning. "This place reminds me of going to the pub as a kid. With mum and dad, of course." Sophie scrunched up her nose. "Come to think of it, I probably always got chicken nuggets and chips. But right now I definitely want a pie."

"Now I kind of want a pie too." Roman smiled. "But the lasagne sounds good."

"Ooh, Lasagne. Maybe we could share?" Sophie said, then suddenly felt shy. As if they were crossing a new line. They'd eaten together before, but this felt different. As if deciding to share half of a restaurant meal with someone was a new level of intimacy.

"Perfect. Best of both worlds. And what about a bottle of red wine? I've had my fill of beer."

"Red wine sounds great."

"I'll order for us," Roman said, standing and ambling over to the bar. Sophie watched as he leaned on the counter waiting for the bartender. She grabbed her phone, about to quickly text Paige, when she remembered she couldn't. Something dropped in her stomach. Was she doing the right thing in keeping Paige in the dark? She pushed it away. Paige had enough to deal with already. They would tell her in due course. Instead, she checked her face and teeth in the camera. She felt flushed and mildly hysterical but also weirdly at peace, and her expression managed to hit both those notes: her eyes bright and her cheeks slightly pink but looking happy.

As she slid her phone back into her bag, Roman took his seat.

"So we need to find Daniel, but I've already tried the normal ways and nothing so far."

Just as Sophie was thinking, *I bet Leo could find him*, the bartender rang a bell.

"Hey, folks," he called loudly, "We've got more heavy rain rolling in and after the last couple of days, some roads are going to get flooded pretty quickly. You might want to think about leaving sooner rather than later, depending on which way you're going. We can fix you up with takeaways. Cheers." His gaze landed on where Roman and Sophie sat at their table and he started over to them. "You two are out-of-towners, right?"

Roman nodded. "Auckland."

"There are a few motels nearby if you don't want to drive back tonight. There are some low-lying spots heading out of town and I wouldn't want to attempt them once this rain has taken hold. If you're going to go, go soon."

"Thanks, mate." Roman turned to Sophie. "Are you able to stay the night? Driving in heavy rain isn't great. I've had two aquaplaning experiences in my life and I'm not particularly interested in another one."

"Aquaplaning?"

"It's when a stretch of road gets covered in water and the car loses contact with the road so instead of driving you're gliding on the water. When there are currents or a water flow, which there are because that's how you got the flooding situation in the first place, your car is moving but you have no control over it." Roman shook his head. "Not ideal."

Sophie grimaced. "It sounds horrible. No thanks." Her stomach contracted and did an excited flip as she uttered her next words.

"And yes, I can stay."

21

Once they'd finished their meals, Sophie realised Roman had already paid for hers. "Oh, thank you. I should give you some money."

"No, please. My treat."

"But—"

"You could buy us breakfast on the way home tomorrow?"

Sophie swallowed. "Sure."

The way he'd said "us" and "home" sounded as if they were driving back to their shared house and it made Sophie feel dizzy. Her entire being ached with yearning for this. Something that felt so close, just within reach, but also still a million miles away.

They paused just inside the door of the pub. Large, heavy droplets of rain now lashed the street outside. "I'll dash out and get the car and drive up to the entrance so you can hop in."

"I can run through the rain with you," Sophie said.

"No point us both getting wet."

In the next moment he'd gone, jogging away with his coat pulled up over his head. Less than a minute passed before his headlights appeared.

Sophie jumped in. "I'm glad we're not driving all the way back in this."

"Me too." Roman glanced at her, his face partly illuminated by the welcome sign in the window of the pub.

Sophie looked away, her chest suddenly tight. What was going to happen next and how on earth was she supposed to keep it together? They hadn't even talked about any of the big stuff yet. Why? Because Roman didn't know what to say? Because he wanted to delay the bad news as long as possible? Because the drive home would then be super awkward? Was he going to fling the news at her just as he dropped her at home? Goodbye and good luck? No, she mentally shook her head. If nothing else, Roman was a grownup, and odds were good he was going to tell her the news in a mature way.

With the rain pelting from the sky, Roman used the drive-through window to check into the motel.

"Two rooms please," Roman said to the woman in the little glass cubicle.

To Sophie, the atmosphere in the car felt loaded. Could Roman feel it too? On the scale from Paige (clueless) to Sophie (far too aware), Roman was closer to Sophie's end, she knew. He seemed very in tune with nuanced and complex social situations. He must not only feel this tension, but his thoughts and emotions had to be contributing to it. They both knew they had to have a big conversation.

She tried to take a quiet calming breath, inhaling slowly then exhaling through her nose. It couldn't have been quiet enough though because she could feel Roman look at her as he drove to their designated parking.

"Units 108 and 109. Any preference?" he said, holding up the two keys. She plucked 108 from his hand. "Thanks."

Roman reached into the backseat to grab his leather satchel, very slightly grazing Sophie's shoulder in the process. Sophie sucked in a breath and kept very still. If she ended up any closer to Roman she wouldn't be able to stop herself from leaning over and smelling his neck like a total weirdo.

With his bag on his lap he looked through the window at the rain and then at the overhang above the rooms. "Only a few more metres," he said.

"I'm ready if you are." Sophie smiled. They nodded at each other, then opened their doors and ran the short distance to units 108 and 109.

"Right, then," Roman said awkwardly.

Oh god, Sophie thought. Was he as nervous as she was? Did that make this better or worse?

"Right." She took a breath. Maybe it was time to just ask him. Maybe she should invite him into her room so they could talk. But was that too much? Too presumptuous?

"Soph, I—"

Suddenly, in a flurry of waving arms and shoes slapping against wet concrete, the motel receptionist appeared, hurrying down the covered walkway towards them.

"You forgot to fill out part of the form," she called to Roman.

"Did I?"

"Here." The woman had a clipboard and a pen. She came to a stop beside Roman. While he took the clipboard she turned to Sophie. "You can go in. Get out of the rain and get under the covers." She tilted her head at Roman. "I only need his driver's license information."

"Erm, right, of course." Sophie swallowed and nodded.

"Towels are inside. Checkout is at ten," the woman added with a broad and completely clueless smile. She nodded encouragingly at Sophie, seeming to be waiting for her to enter the room.

"Thanks." Sophie turned to Roman who was pulling out his wallet. "I'll guess I'll, uh, see you tomorrow."

With an unreadable expression, he nodded slowly. "Yes."

"Sleep well," the woman said. "Let me know if you need anything." She added a beatific smile, as if pleased with her stellar customer service.

And with nothing else to do, Sophie unlocked her door and went into her unit.

· · · · ●· ● · · ·

Inside, she paced the length of the room, almost feverish with pent-up, thwarted emotion.

She went to her bag and pulled out all the contents as if there might be some magical elixir inside, some solution to the scattered hysteria she felt right now. There was not. She dropped the now-empty bag on the floor and sat on the bed. It was only then that she noticed another door, just to the right of the TV. She frowned. She rose and walked over. Where could this lead? Just as she was about to unlock it, she realised. It was an adjoining door to another room. *To Roman's room.* She stared at the off-white wooden panels. It felt like this was a portal to a different dimension. A dimension in which she and Roman were together. It somehow made everything almost unbearable. He was right through there. What if she just lifted her arm and knocked on the door. Then what? What would she say? Was she really going to demand that he tell her everything? Wasn't it up to him to tell her what was going on in his life? With the paternity test and Anya?

She checked the time. It was coming up to ten o'clock. She wanted to call her mum but she couldn't because she lived on a farm and was both an early riser and retirer. Her mother would be long asleep by now. And she couldn't call Paige because not only was Paige herself in the middle of a big conversation with Tim, potentially, but how could she explain being in a motel with Roman? For one brief, insane, moment she thought about calling her flatmate Victoria but quickly snapped out of it.

"Leo," Sophie said suddenly. They'd never had Girl Talk before but she had an inkling he'd be good at it. She scrolled to his number.

"Sophie?" Leo sounded puzzled. "Everything okay?"

"Yeah. No. I mean, I'm fine, but I'm kind of.... Roman is with me."

"He is? What? Why?" Leo sounded both excited and a little put-out, as if he had been excluded from a party.

"We're in a motel."

There was a shocked inhalation. "What are you doing talking to me, then?"

"No, I mean... we're in different rooms, but we're...."

God, how could she explain this? And what did she even want from Leo? What was the point of this call?

"Sophie?"

"Yeah?"

"Did you call to ask me what Roman's thinking?"

Sophie let out a bark of laughter. "Oh god, maybe I am. I don't know."

"Well, in my opinion, I'm pretty sure he's in love with you."

For a moment Sophie was frozen, stunned into stillness. When she let out a breath, a strange, almost strangled noise escaped too.

"'Cos you love him too, right?" Leo said. Sophie could hear his smile through the phone.

"Do you know anything about Anya?" she asked. "The situation?"

"I know the backstory, but not, uh, recent stuff."

"Right."

"But honestly, Soph? Even if he had confided in me, you should probably hear it, whatever it is, from him direct, don't you think?"

Sophie sighed. "Yeah. I know. I guess I needed to hear someone say it."

"Go talk to him."

"I will. Thanks Leo."

Sophie disconnected and threw her phone on the bed. She put her hands on her hips, trying to rally some confidence. No. First she'd take a shower. Then she'd summon the courage to knock on his door.

But when she saw what was in the bathroom, she screamed.

22

"Sophie?" Roman called, banging on the adjoining door. "Did you scream? Was that you?"

Sophie went over and opened it.

"Is everything okay?" he said, immediately stepping inside the room and looking around with obvious worry.

She gave Roman a sheepish smile. "Yes."

He gave her a puzzled smile in return. "What's up?"

"Um...."

"Soph, what is it?"

"It's a bit embarrassing."

"What is?"

"I'll show you." She pointed towards the bathroom and when he walked past her she noticed his hair was wet and he smelled of soap. He'd already had a shower.

Focus, Sophie, focus.

"It's stupid because I know they're harmless, but they kind of freak me out."

Roman took a cautious step up to the door of the bathroom, his head moving as his eyes searched the interior, eventually latching onto something in the shower. When he turned to Sophie he wore a smile.

"A couple of tree wētās got you screaming?" He chuckled.

"I know, I know."

"I thought you grew up on a farm?"

"That doesn't mean insects don't freak me out."

His eyes held hers. "Wētā disposal at your service."

"Thanks. Don't kill them, though."

"I would never." Before he stepped inside the room he turned back. "My bathroom is completely free of insects and the water pressure is pretty damn good. Why don't you use mine while I sort out yours?"

Roman retrieved the two towels from Sophie's bathroom and handed them to her then ducked in again to get the little mini soap and shampoo and conditioner. "Oh, and I got a couple of those little toothbrush kits from reception. They're both in my room. Grab one if you like."

"Oh great, I was dreading going to bed with furry teeth."

"Let me know when you're all done, okay? I'll wait here until you're ready."

"Thanks."

Sophie picked up her bag and took it along with the two towels through the adjoining doors.

Inside Roman's room she went straight to the bathroom. She checked for creepy crawlies, even though he'd already cleared it, and then turned on the shower. Roman was right about the water pressure. For ten minutes she enjoyed a blissful shower, even washing her hair with the crappy motel shampoo—it would probably dry out her hair—because it actually smelled really nice and she couldn't resist.

With one towel turban-style on her head and the other wrapped around her body, she stepped out onto the towel mat. On the sink next to one of the two mini toothbrush kits was a stick of deodorant. Sophie picked it up. Roman must have brought it with him, he must travel with deodorant in his bag. Did Roman get sweaty when he was nervous? Did he think he might get nervous on this trip? She smiled to herself, uncapped the top and brought it close to her nose. Her stomach clenched as the familiar Roman smell hit her nostrils.

She had to do something. She couldn't stay in limbo like this. She had to know what was going on with him. Where his head was. What he felt.

In a rush, she hastily towel-dried her hair, slapped some of the tinted moisturiser she had in her bag on her face, and pulled on her clothes. She started towards the door, then turned back and picked her towels up from the floor. Should she take them back to her own room? Yes. No. Yes. She nodded to herself. God, she felt almost dizzy with nerves.

When she opened the door Roman was standing in the middle of her room, completely still but somehow seeming in motion. As if his mind was racing through something; as if he'd been about to leave, or even as if he'd known she would burst through the door ready to spill the contents of her head and heart all over this terribly decorated motel room.

"Roman. Can we.... I can't... I have to know...."

"Yes." His eyes locked on hers. "Let's talk."

Just then the power went out.

· · · ● ● · ● ● · ·

Roman lit the second candle.

"I'm surprised they had these," Sophie said.

"The lady at reception had a whole drawer full of torches and candles. I get the feeling they might have regular power outages."

"It's actually not so bad," Sophie said, wrapping her arms around herself with pleasure. Rain drummed against the roof, the wind howled outside, and she was in here with Roman. They were sitting on her bed with two feet of space between them and which, oddly, felt too far away as well as too close.

"What do you think?" Roman said. When she looked up he was holding the remains of the bottle of wine they'd started at dinner. They'd both been too full of lasagne and pie and chips to drink much and Roman must have brought it back with him. "Enough for a glass each. What do you say?"

"I say yes please."

Had he thought about this too? About having a cosy drink with her in the room? Did this mean he had something important to tell her? Suddenly, a memory of how Roman had checked his phone just before they had dinner popped into her head. He'd seemed tense before then but more relaxed when he returned. Had he received news? Was he going to tell her now? Was the presence of wine good or bad? Were they drowning their sorrows or celebrating?

But he was smiling at her and she felt good. Optimistic. Could she rely on her skills, her training, her instincts now? Historically they hadn't been great in matters of the heart.

"Roman?" she found herself saying as he handed her a cup of wine. He stopped moving, his eyes searching hers. She let out a breath. "Will you please tell me about Anya?"

He nodded, set down the bottle and turned to face her. "Of course. Starting from when?"

"Whenever makes sense to you."

"I guess the beginning is... when we started drifting apart. A while ago. We were already leading quite separate lives, but when I met you, I suppose that was the catalyst for real change."

With a surge of heat in her cheeks, Sophie looked down. She felt weirdly conflicted about the implications of this.

"And it was as if Anya sensed it," Roman continued. "After that day at the Farmer's market, for sure. She was suddenly all over me. I can see now that she still didn't want me, she just didn't like the idea of *me* moving away from *her*. But at the time, for a while, I thought we might work out after all. Until it became obvious her renewed attention wasn't real. It was a knee-jerk, jealous reaction."

"So she had an affair?"

Roman sighed heavily. "I'm pretty sure she's been cheating on me through almost all of our marriage. Five years ago I think the first one was. I remember the shift in her, in our relationship, but I thought it was just moving out of the newlywed phase and settling into normal married life.

I guess I was too young or not yet cynical enough, perhaps, to understand what was happening." He shook his head. "I didn't want to see it. I couldn't see it. It hurt too much."

"And then?"

"And then it hurt less, and less. And then we were finally in a place in which we both seemed to want the same thing."

"Which was—"

"Our journey together had come to an end."

"But then she—"

"Got pregnant, yes. At first I thought she was messing with me, lying to manipulate me. But... no. She was pregnant alright. And I thought well this is it. If I wanted a sign from the universe, so to speak, then I had it. I wouldn't be abandoning my child."

Sophie nodded, her chest tight.

"But after I found out about Eric." He raised his eyes to hers. "I asked for a paternity test."

Sophie almost couldn't breathe.

"And I got the results earlier this evening."

Sophie gulped. Roman leaned forwards and took her hands in his. "It's not mine. The baby is Eric's."

"Oh my god." Sophie let out a long breath, then abruptly stood up. She didn't want to let go of his hands, but she had to move. She couldn't sit there in stillness, while that news rocketed around her body.

"Sophie?"

Roman's voice was small. When she turned to him his expression was so raw and vulnerable she immediately stepped back and came to sit beside him again. She leaned forwards and took his hands in hers. "I'm so relieved," she whispered. "I'm so, so relieved to hear that."

She dropped her forehead to their hands and took a long slow breath.

When she looked up again, she noticed the sadness in his mouth, the wrinkle between his eyebrows, the clouded pain in his eyes. Suddenly, it hit home how horrible this must have been for him. To be heading towards ending your marriage only to then find out your wife is pregnant. To have to come to terms with that before then discovering she'd been having an affair and it wasn't your baby.

"Roman I'm so sorry."

He blinked. "For what?"

"I'm sorry this happened to you. It must have been awful going through all this only to find out the baby's not yours."

He looked down. "It wasn't great. I wouldn't recommend it." His voice caught and when he raised his eyes to hers, they were wet. He gave her a wry smile.

"And all that time I had to stay away from you until I knew for sure. Because I wouldn't be that guy. I couldn't mess you around even more than I already had. We both needed to know the situation before we did anything, because if the baby had been mine, it would have mattered to me. Anya and I would still have split, but I would still be a father."

She nodded. "It matters, yes. But a horrible ex-wife and a baby wouldn't change how I feel about you."

His eyes clung to hers.

"It was from the first moment for me too, Roman. And I had no right, I knew I didn't. I had no right to expect or hope or anything, but I still did. I tried not to, I tried to make myself stop, but I couldn't. Even when I managed to put you out of my active consciousness, you were still there, under the surface. Always."

"You deserve the best, Sophie." His voice cracked. "I'm sorry it took this long. But... it's been a rough year. The whole of the past year has been kind of a mess. With one exception." His eyes locked on hers. "I met you, Sophie Swanephol. I wouldn't change any of it if it meant I didn't get to meet you. To...." He swallowed, then leaned forwards and tucked her still wet hair behind her ear. She reached up to place her hands on his shoulders and draw him closer until their faces were only inches apart.

"To get the chance to fall in love with Sophie Swanephol," he finished, taking her chin in his hand and kissing her slowly and softly, as if they had all the time in the world.

23

Just after eight a.m. on Thursday morning, Paige banged and slammed and stomped her way into the office. She glared at Sophie's unoccupied desk. They'd agreed to meet at ten o'clock today so perhaps she shouldn't be surprised Sophie was not yet in the office.

What time are you coming in? She messaged Sophie.

I thought we said ten? Is that still okay?

Fine.

Paige made herself a strong coffee, checked for voicemails and emails from clients, then spent the next two hours doing general business administration. When Sophie finally arrived, she floated into the room looking positively radiant.

"Having a day off midweek suits you," Paige said.

"Oh, uh, thanks." Sophie busied herself with her laptop.

"Have you done something different with your hair or something?"

"Oh, uh, different shampoo?" Sophie blushed.

"Hmm."

"How are you? How did it go with Tim in Omaha?"

"Not great."

But Paige was saved further explanation by her phone ringing. "S and S Investigations," she answered. "Yes, Kate, hang on." She put the phone on speaker and got her notepad ready. "Has something happened?"

"We got the coroner report back," Kate said.

"Drowning? At around midnight?" Paige pre-empted.

A pause. "How did you know?"

"We have police contacts."

"Huh," Kate said. "I'm not sure whether I'm impressed or bothered that information like that was made available to you."

"Ah, well," Paige said, eyeing Sophie. "*Whoops*," she mouthed.

"It doesn't matter," Kate said into the silence. "I guess I'm not surprised. Bruce's alcohol levels were very high and he drowned. His death is not being treated as suspicious."

"That doesn't change anything," Paige said quickly. "We've still got heaps of suspicious activity to look into."

"Yes," Kate said. "I agree."

"Hi Kate," Sophie said, moving closer to the phone. "Any updates on the security camera footage?"

"After you left on Monday night I went over to Dad's house and asked him and Natasha point blank. Dad just acted confused, as if he didn't understand why I was asking. As if his best friend hadn't recently drowned in his spa pool right in view of two cameras."

"Is it his system?" Paige asked.

"Sort of," Kate replied. "Dad said the cameras were already set up when he bought the house but he got a new software system installed because that's a good idea."

"Like changing the locks."

"Yeah. But he didn't offer any sort of explanation for why the cameras stopped recording a couple of weeks ago. He said it must have happened automatically. Or a glitch or something. He said he'd basically forgotten about them."

"So according to Don, the cameras weren't switched on when Bruce died and he has no explanation for why they were turned off," Paige said.

"Pretty much. And changing the software system sounds like something my brother would have recommended. Dad wouldn't have thought of that himself."

"What about Natasha?" Paige asked.

"She denied knowing about the cameras at all but I don't know how that's possible."

"We need to talk to your father and Natasha directly," Paige said.

"Jack told them I'd hired you two and also how I ambushed him, so they're now refusing to even speak to me. It's been two days."

"Hmm. Makes it trickier but Sophie and I could talk to Natasha without her knowing who we are."

"Whatever you think is best."

"Kate, I just wanted to double check whether the name Mandy Morris is familiar to you?" Sophie said.

"You asked about her the other night. Is she related to Stacey Morris?"

Paige's eyes cut to Sophie. Sophie shook her head.

"Just something we're following up," Paige said. "Don't forget, if we can get our IT expert access to the camera system we might be able to figure out what's going on behind the scenes."

"Okay. I'll find out if Dad and Natasha are going to be out of the house for any length of time and let you know."

Once Paige had disconnected she turned to Sophie. "Why aren't we telling Kate about Natasha being Mandy Morris?"

"Kate's already a little too invested in Natasha being the culprit, I think it could complicate matters. She might go to Don with the information and then the investigation might be compromised."

"Good point. Okay let's recap the rest of the case. What's your take on Jack?"

"Jack isn't being entirely truthful," Sophie said. "I think he lied when he said he forgot the security system was there, and based on what Kate said about his handwriting on the manual as well as his reaction to your questions, I think he does have the app on his phone."

"Hopefully Don and Natasha will go somewhere so Leo can get at the onsite security console."

Sophie nodded. "And we still have the issue of Natasha's secret identity. Why is she pretending to be someone else?"

"We need to talk to her and Don properly. I think we're going to have to ambush them. They'll just keep avoiding us otherwise."

Sophie nodded. "I also think we may need a more comprehensive list of Don's enemies. The obvious suspects were staying at the house in Waiheke, but that doesn't mean someone else couldn't have done it. The spa pool was outside, after all."

"Good point. Both of the spa pools are outside."

"And a bunch of people must have known where he was going that weekend. Oh, does he have an assistant?"

"I'll ask Kate."

As Paige picked up her phone to send Kate a message, Sophie went to make more coffee. "Uh, Paige?" she called out.

"Yeah?"

"What's this?"

When Paige joined her Sophie was pointing at a large suitcase in the corner of the room.

"Didn't have time to go home."

"From Omaha? You took that big bag with you for an overnight trip?"

"It was two nights."

"And Tim dropped you here instead of taking you home? Why? There's nothing particularly urgent going on today."

Paige's eyes suddenly filled with tears.

Sophie took a step towards her. "What's wrong? Paige, what happened?"

"I moved out."

"What?" Sophie whispered.

"Can I stay with you for a bit?"

"Of course. Are you sure you don't want to talk?"

Paige lifted her chin, pushed back her shoulders and nodded to herself. "I'll be upset later. We have work to do."

Suddenly there was a loud rap at the door. In the next moment two police officers appeared. "Paige Garnet and Sophie Swanephol?"

Paige and Sophie exchanged surprised looks. Apart from Roman, the police had never shown up at their office before.

"Yes?" Paige replied.

"We'd like you to come to the station with us, please."

Paige turned wide eyes from one officer to the other. "Why?"

"We want to talk to you about Natasha Dash."

"Why, what has she done?" Paige asked.

"Nothing. That's the problem. She's missing. And according to one Donald Dash, you two have been harassing her."

24

Thursday night a weary Paige and Sophie left the police station and returned to Sophie's flat in Pt Chevalier.

Victoria, who'd already been warned about Paige's arrival, was waiting in the hall, watching with a less-than-impressed expression as Sophie got the blow-up mattress from the hall cupboard and then handed it over to Paige to take into her room and inflate.

"It's an emergency," Sophie whispered. "She and Tim have sort of broken up."

"They have?" Victoria's eyes went wide.

"Maybe."

She thought for a moment. "Fine, she can stay for a *day or two*. But I don't want to be bothered, okay? This is my home, my sanctuary." She sniffed.

"Of course." Sophie attempted a reassuring smile.

Victoria, seeming satisfied that if she was going to be inconvenienced with a house guest of all things, at least Paige wasn't particularly happy either, turned on her heel and walked loudly back to the kitchen. She then proceeded to, even more loudly, make dinner for herself.

Myra, Sophie's other flatmate, was nowhere to be seen, but Sophie was not surprised. Myra found Paige more than a little intimidating and often made herself scarce when Paige visited.

Sophie's phone buzzed to let her know the pizza she'd ordered was only a minute away. She met the delivery driver at the door and took it straight into her bedroom, knowing that Victoria would continue to hover around the living room and kitchen to assert her dominance over the space. Her territory. Given Paige's personality, an evening spent in proximity to this would almost certainly result in a fight. At the very least it would be an unrelaxing way to spend the evening.

"Thanks for this," Paige said as Sophie stepped into the room. Paige was already in her pyjamas and sitting on Sophie's bed.

"Is it gross if we eat in bed?" Sophie said, setting down the boxes containing the pizza and a side of garlic bread and chicken wings.

Paige shrugged. "Who cares."

"I'll get a tea towel we can put the food on and a few more paper towels," Sophie said, returning briefly to the kitchen to find Victoria loitering in the hallway. At Sophie's approach she leapt back into the living room and grabbed the TV remote, her expression one of determined defiance as if Sophie was about to try to wrestle it away.

"We're going to eat dinner in my room," Sophie reassured her as she moved back down the hall. "Night."

"So," Paige began, once Sophie had shut the door and they'd both settled cross-legged and facing each other on her bed. "Bruce's funeral is tomorrow."

"But Kate put a hold on the investigation."

Kate had been at the police station when they'd arrived, along with a thunderous looking Don Dash. Kate had explained to the officers that she'd hired Paige and Sophie, and their investigation into Natasha had been at her request. They'd told the investigating officer several times that they had no idea where Natasha was, but it wasn't until Roman stepped in and vouched for them that they were released. They were told to go home and not, under any circumstances, to look into Natasha's whereabouts.

Outside the station Kate had told them about Bruce's funeral but suggested they back off for a few days to let the dust settle. Paige had tried to argue that they needed to talk to Don and Natasha more than ever but Don was so enraged about the whole thing Kate was scared what he might do if he discovered the investigation was ongoing. And so, they'd agreed to give it at least the weekend before getting back in touch.

"But it's not as if we can turn back time once Kate reactivates us," Paige argued.

"You think something important is going to happen at the funeral?"

"We still don't know whether his death is connected to what happened to Don at Waiheke. Two friends, who look kind of the same, both drunkenly decide to have a late-night spa. One drowns and the other nearly drowns. It has to be related somehow."

"But Kate's family know what we look like now. Are you saying we should go to the funeral in disguise?"

Sophie had been joking but Paige's face lit up.

"I was kidding."

"But why not?"

"Because...." Sophie trailed off, taking in Paige's tired eyes and earnest expression. The two of them attending the funeral was an unnecessary risk, especially since they had Zelda on the payroll, but it was obvious to Sophie that Paige needed this kind of distraction from her personal life.

"Fine. It's at eleven o'clock tomorrow, right?" Sophie said wearily.

"Epic," Paige said happily, returning to munch on pizza. "What do we think about Natasha's disappearance?" she said after a while.

"I think she's taken herself into hiding because she knows Kate hired private investigators. She's worried we'll expose her real identity."

Paige nodded. "Agreed. Do you think she's got something really terrible in her past?"

"Hard to know. Likely some sort of conning situation."

"Where do you think she's gone?"

"Hiding at one of her friends' houses, I'd guess."

"So we'll wait until Monday and then get Leo to find addresses for them?"

Sophie looked over at Paige. "If Kate wants us to."

"At the very least we should write up a report about who she is. Kate should know. Don should too, really."

"Okay. Monday, though."

"Wait." Paige's eyes locked on Sophie's. "You're not going to like this but... if Don is at Bruce's funeral and Natasha is hiding, then no one will be at their house."

"Paige—"

"Leo could go and look at the security camera console."

"He could get arrested."

"Maybe he's okay with that risk?"

"It's the opposite of what Kate told us to do."

"Fine," Paige said grumpily. "But we have to get at that camera system. I have a feeling it holds the answer to all of this."

"Even if it was turned off?"

"Do we really believe that it was randomly, coincidentally, turned off a week before Bruce's death?"

"No, I suppose not. But we have to be smart about it."

"Oh, I just thought of something else," Paige said, her face lighting up again, but then her mouth twisted. "Erm, never mind." She leaned over and picked up her phone.

"Paige?" Sophie said, watching her type out a message.

"What?" she replied innocently.

Sophie stared at her for a moment, then decided she wouldn't press it. Sometimes it was better to be unaware of what her intrepid and tenacious friend was doing behind the scenes. And god, she could hardly talk, Sophie herself was the one conducting a secret investigation into Paige's father's death.

"Should we watch something?" Sophie said brightly. "Santa Clarita Diet is always good when I need something light and entertaining and soothing."

"Haven't you seen that like three times already?"

"That's part of why it's soothing."

"Whatever. Sure."

They both slept fitfully that night. Paige, Sophie could only guess, was dealing with the situation with Tim. In stark contrast, Sophie couldn't stop reliving her time with Roman, but the lovely memories were marred by two rather large problems.

First, anxiety was starting to creep through her awareness, gaining momentum the longer it was allowed free rein. She hadn't yet properly talked to Roman about their time together, and while she'd felt happy and optimistic on the drive home the next morning, with every inch of distance between the two of them doubt gained ground. They'd seen each other today at the station but Roman had stayed well clear of her. She'd assumed it was because it wouldn't have been a particularly good look if he'd vouched for them as capable professionals, as private investigators he'd worked with before, and then given her a big kiss in front of everyone.

But what if she was wrong about that? What if she'd misread the situation? All her expertise flew out the window when it came to her own heart. What if, now that they'd finally gotten together, Roman was having second thoughts? What if (and this was a looming and insidious fear she'd been dealing with for as long as she'd been dating), now that Roman knew her better he didn't want her anymore? She'd been bumped off the pedestal he'd had in his head and the real Sophie was just not up to scratch. Ugh. Her stomach churned with the thought. She shook her head, clearing it away, only for her mind to latch onto the other unpleasant knowledge she was carrying.

In not telling Paige about what had happened, she was as good as lying to her. Not only about a major event in her own life, but about the investigation into Paige's father's death. Sophie sighed and turned over. She was desperate to talk to Paige, to tell her everything, but she couldn't say anything yet. If she told her about Roman, Paige would immediately demand every detail and then wonder what Roman and Sophie were doing in Te Awamutu in the first place. And even though there were still some big unanswered questions, they'd found enough information now to indicate Terry Garnet's death was not an accident. But to tell Paige that they had evidence her father might have been murdered but still didn't know by whom or why seemed just as cruel as not telling her at all.

· · · · ●·●· · ·

Kate filled her teacup with hot water from the urn, took a biscuit, and then strolled to a quiet spot of the yacht club. She had the beginnings of a headache and would excuse herself soon. Attending the funeral of her father's friend had been a little beyond the call of duty, she thought, but her father was angry with her at the moment and she felt she owed him her presence. He clearly blamed her for Natasha disappearing, and this blame wasn't entirely off the mark.

Kate had at first been mildly worried about Natasha's sudden disappearance (she simply hadn't come home on Tuesday night, nor the next, and while her phone and bag were gone, her car was still in the driveway). But after talking to Paige and Sophie yesterday, she'd learned of Natasha's real name and things had become a little clearer. Now that Natasha was aware private investigators were looking into her, she'd probably rightly assumed they'd discovered her real identity and was hiding out until she could decide what to do. Kate had not yet told her father any of this because he tended to shoot the messenger and she was already right at the bottom of his list of favourite people. There would be a time and a place and right now was not it.

As her eyes idly swept across the room—a decent turnout for Bruce—she noticed two youngish women standing across the far side of the room, both wearing hats and sunglasses. A little over the top given the sky was grey, but not entirely out of place at a funeral. She frowned as she continued to watch them, huddled together in conversation. There was something familiar about them.

"Kate?"

She turned to see Stanley and Russell, two of her father's cronies. "Seen Don in the last ten minutes?" Russell asked.

"I think he's outside," Kate said noncommittally, looking past Stanley to where she'd just spotted Jack and Madison arguing near the tea urn. Tonight, they would get together for a family dinner at her father's house. Jack had thought it necessary given how morose their father appeared to be about Natasha's continued absence. And Jack was right. It wasn't grief over Bruce's death that was causing the normally robust and jovial (loud and arrogant) Don Dash to be so quiet and look so drawn. Kate was starting to think he had real feelings for his new wife. which made Kate's investigation all the more traitorous. But none of that really mattered right now. Because she was on a mission. Last night she'd agreed to Paige's idea and it was rather a good one, she thought.

She just had to make sure she didn't get caught.

25

On Friday afternoon, as Paige pulled into a Pay & Display spot on New North Road, Sophie's phone buzzed. She checked it discreetly. Roman. Mentally, she sighed. Not being able to talk to Roman properly was killing her.

"The funeral was a bust," Paige said as she unbuckled and got out of the car. "I didn't see anything interesting at all."

"Neither."

Wearing sunglasses, wigs and sunglasses—Sophie had watched Paige realise in real-time that they could have a set of disguises on hand at the office to use for stakeouts and that this could be a business expense—they had discreetly attended Bruce's service. They'd decided that talking to people was too risky, instead hanging back and lurking in corners of the yacht club to watch whether anyone unexpected showed up or someone did something suspicious.

"Loitering near Don, I overheard a few conversations that make me wonder how long his list of enemies might be." Paige shook her head. "The jokes he made and the mean things he said about his supposed friends."

"But we're leaving that case until Monday, right?"

"Yeah, it's time to switch focus to the Missing Michael case. Mike's coming in at two."

"Which gives us a little under an hour to get our progress report together."

They let themselves into the office and took their laptops and notepads into the conference room. Paige took up her usual position by the whiteboard.

"Let's go through our notes and clarify our list of suspects, clues and leads and things we have to follow up on."

For a while they both busied themselves going through the case notes, until Sophie looked up. "Michael's housekeeper never called us."

"We'll have to see if Mike has her contact information."

As the sound of footsteps ascending the stairs drifted into the room both Paige and Sophie turned towards the door.

"Mike early, perhaps?" Paige said.

When a conversation between a man and woman became audible, Paige and Sophie frowned at each other. Not Mike, but who? They both rose from their seats and returned to the main office just as their visitors arrived at the door.

"Oh," Sophie said, immediately recognising the woman.

Cassie, her hypnotherapist.

She was with a tall, blond man who looked a little older than Cassie, and looking similar enough to probably be a relative.

"Dr Garnet," Paige said, standing to introduce herself. "Welcome to S and S Investigations. How can we help."

"Paige, this is Cassie," Sophie said, wonderous. "My hypnotherapist."

"Random," Paige said, voicing Sophie's thoughts. "What are you doing here?"

"Sorry, we were in the neighbourhood and Cliff has a situation he might need an investigator for." She nodded at her brother. "Cliff. This is Sophie."

"Hi." He smiled and held out his hand.

"Um, Hi." Sophie shook it then stepped back a little. Looking from Cassie's beaming face to the blush rising on Cliff's cheeks, she started to feel uneasy.

"What's the case?" Paige asked.

"A background check, I suppose. I'm hiring a new person at work."

"He's an architect. He has his own company," Cassie said, nudging Cliff even farther into the room.

"Yes, and there's this guy who has applied but I'm getting a bit of an iffy vibe from him."

"Right," Paige said. "We can do that. We've just got another client coming in this afternoon, any minute, actually, but give us your contact details and we'll send you our fee structure and go from there," Paige said.

Cliff took a business card from his wallet and shyly handed it over to Sophie. "That would be great."

"Uh, right." She took it and smiled. "Thanks. We'll be in touch."

"Nice to see you Sophie," Cassie said, waggling her fingers goodbye.

"And nice to meet you," Cliff added, almost bowing as they exited the office.

"That was your hypnotherapist?" Paige said once they'd gone.

"Erm, yeah."

"Okay, that was super weird, right? Them showing up like that? It wasn't just me getting the wrong vibe?"

"No, you're not. That was weird," Sophie agreed.

· · · · ● · ● · · ·

Mike arrived at S & S Investigations closer to two-thirty, not bothering to apologise for his tardiness.

"How are you?" Sophie asked, taking in his weary tread and more rumpled than usual state of dress.

"Someone was snooping around the house the other night."

"They were?" Paige said excitedly. "Details please."

"Around eight o'clock Tuesday night I got hungry and went into the kitchen of the main house to find something to eat, but there was nothing. Never anything in the pantry these days. I don't know if the maid is slacking off or what." He rolled his eyes. "Anyway. I saw a face at the window. I tried to get a better look but they took off across the lawn."

"They looked through the window and then ran away?"

"Obviously they realised I'd seen them."

"But you feel sure they were specifically looking into the house at you, not just, say, taking a shortcut through the property?"

"Shortcut to where? Next door?" Mike frowned.

"You didn't see their face?" Sophie asked. "Whether it was a man or woman?"

"They wore a hood and a, uh, cloak."

"A cloak?" Paige said. "Not a *coat* but a *cloak*."

Mike nodded. "Yes."

"Anything else? Any other details?" Sophie asked.

"Not about that, but I did recall a clue, yes," he said. "A day or two before Michael disappeared he met with a potential client."

"Michael on his own? You didn't meet with them too?"

He shook his head.

"What was the case?"

"To find her birth mother."

"Oh," Paige said. She and Sophie exchanged a glance.

"I don't know anything else about it but I have an email. It's a generic Gmail account. And I know they met Michael the Monday before last at ten o'clock at Rude Boy café."

"Right, thanks," Sophie said.

"Do you want the email address?"

"Uh, sure," Sophie said.

They already knew this 'potential client' was in fact Zelda. The plan had been to get intel on the SOS Agency operation, but fairly soon after that initial meeting, before Zelda had even provided a proper report on how much of a threat the SOS Agency might be, Mike himself had hired S & S Investigations.

"Hey, did you talk to his ex, Olivia?" Mike asked.

"We're trying to. She's out of town and she's being somewhat evasive, to be honest. She's definitely a person of interest and we're hoping to see her later today."

"Thought so." Mike nodded, seeming pleased.

The receptionist Aaron had already messaged to say he'd asked around and no one knew that Olivia had dated a guy called Michael. He'd also confirmed this morning that she was back at work today as expected.

"What about the housekeeper?" Sophie said.

Mike frowned.

"You were going to pass on our card? Get her to call?" Paige prompted.

"Michael may have had visitors that day," Sophie added. "She might have seen something relevant."

"Right. I forgot." Mike scratched his head. "I was going to talk to her the next time I saw her but that's been a while, now that I think about it. Michael probably has her details written down in an address book he keeps in the kitchen drawer."

"Find it and send it through when you get home, okay?" Paige said.

"You haven't seen the housekeeper in a while?" Sophie clarified. Mike shook his head. She leaned forwards. "When was the last time you saw her?"

"Huh." Mike pursed his lips. "I'm not sure. She's usually there most days. I don't know the exact details, she can't work seven days a week though, right? But she usually stocks the kitchen, cleans, does laundry. It's a full-time job."

"Does she clean your cottage too?"

"No."

"So perhaps you just didn't notice her at the main house," Paige suggested.

"No, I think I would have seen her. I've been spending a bit of time there. Just in case he comes back."

"Try to think," Sophie said. "When was the last time you saw her?"

Mike looked at the ceiling as he thought. "Monday, the day before he disappeared, for sure. After that I'm not entirely—"

"So you can't recall having seen the housekeeper, who is normally there most days, since Michael disappeared?" Paige clarified.

"I guess not, no."

"That is definitely potentially something," Paige said.

"A shortcut!" Mike suddenly blurted.

"Pardon?"

"Desiree!"

"Mike, you're going to have to—"

"The person in the cloak ran across the lawn. I think they crossed over to where Desiree lives next door and she's obsessed with Michael. I can't believe I didn't think of this before. You should definitely talk to her."

"Obsessed?" Sophie asked.

"She always happens to be hanging around her front lawn when he gets home," Mike said, "asking where he's going or where he's been, trying to get him over for dinner. He fobs her off but she keeps trying. She's kind of deluded." His eyes were bright and excited.

"You think Michael's neighbour might have done something to him?"

"She must sit by her window watching for him to come home, the way she ambushes him at his front door, so at the very least she could have seen something."

"The woman with the binoculars," Paige said knowingly, with an almost smug tone. "I just *knew* she was going to be part of the puzzle somehow."

26

As Sophie waited next to the car, Paige walked over to Michael's neighbour's house and knocked on the door. They'd already seen curtains twitching so they knew she was home.

"Desiree? Hello? I only want to ask you a quick question," Paige called out.

From where she stood by the car, Sophie saw the curtains open a little. Skittery eyes peeked through then disappeared again.

"Desiree?" Paige called a little louder. For a full two minutes she tried, knocking every twenty seconds or so, but the door did not open.

"Paige?" Sophie called. When Paige turned around, Sophie shook her head and thumbed behind her. "Let's go."

"But—"

Sophie held up her hand and pointed to her wrist. "Olivia," she mouthed.

Paige gave the door one more rap then let out an annoyed gust of air and marched back to the car.

"She has 'suspicious' written all over her," Paige said once they were both inside the car.

"Based on what Mike said and those binoculars, she certainly seems very attuned to anything happening at Michael's residence, so it's likely she knows something, at the very least. We just need to find an 'in' so she opens the door and talks to us."

"Or...." Paige said as Sophie pulled out of the parking spot.

"We are not breaking into her house to snoop. For one thing I suspect she's home almost all the time. But more importantly, it's illegal and she's possibly done nothing wrong."

"Fine."

For a few moments there was silence.

"Maybe you should message Aaron and let him know we're on our way," Sophie said. "It's Friday. Olivia could be going for drinks or something."

"Sure," Paige said, picking up her phone. A moment later, a surprised "Oh" followed.

"What is it?"

"No need to check with Aaron, she's messaged *us*. She wants to talk. Huh. I gave her my card, remember?" She grinned. "Finally, those business cards have paid off."

"What did she say?"

"Meet me on the ground floor of my work in half an hour," Paige read the message. "Do not come up to reception."

When they got to Olivia's workplace, they dutifully hovered in the elevator bay until the lift pinged open and Olivia emerged, looking tense.

"I can't have you showing up here all the time, distracting Aaron and asking questions. My boss noticed and he's not impressed. I only have a few minutes." She glanced behind her at the empty space, as if someone might have followed her down. "What do you want from me?"

"You already know," Paige said. "We want to ask you about Michael. You dated him a month ago and now he's missing."

She sighed. "Are you sure he's really missing?"

"We're private investigators," Paige said, a tad condescendingly.

"Who hired you? Was it Mike?" Olivia rolled her eyes. "Typical. Ugh, he's so annoying. I won't miss him at all."

"You think Mike is overreacting?" Paige asked.

"You're not worried about Michael?" Sophie added.

Olivia's eyes suddenly went wide. "Should I be?"

"When was the last time you saw him?" Sophie asked.

Olivia looked down, then up again. "Tuesday night last week, okay?"

Paige and Sophie exchanged meaningful looks.

"That's the last night he....right? Look, I didn't do anything to him. It was just a final hook-up, you know? After you break up you often need one more just to seal the deal. And I'd already started seeing Pike so I couldn't have that whole thing come up in front of him."

"Pike?" Paige said.

"The bearded guy who was at the Mt Eden craft thing with you?" Sophie surmised.

"Yes. Pikelet. And yes, he's a little out there. He's barely on social media and I kind of love it."

"If he's not on Facebook why did you delete your account?" Paige asked.

"Because some of his friends are, okay? I thought you might post on my page or something. I don't want him to know. I'm not sure how he'll react and I don't want to find out. Pike's not a big fan of revisiting the past. He thinks we should release all negative energy. Only idiots revisit their trauma."

"Trauma?" Paige said.

"You know what I mean."

"I'm not sure I do."

"It just means we should move forwards, not backwards. Pike's all about living in the moment but with your gaze forwards."

"Right," Paige said.

"So to be clear, there was no trauma with Michael," Sophie said, watching Olivia's face.

"No, I didn't mean... No. It just fizzled out. Or I guess, we weren't on the same page."

"You might have been the last person to see him though, Olivia," Sophie said. "Can you run through what happened on Tuesday?"

Olivia sighed. "I'd been at work drinks for a leaving thing and after a couple of espresso martinis I got nostalgic and I messaged him. I got to his place at around eight and I was home by ten." Olivia nodded. "I left him in bed, completely fine. More than fine. And I got an Uber home. Oh, I can show you."

Olivia fiddled with her phone for a moment and then showed them her Uber trip from St Mary's bay to her house on the Tuesday night in question. As she'd said, she'd arrived home at 21:52.

Paige eyed the phone display then looked at Olivia warily. "That just shows us what time you left. For all we know you were fleeing the scene of a crime."

"Hardly."

"Do you know anyone else who might wish ill of him?" Sophie asked.

Olivia thought for a moment. "I'm not sure about 'ill will'," she said, "but you should talk to his neighbour. I don't know her name, but when she saw me arriving at his house on Tuesday night, she gave me such an evil look." Olivia shuddered. "I can't get it out of my head. It was like she wanted me dead."

· · • •· • •· · ·

Paige and Sophie pulled up, once again, outside Michael's house.

"Do you think my idea will work?" Paige asked.

After leaving Olivia, they'd spent a few minutes brainstorming a way to get Desiree to talk to them. They'd found her full name from Michael's friend list on Facebook, and then quickly discovered that Desiree's main interest in life, apart from Michael, was the TV show Outlander. As the founding member of the *Outlander in Auckland* fan club, she posted almost daily about the series. When Paige messaged her to say she wanted to sponsor an Outlander event this summer and did Desiree have time to talk to her, Desiree replied immediately and agreed. She didn't seem to realise it was odd that Paige wanted to meet her only minutes after sending the message. But perhaps that's what true Outlander fans were prepared to do: drop everything at a moment's notice.

"Yeah, I think it will work," Sophie replied. "The only issue is whether she'll recognise you from visiting earlier today. Or even that first day we met Mike."

"I doubt it. Not being seen is my superpower, remember? And I think both times she had her binoculars trained on you."

"So I guess we're not going in together?"

"I had an idea about that. What if you, while I'm talking to her, go and knock on Michael's door."

"And?"

"And maybe she'll react and say something to me about it."

"The way she watched us walk down to Mike's place and then rushed out when she saw us come out of Michael's house during that first visit? Yeah, I think you're right." Sophie smiled. "You're kind of brilliant, you know?"

"I do."

And so, they formulated the details of the plan.

While Sophie waited in the car with her eye on the ten-minute timer they'd both set on their phones, Paige knocked on Desiree's door.

"Paige?" Desiree said breathlessly?

"Yes. You must be Desiree," Paige replied, as if she'd never seen her before.

From Paige's estimation, Desiree was in her mid-thirties but she had an oddly matronly manner about her. With her round face and distracted air, she reminded Paige a lot of her mother's friend Millie.

"Come in, come in." Desiree opened the door wider. Paige smiled. Her plan had worked. To a fellow Outlander fan, Desiree was more than happy to let down her guard.

As she entered Desiree's simple and neat bungalow, Paige spotted what looked like a hooded cloak hanging on a hook near the door. Well, well, well, she thought. As they took seats in the living room, Paige's attention was drawn away from the binoculars sitting on the window ledge, to Desiree's hands excitedly picking at the cloth of her trousers.

"What happened there?" Paige asked. On Desiree's left wrist a rather clumsy-looking bandage was visible just beyond the cuff of her jumper.

"Oh, uh, my cat scratched me."

"Huh." Paige looked around the space. There was no evidence of a cat. No toys, no cat hair, no actual cat slinking into the living room to see who had come to visit. A little bubble of excitement rose in her chest.

"So," Paige began.

At this apparent invitation, Desiree launched into a detailed spiel about Outlander's most recent episode. As Paige listened she checked the time on her phone and then at the appropriate moment stood abruptly and walked over to the window. "Who's that?" she said innocently, hoping Desiree wouldn't notice Paige couldn't see the window from where she'd been sitting and had no reason to go over there.

"Pardon?"

"There's a woman next door."

"What?" Desiree rushed over to the window, jostling Paige from her spot and picking up the binoculars even though Sophie was clearly visible (no magnification necessary) as she stood at Michael's front door, knocking and waiting.

"Who is that?" Desiree hissed. "Another one?"

"Another what?" Paige said.

"Of all the nerve. He promised."

"Who promised what, Desiree?" Paige asked, even though she wasn't entirely sure Desiree had remembered Paige was even there.

"We were going to watch together." Suddenly she whirled around. "He likes Outlander too," she said earnestly. She went back to the window. "He's been gone so long."

"Michael?"

"It's been over a week. He didn't say anything."

"You don't know where he is?"

"No." She turned panicked eyes to Paige. "I'm starting to worry."

"Should we go over there and have a look?"

Desiree's eyes flickered. "Yes." She nodded eagerly. "I usually go out the back way." She pointed down the hall.

"I'm right behind you," Paige said, surreptitiously texting Sophie to tell her to leave and hide in the car.

Paige followed Desiree out the back, across the lawn, through the gap in the hedges separating the property, up to Michael's back door, and proceeded to do one full circuit looking in every single window.

At the one near the front, Desiree stopped to try to slide it up. Paige watched with amazement. Did Desiree not realise it was illegal to force your way into other people's houses?

"It's sometimes open," Desiree explained, not seeming aware of what she was admitting. After a moment, she gave up and turned away. "No luck."

"I guess he's not home," Paige said sympathetically. "Okay, I better go. I'll message you later about the, uh, details." She then scampered away before Desiree could detach herself from her fixation on Michael and return to her fixation on Outlander.

Paige hurried across the lawn and leapt into Sophie's car. "Let's go."

Sophie started the ignition. "Well?" she prompted.

"Let's just say it went very well."

"Um, let's say a little more than that, please."

"I have a theory about Michael."

"What is it?"

"Actually, it's only part of the story. We need the rest."

"The rest?"

"Yes."

"Paige!"

"We need to find Michael's housekeeper."

27

When Laurie Jefferies entered the Lord Kitchener pub, just off Sandringham Road, Roman caught his eye and waved him over to his table.

"Thanks for meeting me," Roman said once Laurie had landed opposite him with a wheezy thump.

"No worries. Just finished work and this is on my way home. I'm gasping for a beer."

"I'll grab you one." Roman rose from his seat.

"An IPA would be great. Cheers."

"Back in a sec."

When Roman returned he slid the beer over to Laurie who immediately took a long pull.

"Long day?"

"Sometimes I wonder why I chose to be a lawyer," Laurie said. "Honestly, it can be like beating your head against a brick wall."

"I think most jobs are like that aren't they?" Roman chuckled.

"I suppose." Laurie took another sip then set down his drink. "Anyway, what can I do for you?"

Roman pulled out his small notebook. "I wondered if there might be someone else at your firm I could talk to. Terry was there for quite a while, right? He must have worked with a bunch of people."

"True." Laurie nodded. "I don't know if I could pull out a list for you, but you know who could?"

After thinking a moment, Roman nodded. "Your assistant Jenny?"

"Yeah. She's been there forever and she used to work for Terry. And she's got an excellent memory. Did you talk to her last time?"

"Briefly. She didn't say much."

Something flickered across Laurie's face. "No? Huh. I thought she'd be able to help you."

"She couldn't think of anything that might be relevant. She didn't seem to want to talk about him at all. Did they get on okay?"

The Terry Garnet Roman had known from working on a few cases together got on with just about everyone. Thinking back, Jenny's lack of interest in the matter had been a little surprising, but her phone had rung ten times during the short conversation they'd had so he doubted she'd been able to give the question her full attention.

"As far as I know, yes. I certainly didn't see anything to indicate an issue." Laurie shrugged. "I guess she's pretty busy."

"That's the impression I got." Roman took a sip of beer. "I'm not having any luck finding Terry's old mate Daniel. He's probably the key. I did manage to track down Chris Connolly."

Laurie frowned. "Connolly?"

"The DS who ran Terry's investigation."

"Right. And what did he say?"

"Nothing much, except confirmed that I need to talk to Daniel."

"Still no luck, I take it?"

"I'm surprised it's possible to go off the grid in this day and age. But I guess all you need to do is not use the internet, huh?"

Laurie laughed. "Yeah." He scratched his head. "All I know about Daniel is that he likes his fishing." He shrugged. "Sorry, not much help."

"Thanks for trying."

Laurie said goodnight and left but Roman stayed at the pub to finish his beer. His thoughts, like they always did, shifted to Sophie. He picked up his phone and sent her a quick message to let her know how his meeting with Laurie went. He then set down his phone, no longer feeling any sort of panicky anxiety about whether she would reply or not, whether he'd chosen the right thing to say or whether the woman he now knew to be *the one* would slip away, and smiled. All they had to do was wait until this case could be resolved and then they would be together properly.

Soon.

· · · • • · • • · · ·

Leo and Zelda reached the top of the brightly lit, neon-encased stairs. Zelda spread her hands as if to say Ta-Da.

"Bowling? I would have thought you're too cool for something like this." He gave her a small smile.

"We're being ironic," Zelda replied, grinning. "You can do anything uncool as long as you do it ironically. Or like, as a retro thing."

"Gotcha."

"So you're into it?" Zelda said, suddenly unsure. She mentally shook her head, trying to rid herself of this weird feeling crawling through her insides. For the first time, maybe ever, she understood the *butterflies in my stomach* expression. And she knew the reason for the sensation. Because she'd brought Leo here to say the thing she'd wanted to say for ages. She used to think of herself as something of a *cool cucumber* (her aunt had once said this to her and she'd loved it), but this whole Leo thing was proving her wrong. And she'd chosen this loud, crowded, neon-tinged environment because if things didn't go the way she planned, then at least they wouldn't be sitting at a two-seater table with nothing to do but stare at each other awkwardly.

"Sure. I won't say no to a bit of bowling."

They started toward the admission and shoe-hire counter.

"Hey, going undercover to suss out that SOS Agency thing was pretty cool, ay," Leo said.

"Yeah, I'd love to do more undercover work."

"I'm sure there will be other opportunities," Leo said. "Sophie told me she thinks we'll be entering a new Costumes And Disguises phase soon."

"She thinks?"

"Yeah. She predicts that Paige will start coming up with ambush plans that involve disguises. She said it's the natural evolution of Paige's detective schtick." Leo laughed.

They joined the short queue of people at the counter.

"Hey, so what's your plan?" Leo said suddenly. "Are you going to carry on with uni next year?"

"Random question."

He shrugged. "I've been wondering. If you do postgrad won't you be too busy to work?"

"I haven't decided yet. But a lot of people work. Up to ten hours and your scholarships etc won't be affected." Zelda was thoughtful. "I still need to find a programme or a project that makes sense. But I can always work for a bit and then go back to postgrad in a few years."

Leo nodded. "Yeah. The way S and S is going, we're probably going to need you working more hours."

"You think?" Zelda raised her eyebrows then made a face. "I'm still not sure Paige is happy about me being there."

"I think she's warming to you."

Zelda was suddenly struck with an unpleasant realisation. Leo was Paige's friend. Her associate. She was clearly protective of him. So what would happen if—

"Do you want me to ask them about future work?" Leo said into the silence. "I could talk to Paige and Sophie. Make sure they know you're keen."

"Ah, yeah." Zelda looked down, picking at the skin on one nail.

Leo frowned. "What's up?"

"I just, uh, I wanted to talk to you about something else, but—"

Just then, Leo's phone buzzed loudly. "Sorry, hang on." He checked the message. "It's Paige. They've got an urgent job on." He looked up to waggle his eyebrows at Zelda. "For both of us."

· · • • · • · · ·

At S & S Investigations, Sophie and Paige sat at the conference table with the remnants of their dinner pushed to one side and the relevant case files and notes in front of them. It was late, but they were so close to cracking the Case of The Missing Michael that they'd agreed to keep going until they did.

"Anything from Zelda or Leo yet?" Paige asked.

"Nope."

Both Zelda and Leo had been sent to follow up on the two angles that Paige believed would solve the case. Meanwhile, Paige and Sophie were going through the details one more time to make sure they hadn't missed anything, as well as writing up the final report to send to Mike once the confirmations came in.

After nearly an hour of quiet work, both Paige and Sophie's phones pinged.

"Leo or Zelda?" Sophie said before they'd picked up their phones to check the incoming message.

Paige lifted her eyes as she thought. "My guess is it's Leo."

"I bet Zelda," Sophie said.

They both checked their phone display.

"Why do I bet against a behaviour expert," Paige said, rolling her eyes.

Sophie read the message. "Part one of your theory is confirmed."

"All we need now is—"

Their phones pinged again.

"Leo." Paige smiled. "I was so close."

Paige jotted down the phone number Leo had sent for the case file, then clicked on it to call. There was no question of whether she or Sophie would make the call. It was always going to be Paige.

"It's ringing," she said to Sophie, who could already hear the ringing tone through the phone. "Hello," Paige said, her voice smooth and friendly. "This is Doctor Paige Garnet," she replied. "You don't know me, but I have something important to ask you."

After ten minutes, she disconnected and without saying anything, raised one hand for Sophie to Hi-Five.

"Another one cracked," Sophie said.

"Now all we have to do is tell Mike."

Paige and Sophie exchanged a grimace.

Because the news wasn't great.

28

Saturday morning, Mike opened the door to see Michael standing on his doorstep wearing a sheepish expression. His best friend, who he'd been worrying about for almost two weeks now, had never been missing. He'd never been in any sort of danger at all. He'd just left on his own volition. But worse than that, perhaps, was the reason why.

"I'm sorry," Michael said immediately.

Mike stared at him. "Is that it? Is that all you have to say?"

"Of course not, but it's where I want to start."

Mike sighed and opened the door wider for Michael to enter. "Beer?"

"Thanks."

He retrieved two bottles of pale ale from the fridge and took one over to Michael, who'd taken a seat at the small dining table. "So," he said, letting out another sigh.

Mike already knew what had happened from the report the S & S Investigators had sent through—that had not been a fun read—but there were still a few pieces to fill in. And he wanted to hear Michael's version of events. He wanted an explanation. Because all this time Michael had been hiding from Mike himself. And the betrayal was like a punch to the gut.

On that Tuesday night, Michael had been visited by an amorous Olivia, who had already moved on to someone else but wanted one final roll in the hay. Michael had been happy to oblige. But it happened to be the same night that he'd intimated he would spend with his neighbour Desiree—at least, that was Desiree's take on the situation—so when Desiree saw Olivia entering his house she'd been rather (understandably) upset. She'd gone over to his house but chickened out of actually knocking on the door and talking to him. She'd instead done a circuit of the house and found a window she could climb through. She was the one who'd knocked over the plant and the lamp and cut herself in the process, bleeding on the hall runner.

Michael, who'd been oblivious to all of this, had stayed upstairs that night and then left early the next morning, as planned. Not the most observant chap on a good day, that morning he'd been too busy trying to get away before Mike showed up at the house, uninvited as always.

Michael had been formulating a way to break free from Mike for quite some time now, and while most of it was already set up, he had in more recent weeks realised that things would be simpler if he implemented the final phase of his plan from a distance. Tauranga, to be precise. He would stay with his sister as he completed the necessary steps to make his move to Australia.

He'd told his housekeeper about his departure date and asked her to make weekly instead of daily visits to keep things ticking over until his father decided what he wanted to do with the property. He'd instructed both his father and his sister, should Mike reach out, not to tell Mike any of this. Not until Michael had a chance to find the words…. and to be ready to scarper very soon after.

Paige and Sophie had learned all of this after speaking to the housekeeper and then to Michael himself once Leo had located his new phone number.

"So…." Michael began.

"Why? That's all I need to know," Mike said. "Why did you disappear like that?"

"Because I'm moving to Australia on my own." Michael pressed his lips together. "Because I want a fresh start."

"That doesn't—"

"I had to leave without saying goodbye because it would have been too difficult otherwise. You would have made it impossible to leave, or you would have invited yourself along and ended up coming with me. And, I'm sorry to say this to your face, in fact the whole point of this was to avoid having to say this to you directly...."

Mike swallowed. "Yes?"

"The whole point of moving is to make a fresh start. I'm not saying we're never going to be friends again, but we need a break from each other. We're co-dependent. Or at least, you're too dependent on me. You need to find your own feet. Once you've done that, we can reconnect, okay?"

"So you disappeared because you couldn't tell me you wanted to leave?"

"Yes."

"But—"

"Your family is here, Mike. All of them. You've neglected them for a while now and I really think it's time you reconnected with them. You and I can still be friends across the Tasman. We'll be fine. I just need this, right now, and I think you do too. Everything will work out in the end."

"I see." Mike was quiet for a moment. "And what about this cottage?"

"That's up to my father," Michael said. He grimaced. "But if I were you I'd start looking for a flat. And a job."

"Great."

Michael smiled brightly. "Honestly, things are going to work out for the best, you'll see."

"And what about you, are you getting a job in Oz?"

Michael's eyes shifted to one side. "Dad's got a friend who could do with an extra pair of hands." He shrugged and smiled. "It'll work out, I'm sure."

Mike nodded slowly. "Yes, I'm sure."

Maybe Michael was right. Maybe it was time for a change.

· · · · ● · ● · · · ·

Paige and Sophie were back at the office, both losing steam and feeling a little frayed around the edges, but they were nothing if not dedicated to their work.

"Right," Paige said, standing up. "Now that we've solved the Michael case, we can turn all our attention on the Black Widow. AKA, figuring out exactly what Natasha/Mandy is up to. When is Leo getting here?"

"He's on his way," Sophie replied.

"Let's go through what we know until he gets here. He's probably going to bring a piece of news that could shake up everything but we might as well recap while we wait."

Sophie lifted her gaze to Paige. "What news?"

"Um, it's unconfirmed. We'll have to wait for Leo."

"Paige."

"Natasha being on the loose is making me uneasy," Paige said to change the subject. "If she's *not* the culprit, she's away from the house, so someone might try to kill Don this weekend. He's kind of a sitting duck."

"Maybe Kate and Jack are with him?" Sophie said.

"They're not, I asked Kate. Don banished them. He said he's had enough of his family flapping around and they're the reason Natasha is staying away."

"So you've had a whole conversation with Kate about this?" Sophie raised one eyebrow.

Paige made a guilty face.

"Are we on or off the case at the moment?"

"We're on," Paige said with confidence, then turned to the whiteboard. "We have to go through the timeline and each of the suspects." She paused to gesture at the photographs she'd downloaded and affixed to the board. "We need to talk about possible means, motives and opportunity, right?"

She turned back to wait for Sophie's nod. "Okay, start reading," Paige said, waiting at the whiteboard.

"According to Kate, the very first suspicious events were the car accident and the electric fence thing. Natasha was sort of responsible for both the car hitting the tree and Don grabbing the fence and getting an electric shock."

"Both could have been accidents, but in the context of everything else, possibly are not," Paige said.

"And then we have the dinner in which Natasha put sesame seeds on the salad and encouraged Don to eat it. There's no question of who did it, but Natasha's explanation was she didn't realise Don was allergic."

"But Kate is adamant Natasha knew," Paige said.

"It's still not concrete. Natasha may not have absorbed that information."

"But one of the EpiPens was missing."

"And you think that's not a coincidence," Sophie said.

"Maybe not."

"Natasha hid it?"

"I guess anyone could have hidden the EpiPen. It sounds like the family was at the house regularly. All six of them were there that night. Don, Natasha, Kate, Tina, Madison, and Jack."

"Hmm," Sophie said, looking thoughtful. "Something is sliding around my brain right now."

"Yeah?" Paige said excitedly.

"An unformed theory."

"Well?"

"It's not ready yet. It's still only an amorphous blob. I don't even know if I can put it into words. Let's keep going."

"When Bruce died only Natasha and Don were at the house. At least, that we know about. Without security footage, who knows who else showed up."

"Bruce's death was ruled accidental."

"I know but I still think it should be on the timeline. It feels relevant to me. I can't quite explain it," Paige said.

"You don't need to, I get it," Sophie said. "It feels significant to me too."

Paige wrote *Bruce Drowning – Accidental?* on the board.

"But it's the Waiheke event we're really interested in," Paige said. "Because it's pretty likely someone did try to kill Don."

"We need Leo to do a background check on each person."

Just then, the downstairs door slammed and footsteps bounded up the stairs.

"He's got a knack for timing, doesn't he," Sophie said, smiling.

Leo burst through the door, his face bright. "Ladies!"

"Hey, Leo," Sophie said.

"You got it?" Paige asked.

"I got it."

"Got what?" Sophie asked.

"Actually, I've got some other news too."

"Other than what?" Sophie said, getting a little frustrated.

"You do?" Paige said.

"It's about Natasha. From a year ago. Before she met Don."

"She's a black widow?" Paige cried. "I knew it."

"Let's just say she definitely could be."

"Tell us everything."

Leo took a seat and slid his laptop from his bag. "Remember how I told you that last year she dated a guy who was kind of the same as Don."

"Right, and then she met Don at a charity event and she posted about meeting the one or something," Paige said.

"Yeah, but I just found out that guy before Don is dead."

Sophie made a face. "Not by natural causes I take it."

"A heart attack, but not everyone thought so. His sister did an interview with a tabloid-ish paper and basically said she thought someone killed him."

"Was Natasha mentioned?"

"She didn't say anything about Natasha or his love life. Given the vibe of the article, I think if the sister had known, it would have been included." Leo typed for a few moments, then looked up. "I've sent it to you both."

"So what does the sister think happened?"

"That someone spiked his drink with some drug that interacted with his heart medication."

"The coroner report?"

"She said they didn't test for that. It's all a bit vague," Leo said.

"But Natasha didn't inherit anything from him, right?" Sophie said.

"No, I checked." Leo seemed pleased with himself.

"So what would have been in it for her?" Sophie continued.

"The dude was old, he had a heart condition and he died of a heart attack," Paige said. "What was the sister's theory based on?"

"She's a wealthy socialite lady, and I—"

"Wait," Paige said. "How old is she?

"Uh," Leo checked his notes. "Fifty-eight."

"Oh." She frowned.

"You can be a socialite even if you're older," Sophie said.

"She's newsworthy over there," Leo continued. "And she had a suspected rehab stint a few months before her brother's death. I think the reporter indulged her theory to get her to talk. To get a scoop."

"Hmm." Paige and Sophie eyed each other.

"Not sure what to make of that, really," Sophie said.

"It's definitely possible Natasha was involved but it's all a bit too vague to put on the murder board," Paige said. "But we'll add it to the file and keep it in the back of our minds."

"Now will you two let me in on the other thing you've been doing? Behind my back?" Sophie said a little grumpily.

"Kate took her brother's phone," Paige said.

"She stole it?"

"Borrowed," Leo clarified. "So I could look at it."

"Where does Jack think his phone is?"

"Earlier, Kate popped over to Jack's house to say hello, and she 'accidently' picked up his phone and took it with her. She dropped it off to me instead," Leo said. "He's already noticed so Kate told him she'd get it back to him soon."

"Soon?"

"She reckons she can delay him for another hour or two."

"Is this what you were engineering on Thursday night?" Sophie said, throwing a look at Paige. "Kate getting Jack's phone?"

When Paige smiled, Sophie didn't know whether she was annoyed or impressed.

"Guess what I found straight away," Leo said.

"Leo, we've been through this. Guessing is annoying," Paige said.

"Okay, fine. Someone has cloned Jack's phone."

Sophie and Paige both gasped.

"I know, right?" Leo said, again looking pleased. "And Jack has definitely accessed the security camera app. Several times in the past few months."

"Wait, the clone did or Jack did?" Sophie asked.

"Jack. I can't tell what the clone looked at, but they would have seen everything he saw. Guess what?"

"Leo!"

"Someone deleted footage from the cloud the Sunday before last."

"The day after Bruce was found."

"Yep."

"No way," Paige breathed.

"Way."

"What did they delete?" Sophie asked.

"That, I can't tell, but the files from the months before that are still there so it seems like it was targeted deletion. Someone deleted the files from the actual computer in Don's office as well as from the cloud."

"Which means the system *was* recording that night?" Paige said.

"I'd say so, yeah."

"Was the person who deleted everything the same person who cloned Jack's phone?" Sophie asked.

Leo shrugged. "Could be three different people for all we know. If I could get into Don's home office, I might be able to learn more, I think."

"Ooh, maybe we could lure Don out of the house," Paige said, sitting up straighter. "We could pretend to be Natasha and say we want to talk and then while he's waiting for her, Leo can nip in and get what he needs."

"Nip in?"

"You know what I mean. And we need to try to find Natasha," Paige said. "Any ideas, Leo?"

"Can we get her phone number? If it's turned on, then yeah I can probably find her." Leo made a thinking face then pulled a phone out of his satchel. "Hang on, I think I saw her name in Jack's phone." He scrolled for a moment, then smiled. "He has her number." He got out his notepad and wrote it down.

"We need to see what communication has gone on between Jack and Natasha," Paige said.

"Not much on text, just a few messages. They're all like, "*Is Dad with you?*" and, "*What time are you coming over on Sunday?*", that kind of thing."

Paige held out her hand for the phone. "I'll check all the messaging apps."

Leo handed it over.

"Can phones be cloned remotely?" Sophie asked Leo. "Whoever did that to Jack's phone, did they need to get their hands on it?"

"It's easier if you have access to the phone, but not impossible."

"So it could have been any of the suspects."

"Technically it could have been anyone at all."

"Oh," Paige said. "Here's an interesting message thread." She held up Jack's phone so the other two could see. "Very interesting indeed."

29

Sophie pulled up outside the bungalow on Richmond Road in Ponsonby. According to Leo, Natasha's phone was in here, which meant she probably was too.

"So what's our plan?" Sophie said as she turned off the engine and unbuckled.

"We knock on the door and tell Natasha the jig is up."

"Really?"

"Do you have a better idea?"

"I suppose not."

"We can threaten to expose her if she doesn't tell us everything."

Sophie conceded a nod. As these types of plans went, it was as good as any.

Their knock was answered fairly promptly by one of the women Natasha had been with at the mall. Her hair was piled up in an artfully messy bun and she wore leggings and an oversized jumper, but her makeup was immaculate.

"Yeah?" she said, her eyes immediately latching onto Sophie. They narrowed. "Who are you?"

While she was distracted by Sophie, Paige scuttled down the cluttered hallway into the living room. The woman wouldn't have noticed except Paige clipped her elbow as she passed.

"Hey," she said, glaring at Paige's departing figure.

"Erm, sorry," Sophie said, hurrying down the hall after Paige.

On the couch in the living room, facing a ring light and holding up her phone to take a selfie, was Natasha. She wore a pink facemask and in her hand was a cocktail. The colour of her long, false fingernails matched her facemask almost exactly.

"Um, hello? Who are you?" Natasha said unconvincingly.

Sophie, now standing next to Paige, thought Natasha knew exactly who they were. Natasha had probably googled them as soon as she'd learned Kate had hired investigators. That's what Sophie would have done.

"So you're not *missing* so much as taking a break from your husband," Paige said.

Natasha frowned. "Things not good for me now."

"Yeah, you seem really worried," Paige said sarcastically.

"No. I scared," Natasha said, pouting.

Paige rolled her eyes. "You can drop the accent, Mandy. We know you're from Lancashire."

She stared at Paige for a moment, then sighed. "Yeah, I figured."

"But the Russian was real, right? Your mother taught you?"

Her eyes widened. "How do you know about my mother?" Her voice was loud; harsh.

"We know everything," Paige said.

"Everything?"

"We know your real name isn't Natasha, that your dad died in a house fire and you and your sister got plastic surgery afterwards, and that you use your Russian heritage to ensnare wealthy men." Paige tilted her head. "Okay that last bit is more of a guess, but we're right, aren't we?"

Natasha's mouth pressed into a line and her eyes narrowed. "Have you told Don my real name? Or Kate?"

"Not yet, no."

"Really?" She sounded surprised. "Why? What do you want?"

"You all good, Babe?" her friend said, finally appearing in the living room, her phone dangling from one hand. Natasha nodded. "I'll give you some space to sort this out, yeah?" She waved her fingernails in the direction of Paige and Sophie. "But I'm just in the next room, and not being funny, but I will *do you in* if you hurt a hair on her head, alright? She's my girl, okay? Ride or Die."

"We just want to talk," Sophie said, a little alarmed at the intensity in Natasha's friend's eyes. She'd seen the fights on Love Island and she had neither the training nor the temperament to deal with that kind of situation.

"Are you trying to kill Don?" Paige said suddenly, her eyes fixed on Natasha. Sophie also watched her face.

She sighed. "Honestly, I'm not. He's not so bad."

"But you did marry him for his money."

"Of course I did. A girl's gotta work with what she's got. She's gotta look after herself, you know?"

"And by look after herself you mean marry a rich guy so he can look after her?"

"Yes." Natasha frowned as if Paige was being dense.

"What about the sesame seed salad and the electrocution stuff."

Immediately, Natasha looked guilty. "Oh, you know," she waved her hand, "those were accidents."

"I don't think you're being entirely truthful," Sophie said.

"She's a human lie detector," Paige said, nodding at Sophie, "and if you don't tell the truth now it will look bad later in court," she bluffed.

Natasha's eyes widened at the word 'court', then narrowed and became sceptical. She raised her hand to touch her facemask.

"Yes, even with that crap on your face," Paige added. "Listen, the quicker you tell us what you've been up to the better this will go for you."

"Okay fine. It was only sort of an accident. I saw the *Beware Of Electric Fence* sign, but I knew it wouldn't be that bad. I've been on farms before. And it was so funny when he started jerking and shaking like that." She snickered at the memory. "You would have laughed too. And he deserved it."

"He did?"

"He stayed out until two a.m. a couple of nights before. No text, no explanation, nothing. He does something wrong, he gets zapped." She snapped her fingers and cackled. "Isn't that a famous experiment? To train behaviour?"

"Actually, yeah, sort of," Sophie said.

"And he was fine," Natasha scoffed. "It's just a bit of fun, alright?

"What else have you done for 'fun'," Paige asked. "For 'training purposes'."

"It's no big deal," Natasha huffed. "Just messing around."

"An example?" Paige pressed.

Natasha rolled her eyes. "Fine. Like, he came home plastered one night recently and he hadn't even told me he was going out. He didn't say anything about it and he didn't answer his phone. So when he got home I made him a nightcap and slipped him a sleeping pill and then before he passed out I got him into his car and left him there so he'd wake up all cold and uncomfortable and freak out and wonder how he got there." She giggled. "And he did. You should have seen his expression the next day. Creeping around, wondering if I knew he'd slept in the car. Trying to piece together his evening. And he was so sweet to me for days after that." She laughed again. "And it's kind of funny. C'mon." Suddenly her expression turned sour. "If he doesn't want that stuff to keep happening then he should stop acting like a teenager."

"What about the allergic reaction?" Paige asked.

"He left me waiting at a restaurant on Saturday night. For ages. I felt like such an idiot. All the wait staff were laughing at me." Her eyes flashed.

"So you poisoned him?" Paige said, lifting her eyebrows.

"No, I just wanted him to... I don't know, I guess I didn't think that through properly," she conceded. "I thought his face would just go all puffy or something. But it was fine," she repeated, her apparent mantra. "We have those pen thingies around." She waved this off too.

Sophie frowned as she watched Natasha airily explain her rather serious misdeeds.

"So when Don does something you don't like you punish him with mild electrocution or give him things he's allergic to or drug him or drive him into a tree?" Paige sounded awed more than anything else.

"I get bored easily." Natasha shrugged.

"So you didn't attempt to drown Don? You didn't successfully drown Bruce?" Paige continued.

Natasha narrowed her eyes. "I never touched Bruce. But I wasn't exactly sad about his death. Don was so much more of a wanker when Bruce was around."

"So you didn't try to drown Don when you were in Waiheke," Sophie repeated the question.

Natasha's eyes fixed on hers. "No."

"And the security system? Did you know there are cameras on the property?"

Natasha sipped at her drink. "Of course, I'm not stupid."

"Did you turn them off?" Sophie asked.

"It's not a crime. Who wants to be recorded all the time?"

Paige stepped forwards. "Did you delete files from Don's home computer?"

"What files?" Natasha said innocently.

"From the camera system. Of the night Bruce died."

She shrugged. "I don't know anything about that." She took another sip of her drink.

Paige looked at Sophie who made an uncertain face.

"So you're not trying to kill Don," Sophie asked, watching her carefully.

"I haven't checked his will yet, have I?" Natasha gave them a sly look. "No point in him being dead if I don't get his money." She cackled.

"Do you think someone else is trying to kill Don?" Sophie asked.

Natasha looked away. "Not sure, really. Maybe?" She sighed. "I'm bored. This is boring. What do you want?"

Paige and Sophie exchanged glances.

30

Back at S & S Investigations, Leo and Zelda had joined Paige and Sophie in the conference room. It was time to figure out the Dash case. They were so close to a solution, Paige and Sophie agreed, but they had just one more piece of the puzzle to slot into place. Namely, identifying the culprit.

"Right," Paige said officiously, shuffling her papers as she stood in front of the whiteboard. "If we just go through everything one more time, I think we'll get there."

Paige turned to Sophie and nodded. "Sophie, what's the theory that's been brewing in your brain?"

"I think there are two related but slightly different things happening here." Sophie said, mostly to Leo and Zelda since she'd already shared this theory with Paige. "First off, Natasha has been messing with Don, for fun, essentially."

"Behaviour training," Paige said. "Classical conditioning with a sadistic paradigm."

Sophie chuckled. "Pretty much."

"So that's one part," Paige said.

"And the other is someone else noticing what Natasha was up to and using it to their advantage."

"Who?" Zelda asked.

"That's the question," Paige said, turning to point at the whiteboard on which photos of the suspects were posted. "I believe one of these people is our would-be murderer. Let's go through each one again."

"Oh my god," Leo said, lurching to stand.

"What is it?" Paige said eagerly.

"Wow," Leo said. "I didn't properly look at the board before."

"Oh good, I'm glad I went to all the trouble of making it perfect, then," Paige said grumpily.

"Leo?" Sophie said.

He pointed at the whiteboard. "I know that person."

"Who?" Paige said.

He went over to tap one of the photos. "And they're totally capable of cloning a phone and hacking into security cameras."

For a moment, everyone was quiet.

"And that was the final bit we needed," Sophie said, a smile growing on her face. "I'm almost certain I know what has been going on."

A few minutes later, she'd explained it to the others.

"Nice," Zelda said with a grin.

"But how do we prove it?" Leo said.

"I have an idea," Paige said. "It's a bit tricky. It's going to require a *dash* of finesse." She looked around the room, eyes sparkling at her own wit.

"That's puntastic," Zelda said wryly. "What's your plan?"

"We're going to *Murder She Wrote* this one," Paige said happily.

"Huh?" Leo said.

"We set a trap for the potential killer." Zelda grinned.

"Exactly," Paige replied. "And I think I know the bait we can use."

Once Paige had explained herself she looked around the room. "Any feedback?"

"How do we know it will work?" Zelda asked.

"We don't. We just have to try," Paige said. "But it always worked for Jessica Fletcher."

· · · · ●·●· · · ·

At a little past midnight, Paige's Walkie Talkie crackled.

"This is Oscar and Elmo," Zelda whispered. "I have eyes on the target."

From their hiding position, Paige and Sophie exchanged excited glances. "Roger that," Paige replied. "Squirrel and Swan are in position."

Zelda and Leo were in Leo's car, parked outside Don and Natasha's house, while Paige and Sophie waited inside, hiding behind the large couch in the living room.

"Which of them is Oscar and which is Elmo?" Paige asked, grinning.

Sophie smiled. "Leo is Elmo and Zelda is Oscar. Obviously."

Paige lifted the Walkie again. "Is the target alone?"

"Affirmative," Zelda replied. "Creeping up to the front door right now. About to enter the property."

"Radio silence from now on. Until I give you the signal."

"Roger."

Paige set down her Walkie Talkie then made a two-fingered fist to (unnecessarily) make the *Watching You* gesture at the front door, at which both she and Sophie then trained their eyes.

In the next moment, the sound of the front door being quietly unlocked drifted across to them and a figure clad completely in black eased the door shut then tiptoed down the hall towards the stairs. Paige and Sophie silently rose and went to follow the person. At the foot of the stairs, Sophie activated the camera on her phone and started recording.

When Paige and Sophie rounded the door to the master bedroom, they saw what appeared to be Don sleeping in the middle of the bed and the black-clad figure creeping up to him.

"A-ha!" Paige cried slamming on the lights.

The figure lurched upright and let out a shriek. The door to the walk-in wardrobe banged open and Kate rushed out, tackling the intruder onto the bed, landing on the pile of cushions that was supposed to be Don.

"Got you," Kate cried.

After a brief struggle, Kate successfully wrenched something out of the intruder's hand, who then gave up. "Fine, fine, get off me, okay?"

They both sat up and Kate pulled at the hood covering the intruder's head.

Madison scowled at her. "You broke my nail."

· · · · ●● · ●● · ·

Downstairs, Kate, Madison and the four S & S investigators took seats in the living room for the final denouement. Don and Natasha would not join them for this reveal, as they were currently holed up in a hotel room having a serious talk about whether they could salvage things. Jack had been completely left out of the plan because of his relationship with Madison, as had Tina for the same reason. The police (Roman) had been called and were on the way. But no one would deny Paige her moment in the sun.

Paige held up the vial of sesame oil that Kate had wrested away from Madison just moments before. "The murder weapon."

"No one was murdered," Madison said scathingly.

"The attempted murder weapon," Paige adjusted quickly. "This much sesame oil poured directly into Don's mouth would definitely have killed him. You're going to find it hard to explain why you were sneaking into his bedroom in the middle of the night with that in your hand."

"What is this?" Madison said not particularly convincingly, her eyes darting around the room.

"Good question," Paige said, waggling her finger. "A question you know the answer to, Madison, but a question I intend to answer nonetheless." Paige walked across the room, all eyes moving with her as she took slow measured steps from one end to the other.

"Earlier today we set a trap for you."

"Really?" Madison said sarcastically. "I hadn't noticed."

"Once we told Don that it wasn't Natasha trying to kill him, he admitted that yes, someone had pushed his head underwater in the spa that night on Waiheke. He finally allowed himself to acknowledge that he'd clearly felt the hand on his head. He hadn't wanted to before because he'd felt fingernails, long, fake fingernails on his scalp and he'd assumed the worst. That it was Natasha who'd pushed his head under. He must have been worried about her motives for marrying him too because he thought his new bride had tried to kill him and his reaction was to immediately go into denial about the whole thing."

"A classic Don Dash approach," Kate said. "Anything he doesn't want to deal with, he just pretends it didn't happen or it doesn't exist. It's actually surprisingly effective most of the time."

"Indeed," Paige said, as if only she could confirm such things. "But Don was wrong. It wasn't Natasha who held his head under. He was right about the fingernails though." Paige looked pointedly at Madisons long, glossy, mint-coloured nails. "We knew someone had been interfering with the camera security system here at the house, and once Leo identified you, Madison, as someone he'd come across in computer science circles a few years ago, things started to fall into place. But we needed to catch you in the act."

"So that message you sent about Natasha going back to the UK on Monday was a lie," Madison said to Kate. "All that stuff about Don spending the weekend packing up her belongings. That he was done with her and she'd be gone soon, it was all fake?"

"Yes. We wanted you to think she was leaving. Because once Natasha left this country, you wouldn't be able to frame her for Don's murder. Which meant you had to act quickly."

Madison stared at Paige. "Why would I want to frame Natasha?"

"Because Jack and Natasha getting together was only a matter of time," Sophie answered this one. "Because they were clearly attracted to one another and had progressed to flirting and talking on WhatsApp and you knew about this. You were worried he would stray and you wanted her gone."

Madison looked away.

"You cloned Jack's phone to keep track of him. You knew, for example, that he'd downloaded security footage of Natasha using the spa and the pool."

"She put on a show for him," Madison spat. "She knew the cameras were there and it looked as if she knew she had an audience. Not to mention the way she walked around half-naked whenever Jack was here."

"But why try and kill Don? Why not go for Natasha, the source?" Paige asked.

Madison didn't reply.

"Because you hate Don, don't you?" Sophie said, taking in Madison's bitter expression. "He's not the most charming man in the world and not particularly fun to have as part of your family. You wanted him gone and Natasha out of the picture."

"Not to mention a sizeable inheritance, right?" Paige added. "And then your life would be perfect."

Leo and Zelda, sitting on either side of Madison (ready to leap into action should she try to do a runner), were following the unveiling like one follows a game of tennis.

"He's awful," Madison said finally. "And because of him, Jack is always working. We hardly ever do anything fun. We can't go on proper holidays. But he won't slow down because he's trying to impress his awful, misogynistic, father. And then when Natasha pulled that sesame seed stunt at dinner, it gave me the start of an idea. When Bruce drowned in the pool and Kate blamed Natasha, everything clicked into place. I knew what I was going to do."

"And what was that, exactly?" Paige said excitedly.

Madison, as if realising that she perhaps didn't need to confess to anything, folded her arms across her chest and clamped her mouth shut.

"We all knew Dad was having a spa and a drink that night," Kate said into the silence. "Everyone went to bed so you must have pretended to fall asleep, waited until Jack nodded off, then crept out of your room. When you saw Don still there, drunkenly sitting in the spa, you must have thought *what a perfect opportunity*, right?" Kate's eyes bored into Madison. "So you pushed him under but then I came into the kitchen, probably making a lot of noise, and you immediately ducked down and crawled back through the sliding doors. It would have been easy to hide yourself. And when I went out to the spa, you ran back to bed and pretended to wake up with everyone else."

Madison looked away.

"Did Tina know?" Kate said, a tremble in her voice. "About your plan?"

Madison turned back to Kate, her expression now resigned and almost indifferent. "Tina knows nothing."

Kate abruptly stood and walked over to the window to gaze out through the glass, obviously working through some emotions.

For a moment no one said anything.

"Hang on," Leo said. "Don thought his wife was maybe trying to kill him but he didn't do anything about it? Didn't even acknowledge it? He must have realised she was the one who turned off the security cameras and he didn't worry about why? That doesn't make sense."

"Cognitive dissonance," Paige and Sophie said at the same time.

"Huh?"

"Our brains really don't like trying to hold two conflicting beliefs," Paige said. "Don was more invested in believing Natasha loves him, so he had to discard the information that she might be trying to kill him. Who knows what mental gymnastics he did to make that possible in his head, but based on his actions, he obviously refused to acknowledge that she could try to kill him."

"I think Dad really loves Natasha," Kate said, staying where she was but turning back to the group.

"But she lied to him about who she is," Zelda said.

"Yeah, I guess they're sorting that out right now," Kate said.

There was a knock on the door.

"That'll be Roman," Paige said.

As she and Sophie followed Kate to answer the door, Madison leaned over to urgently whisper something in Leo's ear.

31

Monday morning, Kate took her coffee out to the balcony. The morning was chilly so she wrapped her cardigan tighter around her shoulders. She could hear Tina moving around inside, treading carefully as if she didn't want to disturb Kate, but it wasn't so much about noise as it was the argument they'd had last night.

Kate had wanted to have an intervention for her father, but Tina thought that Kate should just let her father live his life as he saw fit. But how could he stay married to Natasha when she lied about who she was? No wonder she'd seemed like a character from an eighties movie. She kind of was. She'd even admitted to punishing her father for his pretty typical less-than-ideal behaviour in borderline sadistic ways. The sesame oil on the salad, the 'accidental' electrocution. Part of Kate couldn't wait to tell her mother about this; she'd probably take great pleasure in the news. But another part of her felt shocked about the whole situation. And she still couldn't believe the casual way Natasha had confessed to these deeds and the relaxed way her father had taken the news. Her father didn't care that she'd artificially enhanced her Russian heritage and donned a fake name. He seemed almost proud of what Natasha had done; of how she'd behaved. As if it was some sort of testament to her love or commitment to him. Was this some sort of Later Life Crisis her dad was going through? Some sort of irrational behaviour akin to buying a ridiculous sports car? Was Natasha the human version of an impractical, dangerous, flashy sports car that would definitely cost him a lot of money and of which he'd probably ultimately lose control? Because if you were going to go out, you might as well go out in a dramatic fireball?

Kate sighed. It actually made sense. Especially for someone like her father.

"Tina?" She called behind her.

"Yeah?"

"Want to join me?"

She turned her head so she could see Tina's face.

"Sure." She smiled. "I'll bring more coffee."

"And a blanket?" Kate called back. "It's pretty cold out here."

As Tina clattered around the kitchen, seeming to have gotten the message Kate was hoping she'd receive: that all was well and Kate now agreed with her.

Kate turned back to gaze out over the city. She unclenched her jaw and pushed her shoulders down. She had to let her father lead his life, no matter how foolish, impractical, or dangerous it might be.

· · · · ·· ·· · ·

Professor Richard Thinton eyed his ringing phone warily. It wasn't going to be that human mosquito Mike again would it? He picked it up and eyed the display. No, but it was another nuisance in his life. The whole point of staying late at the office was to avoid *this*.

"Yes?"

"Don't answer the phone like that," his wife hissed. "We haven't even started the conversation and you've already got that 'I'm being nagged to death' tone in your voice."

"You're overreacting."

"My god, you're irritating. And I don't nag you, we barely even talk to each other these days."

"Listen—"

"Ugh, whatever. The mechanics called. Your car is ready."

She slammed down the phone.

Good god, she was driving him insane recently. What on earth could he do about this situation? Was it time to talk to his lawyer? Richard nodded to himself. Perhaps it would be wise to get the ball rolling, to start shifting some things around. He couldn't have her stepping away with half of everything he'd built up over the years. He turned to his computer and made a note in his diary.

When his computer pinged with an email, he went to his inbox. Four hundred unread messages that would never see the light of day, but four new ones at the top of the feed would get some attention for the next while. Because if he left the office now he might arrive before his wife went out, even with the added step of picking up his car on the way.

The first two emails were from colleagues, boring administrative matters. He chuckled to himself as he sent two rather jaunty replies. He was rather witty on the old email, Richard thought to himself. (He was not.)

The next one gave him pause at first. He didn't understand the significance until the second read-through. "Ah," he said out loud.

Once he had realised that the SOS Agency was a waste of time he'd banished it to the archives of his mind (filed under *failures that had nothing to do with me*). But perhaps something good had come out of it after all. When he first looked into the logistics of setting up a private investigator business, he'd done his due diligence, reaching out to his contacts here and there as appropriate, including asking about what certification was expected. And now, an inside contact at the Ministry of Justice had just let him know of a new requirement. Private Investigators now had to be licensed by the Ministry of Justice, pursuant to the PSPLA Act.

"Ha!" Richard crowed. Was Paige aware of this? It was brand new legislation so he suspected not. Could he get them struck off the registry, or whatever it was called, because they were operating without a license? At the very least he could get them some bad publicity and it was certainly worth a shot. He opened a new email and sent one to his reporter friend

Andrew Finch. Had he used up all his favours with Finchy by now? No matter, he could earn new ones.

Once he'd sent the email suggesting they get together for a beer, he sat back and smiled. This could be it. This could be the way to taking down S & S Investigations.

Just then there was a knock at his office door. He turned to see a familiar face. "Oh, hello." He squinted at her. "Sorry, I know we've met but I can't remember...."

"Zelda," she said. "Can I talk to you?"

32

Paige fixed amazed eyes on Leo. "Madison told you where to find the deleted footage?"

"Basically, yeah."

"But why?"

"That's why I'm here," Leo said, pulling his laptop from his bag as he took a seat at the conference table. "To show you."

"Why didn't you tell us this that night?" Paige demanded.

"Because I had to first access then clean up the footage. I didn't want to get you all excited and have nothing to tell you."

"Should we get excited now?" Paige said.

"I'm not sure excited is the right word." Leo made a face. "The cameras were recording when Bruce died."

"They weren't turned off after all?" Sophie said.

"Actually, they were, but not until after he died. And then Madison hacked in and turned them back on but redirected the file footage to be sent directly to her own storage area in the cloud. The files weren't stored in the normal place so it looked like nothing had been recorded."

"For how long? When did she hack in?" Paige asked.

"She'd cloned Jack's phone, remember? So she'd had access to the system for months, but those diverted files start from the weekend Bruce died."

"So she kept footage of what happened, and kept recording," Sophie said.

"Yeah."

"Why?" Paige asked.

"Probably because she wanted to keep watching what Natasha was doing," Sophie said. "Gathering evidence."

"Right, because of the framing plan," Paige said.

"So if Madison told you to access the footage, that suggests it doesn't incriminate her."

"Yeah." Leo made a face then turned his laptop around so they could all see his screen. "Let me show you."

Paige turned to Sophie. "This is number one."

"Huh?" Sophie replied.

"You said if we need to project footage or clues or whatever onto a screen four more times, then we can get a big screen. This is number one. Three more to go."

Sophie eyed her friend. Paige lifted her palms to the sky. "You made the rule."

"So, my image resolution enhancement skills are a bit rusty, but I got there in the end," Leo said.

"And?" Paige said impatiently.

"You know how there are two cameras out on the patio?"

"The one right near the pool house, facing the pool, had the best angle to show what happened to Bruce," Sophie said.

"Right. And that one shows him drowning without anyone else in frame. No one touched him."

"But?" Paige prompted.

"But when you look at the other camera, from the other side of the deck, you can see some of the French doors that lead into the house." Leo pressed play on his laptop.

Paige and Sophie both leaned closer and watched Bruce stumble out to the spa pool holding a bottle of something, then sit on the edge and dangle his feet in the water.

"There's something kind of morbid about this," Paige said cheerfully.

"I agree," Sophie shivered. "Knowing at some point in the near future he won't be alive anymore is grim."

"Okay, I'll speed up the next twenty minutes."

Leo fast-forwarded through Bruce doing almost nothing at all except sitting and drinking, until he leaned forwards a little, his chin tucking into his chest, then fell face first into the pool.

Sophie averted her eyes. "Okay, this is now officially horrible. I don't want to see this, Leo."

"Okay, don't look at Bruce," Leo used his hand to cover part of the screen. "Look at that instead." Leo paused the frame and pointed to the lefthand side.

"Holy crap," Paige exclaimed.

Sophie sucked in a shocked gasp. Visible through the French doors, looking out at the pool, seeming to watch Bruce as he slid into the water and ultimately drown, was Natasha.

"Wow," Paige breathed.

"She knew," Sophie said. "She watched and she didn't do anything. When we asked her about deleting the footage the other day I got a bit of a dishonest vibe, but she's one of those people, I suspect, that can lie without giving off any indicators. Because she's kind of disconnected from the truth, if that makes sense. In her narrative, she didn't do anything wrong."

"It was Natasha who deleted the files from the home system because she was worried she could be seen letting him drown, right?" Paige said. "And then she probably turned off the whole system so she was free to do whatever dodgy stuff she wanted."

"Yeah, the files were deleted at four a.m.," Leo said. "She must have gone to bed then woken up again when she remembered the cameras. She must not have realised that the footage was almost immediately uploaded to the cloud."

"Which is where Madison saw it," Sophie said.

"But why would Madison remove the evidence? She wanted Natasha out of the picture," Paige said.

"She wanted to frame Natasha for *Don's* death, right?" Leo said. "Not Bruce's."

"Right," Sophie said. "Because if Madison had turned over to the police the footage of Natasha watching Bruce drown, then Natasha might have been arrested immediately."

"And then Madison couldn't frame Natasha for Don's death," Leo said. "Because Natasha, in jail, would have a rock-solid alibi."

"You can't frame a woman who is locked up," Paige finished.

"Madison kept the footage of what Natasha did, or didn't do, I suppose, in case she needed it as evidence that Natasha is capable of murder," Sophie said.

"And Madison hacked in and turned the cameras back on so she could catch Natasha doing other dodgy things," Paige said.

"And she changed where the feed was sent so no one knew except her," Leo finished.

"Oh," Sophie said, nodding to herself. "That's why she recognised me when we met her at Kate's place. She'd seen us on the cameras snooping through the house that night."

"It all tracks," Paige said happily.

For a moment, the three of them were quiet, processing this rather macabre discovery.

"So what do we do with this information?" Sophie asked.

"We take it to Roman," Paige replied.

"And we should tell Kate to warn her father too."

"Roman will ask how we got it. This isn't legal." Leo looked alarmed.

"Okay fine, we'll send it in anonymously. They'll assume it was Don or his family."

Paige stared at the image. "Even with this footage, I'm pretty sure she's going to be able to argue that she didn't see what happened to Bruce. She'll say she just happened to be standing there and she wasn't looking at him at all. He didn't cry out or make a splash or anything."

"We still don't know why she's been using the name Natasha," Sophie said. "Was it really just to seem more exotic?"

"I think she was pre-emptively using a fake identity so she could abandon it if she needed to run." Paige nodded.

"Do we still do the whisky celebration?" Leo asked, looking from Paige to Sophie.

After a moment, Paige shrugged. "We solved two cases and we got paid."

As she went over and got out the whisky and three tumblers Leo turned to Sophie. "I've been meaning to ask you for ages. How is it going with Roman? Going away together is a big deal."

"*What*?" Paige cried, turning to Sophie. "You and Roman went away together?"

Sophie cast a panicked look at Leo who made a clueless face in response.

"I was going to tell you, there's just been so much going on."

"Oh my god, Sophie, that's epic. Tell me everything!"

Before Sophie could say anything, Paige's phone rang. She looked at the display. "I don't know this number," she said, then shrugged and answered the call. "Doctor Garnet, S and S Investigations. Yes?" She started walking slowly into the main office. "Oh, right. Random. What? Yeah, I do. What's going on?"

"Leo," Sophie hissed once Paige had moved away.

"What?"

"Why did you say that?"

"Say what?"

"About me and Roman."

"It's a secret?" Leo's eyes went wide. "I had no idea."

"No, I suppose you wouldn't. Sorry, I just haven't—"

Suddenly, Paige was back, her face thunderous. "That's what you and Roman were doing? Sneaking around behind my back, asking questions about Dad?"

Sophie could only stare at Paige's furious expression.

"That was Laurie Jefferies on the phone, a guy Dad used to work with. He wanted to know if I needed any help with my investigation into Dad's death." Paige's mouth was set in a tight white line.

"I'm sorry, Paige, I was keeping it low key until we knew whether—"

"Keeping *it* low key? How could you?" Paige's eyes were bright and wet. "I can't believe this. First you finally get together with your dream guy and you don't even tell me. And then I find out the reason is because you're sneaking around behind my back, digging into Dad's death."

"Paige, I'm sorry."

"How did Leo know?"

"What?"

"How. Did. Leo. Know?" she repeated, her jaw clenched. "About you and Roman. About going away together?"

"Oh, I.... I called him. But only because—"

"Because you were too busy lying to me about *everything*."

"Paige, please—"

Paige held up one hand, her face turning red, then picked up her bag and stalked out of the room. Sophie followed her progress with shocked eyes.

"What have I done?" she whispered.

33

Nearly one week had passed since Paige had stormed out of the office. She still refused to speak to Sophie, Leo, or Roman. She wouldn't talk to Tim either, except for sulky replies to his "at least let me know you're alive" messages.

Sophie had known Paige wouldn't react well but the situation had been exacerbated by terrible timing. Right in the middle of her separation from Tim was maybe the worst time to find out that Sophie had been lying to her.

Sophie knew from Alice Garnet's Instagram feed (she'd really taken to social media), that Paige was staying with her but from the increasingly forced smiles and passive aggressive captions documenting their time together, Sophie suspected that this arrangement might come to an end soon. What then for Paige? Would she go home to Tim to sort things out? Would she reach out to Sophie? Or would she stubbornly refuse to let her apologise (again) and find someone else to stay with. Or would she do something more drastic like find a new flat. The latter was possible. Paige could be stubborn. Sophie knew she deserved this radio silence, but it couldn't last forever, could it? And how was Paige spending her time? Without an active case to work on and nowhere to go every day, she and her mother had to be driving each other absolutely nuts.

"Sophie?" Leo said, sitting across from her in the conference room. "Are you okay?"

"I was just thinking about...." Sophie trailed off. It wasn't necessary to explain what she'd been thinking about. She had called this Sunday afternoon meeting because she couldn't spend another day doing nothing. They had to figure out a way forwards.

She'd asked Roman if he could make it here but he had been called in to work as well. The only upside to the whole Paige situation was that she and Roman had had a chance to properly connect over the past week, and that horrible creeping doubt about whether he still felt the same about her had finally been put to rest.

"Do you think she'll come back to work soon?" Leo asked. "Should we try going over there again?"

Sophie thought for a moment. "I don't think she's going to talk until she's ready. It's not so much us making a case for ourselves and apologising as her coming to terms with the situation and deciding how she wants to proceed."

"What if she decides to move to a different country and make new friends?" Leo said in a small voice.

Something churned in Sophie's stomach. "We won't be able to stop her."

"But...." Leo trailed off.

"If Paige had learned what I did, that there are some big questions about what really happened to her father, then she wouldn't have let it go either. It's painful now, but I think this needed to happen. We just didn't go about it the right way."

"I agree. But I still think we should try to find Daniel Crane," Leo said. "If that turns out to be a dead-end we can drop it. Or at least, let Paige decide what she wants to do."

Sophie nodded. "I doubt Paige could cope with being actively involved in the investigation. I can't imagine her being able to go through the details of his death, trying to determine whether someone did it on purpose. It would be excruciating. No. If we can find this Daniel guy, he might have a major piece of information. If we can't find him then there are no other avenues to follow up, right?"

"Right," Leo said.

"So let's at least finish what we started. Otherwise it will all have been for nothing."

· · • • • • • • · ·

Alice Garnet put away the vacuum cleaner then walked over to where her daughter was lolling on the couch and staring at the television. From the coffee table she picked up the remote. As the screen went blank, Paige lifted her head.

"Hey! I was watching that."

"You were watching a documentary about steam engines?"

"It was riveting."

Alice moved Paige's legs and sat down on the couch. She smoothed the material of her neatly ironed trousers across her knees, picked off a stray piece of fluff, then turned to her daughter.

"Paige, darling, you've been here a week now."

"I'm aware of that."

"Well...."

As nice as it was to have someone to eat dinner with (and it was quite nice, Alice had to admit), Alice was an independent woman used to living an independent life. Having her daughter moping around the house without doing anything remotely useful (was Paige under the impression dishes magically washed themselves? That laundry cleaned and folded itself?) was cramping her style. In more ways than one.

"Isn't it about time you got things sorted out?"

"Sure." Paige snapped her fingers angrily. "There. Done."

Alice rolled her eyes. "Good lord, did I really raise you to be this immature?"

"Seems like it. I've got your genes and I'm the product of your parenting. Not sure who else you could find to blame."

"Not just *my* genes."

At this, they both fell silent. Alice had been told of the reason for Paige and Sophie's falling out. At first by Paige, in a barely coherent stream of words that had tumbled out as she'd stomped into the house and marched up the stairs, uninvited, to set up camp in the spare room. A more comprehensive version of events had then been offered by Sophie when Alice had called her to ask what on earth was going on.

"You're not happy like this. Sophie didn't go about things the best way—"

"Ha!"

"... and you've hit a bit of a hurdle with Tim, granted, but ignoring both of those problems like this isn't going to fix anything."

"But I didn't do anything wrong," Paige said in a small voice.

Alice took a breath and steeled herself. "I have a date tonight."

"*What*?"

"I thought you'd be gone by now."

"But I'm not."

"He's coming over. I'm cooking him dinner."

Paige's eyes went wide. "You can't."

"Yes I can."

"But—"

"Paige, darling, this is hardly a new development. I've been on several dates over the past year. I've even had—"

Paige held up her hand to stop her finishing the sentence. "But not in my presence. For the most part, anyway."

For a moment they both fell silent, acknowledging the couple of times that Paige had unfortunately borne witness to her mother's romantic life.

"It was your decision to move in here. Not mine. You have other options you know."

Paige crossed her arms grumpily. "Do I?" She looked down, then up again, sitting up properly as her eyes suddenly became wet with tears. "It's only been five years since Dad died. How can you disrespect—"

"Paige Garnet!" Alice set her lips in a firm line. "Not a day goes by that I don't think about your father. Not a single day. But I get lonely. And I do enjoy the occasional date. The company of a gentleman."

"Mum, oh my god, don't—"

"Don't shush me. Don't you dare. You are in my house, remember."

"Dad's house," Paige mumbled.

"I listen to the last message he left, right before he went on that infernal fishing trip, every day." Alice's voice shook and tears sprung into her eyes. "Every single night before I go to sleep. Do not accuse me of being unfaithful or disloyal to Terry. I will always love him. Always. But I can't just rattle around this house for the rest of my life." She fixed her eyes on Paige, her expression both furious and sad.

Paige sighed heavily and dropped her head forwards so that it rested on her hands. "I don't know what to do, Mum." Her voice was small. "Everything is such a mess."

"I know." Alice leaned across to rub her daughter's arm. "I know it feels like they betrayed you, but everyone has your best interests at heart. No one is doing anything to hurt you intentionally."

"It still hurts."

"I know. And that's okay. You let it hurt for a while, and then you refocus your mind on the intentions behind the actions. Think about what Sophie, and Tim, want, what they're trying to do. And then you go talk to them and you figure it out."

34

At S & S Investigations, Leo and Sophie sat across from each other, both working on their laptops.

"This is weird without Paige," Leo said after a while.

Sophie stopped reading and looked up. "I know. I almost can't stand it. I keep waiting for her to come back with dinner or a case update. It feels wrong."

"Should we change location? Get dinner and work at the restaurant?"

Sophie thought for a moment. "But what if she shows up and we're not here?"

"True."

Sophie gestured at Leo's laptop. "How are you getting on?"

"Nothing yet. Anything from Roman?"

"He's taking another look at police databases."

Roman, grabbing moments while working his actual job, was trying official channels again while Sophie and Leo went through all the social media and general internet avenues they could think of to find Daniel Crane.

"Okay, what about a reverse image search," Sophie said. "We have that photo that Roman downloaded from the database."

"Already tried. I got a bunch of hits but nothing recent. Five years ago Daniel pretty much disappeared. Not hard to do when you sell your Auckland property for a bunch of cash you can live off of."

"Which he did right before he disappeared."

"But then what?"

"He's renting somewhere and paying cash?"

"Staying with a friend?"

"Maybe his friend bought a house under their name but used Daniel's money."

Leo nodded. "Definitely possible."

"So how do we find him?"

They thought some more.

"Wait. What if he didn't disappear? What if someone *disappeared* him," Leo said. Their eyes met.

"Then we're at a dead end."

"Literally." Leo grimaced.

Just then Leo's phone rang. Sophie and Leo locked hopeful eyes.

"Is it her?" Sophie said. It was completely within Paige's M.O. to reach out to Leo instead of Sophie.

Leo grabbed at his phone to check the display, then frowned. "No."

Sophie's shoulders slumped. Leo continued to eye the display. Sophie watched him. "Who is it?" she asked, taking in his uncertain expression. His eyes shifted to hers. They looked almost guilty.

"Leo?"

"Hang on."

He stood and moved into the other room, shutting the door behind him as he answered the call. Sophie watched him go, frustrated. If Paige were here she would have jumped up and pressed her ear against the door so she could eavesdrop on Leo's mysterious call. But that wasn't Sophie's style, so she would just have to hope that Leo would tell her what that was all about when he returned. Sophie turned her attention to the whiteboard. It sat unused in the corner, abandoned and forlorn. She sighed.

"Sorry about that," Leo said as he opened the door and took his seat across from Sophie.

"No worries." She studied his face, trying to make sense of his expression. His eyes met hers. He gave her an uncertain smile.

"Everything okay?" she asked.

"Yeah, I...."

"Was that call bad news?"

"No. Someone I...." Leo looked down. "This is weirdly hard to say."

Sophie felt a pulse of worry rocket through her body. "Leo? What's up?"

His eyes met hers. "Everything's fine," he said quickly. "I guess it's just this thing that I.... but now with Paige and... I don't know." He shrugged. "I'm feeling the urge to tell you something I thought I never would."

"Yes? You can tell me anything." Sophie was holding her breath.

What could this be?

"A while ago, I, uh, after Alice and I...."

"Broke up?" Sophie finished.

"Yeah," Leo said. "And we had that Murder At The Reunion case with that guy Wade who worked as an escort?"

"Of course."

Wade and Sophie had gone to the same high school, unexpectedly reconnecting at a different high school reunion.

"He worked as an escort and I kind of got the idea to...."

Sophie's eyes went wide. "You got a side hustle as a male escort?" She clapped one hand over her mouth.

"See, this is why I didn't want to say anything."

"Sorry, sorry. I'm not judging. I dated Wade, remember? It's just... unexpected."

Leo, who'd enjoyed a confidence surge after a bit of a glow-up, had ridden this wave into the books of Yvette Collier, who was, for lack of a better word, a madam. She owned a male escort agency at which nice young men like Leo could be paid to take older ladies on dates. Nothing more, just simple excursions to dinners and events that women might want to attend with a date who offered no stress nor complications.

And so, Leo explained this to Sophie.

"I didn't really get very far. I mean, I got onto her books and even went on a couple of dates, but as S and S got busier I didn't need the extra money."

"But you could carry on doing that if you wanted to. If you enjoyed it. Did you enjoy it?" Sophie asked, genuinely curious.

"I guess I did, sort of. But life kept getting in the way. And it feels a bit off to do that while I'm dating someone in real life."

"And are you? Dating someone?" Sophie asked.

"No."

But you'd like to be, Sophie thought but didn't say.

"So yeah." Leo sat back. "I kept it a secret from you all this time and that felt wrong. Plus you knew I was keeping a secret, right?"

Sophie nodded. "I picked up on it, yeah. I figured you'd tell us when you were ready."

"I don't know why it matters." He lifted his shoulders. "It just seems like something you should know. All this stuff with Paige, I guess. Keeping secrets from your friends doesn't feel right."

"Tell me about it." Sophie grimaced. "But thank you for sharing," she added with a smile.

· · · • · • • · ·

At the knock on the front door, Paige grabbed her now-full drink bottle, the reason she'd come down to the kitchen, and ran quickly and quietly up the stairs.

"Paige, are you not going to say hello?" her mother asked as Paige whizzed past her on the stairs.

"To your *date*? Nope."

She would *tolerate* her mother entertaining a gentleman caller tonight, but she refused to participate in the evening. To shake his hand and smile and make small talk with an interloper? No, thank you.

Paige took her laptop into bed and got under the covers and after scrolling through options on three streaming platforms, decided on *The Nice Guys*, a seventies P.I. comedy starring Russell Crowe and Ryan Gosling. She'd watched it before but for maybe the first time in her life she understood why Sophie watched TV shows and movies that she'd already seen. Because it was comforting to know what to expect. Because you knew you wouldn't be hit with a horrible, triggering scene that slammed into your chest and eviscerated your heart just when you were feeling at your most vulnerable.

Paige pushed away the image of Sophie's apologetic face that had popped into her head and pressed play.

Halfway through, after one particularly sweet scene between Ryan and his onscreen daughter, Paige paused the movie and wandered out of the room she'd been sleeping in. Her childhood bedroom had long been converted into a yoga and crafts room for her mother. She paused at the top of the stairs, hearing her mother's laugh ring out. Wincing, she stepped back and entered her parents' room.

Then, like she'd done many, many times before, she went to the double closet and pulled out a photo album from a box nestled in the bottom. Paige found her favourite photo of her and her father, taken at the beach. Him grinning through his moustache and Paige on his shoulders, squinting into the sun with her little paws firmly gripping his forehead. A lump appeared in her throat and she swallowed it away. She sighed a heavy sad sigh. It was time.

• • • • • • • • •

Sophie and Leo, having now acknowledged that Daniel Crane might already be dead but latching onto the possibility he wasn't, had carried on with their search.

"Shame Roman can't pull strings and access Daniel's bank information," Leo said.

"I'm glad Roman isn't able or prepared to do that," Sophie said. "That's basically corrupt."

"True."

Sophie tapped her pen against her notepad. "Okay, so he's living life off the grid. He doesn't have a current driver's license so he's either taking taxis everywhere—"

"Or he's walking."

"Or biking." Sophie nodded. "In which case he lives in the type of place you can get around easily without a car."

"Would that be a smaller city?"

"I mean, it's possible to get around Auckland without a car, but maybe...." Sophie trailed off, her eyes going wide.

"What is it?"

"Fishing."

"No thanks, not really a fan."

"Daniel was super into fishing. He's the reason Terry went on that trip at all."

"And?"

"What is Daniel doing all day if he's retired and living off the grid?"

Leo smiled. "Fishing."

"So he'd go somewhere that had good fishing, right?"

"That doesn't narrow it down much, but.... is it crazy to think that he moved to Whangarei, the place they went fishing the night Terry disappeared?" Leo said.

"No, that's not crazy. It's completely logical. So do we go there and just walk around and look for him?"

"We could, but Whangarei is pretty big. Let's first try something easier."

"Yeah?"

"Search the internet."

Sophie smiled. "Of course. Fishing plus Whangarei plus his name."

And finally, they got a break.

35

The next day at around three o'clock, Sophie pulled on her coat, packed her laptop into her bag, then hoisted it onto her shoulder. After finding reference to a Daniel in a fishing magazine, and then another one in a local fishing blog, they were able to hone in on a suburb of Whangarei. Today, she and Roman were going to drive there, about an hour north of Auckland, and essentially ask around until they found him. Neither of them expected to find success at first go, but they were prepared to stay overnight and try again tomorrow. At the thought of more time with Roman, despite the messiness of the Paige situation, Sophie's stomach did an excited (and nervous) flip.

Her phone beeped. A message from Roman himself.

Leaving work now. Ready to go? x

But before she could reply 'yes', Paige walked through the door.

"Oh." Sophie stopped.

"I'm here." Paige paused by Sophie's desk and started to fiddle with the pen holder, her eyes down. "What're you doing?" she mumbled, still not looking up.

"Um." Sophie swallowed. "Nothing." She eased off her coat. Her overnight bag sat by her feet waiting, but out of Paige's eyeline. Sophie couldn't tell whether or not Paige had noticed Sophie had been about to exit the office, but it didn't matter. Paige was here and Sophie wasn't about to leave.

"What's up?" Sophie asked casually.

"Nothing." Paige selected one of the pens and started clicking the end up and down, up and down, her eyes fixed on her pointless task.

"I, uh, I'm glad you're here," Sophie said tentatively.

"Whatever." Paige shrugged, then abruptly turned and walked into the other room. Sophie watched Paige set her bag on the table then heard her turn on the coffee machine.

Sophie, heart racing, pulled out her phone and sent a quick text to Roman.

Paige just showed up at the office!

Great news.

I have to stay and talk to her.

We could go to Whangarei tomorrow instead?

Love to but it depends on what Paige says.

I understand. I'll keep working on getting an address for Daniel in the meantime and chase down any other possible leads.

OK. Message me later. X

XX

Sophie walked through to the second office. Paige was standing at the whiteboard, staring at the notes from The Case of the Missing Michael. On the flipside was The Case of the Black Widow. (She hadn't been Don's black widow but she definitely had the potential.) They'd solved both already but Paige always liked to keep the notes until the whiteboard needed to be cleaned off for another client.

"Mum had a date last night," she said finally.

"Really? Who with?"

"Just some guy." Paige shrugged. "She made him dinner."

"Did you...?"

"I stayed in my room." Paige gave her a small smile. "I didn't even meet him."

Sophie nodded. "Fair enough."

Silence fell.

Sophie swallowed. "Paige, I'm sorry. I'm sorry I didn't tell you. I honestly thought it was the best way. But I can see now it wasn't."

Paige looked down, not saying anything. She traced her fingers across the smooth wood of the table. "I feel so... raw."

Sophie nodded. "I get it."

"It's just brought everything up again."

"I know. That's why we kept it from you."

"How did it even start?"

"Roman always thought something was off about that investigation. Seeing you at the Dixon's house for our very first case brought it all back. He started looking into it just kind of sporadically and then..."

"He asked you to help?"

Sophie swallowed again, a hard painful lump of deceit. "Paige, I have to be honest with you. If we're going to move forwards, I have to tell you the truth."

Paige looked up, her expression suddenly stricken.

"Part of it was just being close to Roman. It was an excuse to hang out with him. I knew I shouldn't but I couldn't resist. He was married. And he knew he shouldn't be spending time with me but he couldn't resist either. So all that got tangled up in hiding the investigation. It wasn't about hiding it from you, although we both wanted to protect you, but it was also kind of an act of denial, you know?"

"You and Roman had an affair?"

"No. God, no. He and Anya are done. The baby is Eric's."

"Oh." Paige's eyes were bright. "That's great. I'm so happy for you."

Sophie took a step towards her. "That trip to Te Awamutu was to talk to the retired cop who worked on your dad's, uh, investigation. That's when we, uh, kind of ...." Sophie felt her cheeks warm.

"I'm glad you weren't secretly seeing him this whole time. I mean. In that way."

"I couldn't have kept it from you for that long. It was eating me up not being able to share it with you for even that short amount of time."

Paige gave her a small smile. "I'm happy for you, Soph. Honestly. You two were always meant to be together."

Sophie gave her a shaky smile. "Thanks."

Without warning, Paige lurched forwards to pull Sophie into a fierce hug. Sophie returned it, just as fierce, until Paige whimpered. "I can't breathe."

Sophie released her. Sorry. It's just…. you've forgiven me now?"

"Yeah. But this means you have to forgive me too."

Sophie's eyes went wide. "What did you do?"

"Nothing. But I will. Probably. Right?"

Sophie smiled. "Deal."

They took seats at the conference table.

"How are you feeling?" Sophie asked.

"All of this has brought up all the old emotions I thought were gone."

"I know. And I'm sorry about that."

"Maybe it's for the best. Maybe I needed this to properly let go."

"Maybe."

"Mum told me she still listens to the last voicemail Dad left her every day. Every single day."

"Oh. That makes me sad."

"I know. I've been a bit mean to Mum, I think."

Sophie gave her a small smile. "Yeah?"

"I used to blame her. Like, I used to rant at her in my head. Why did she let him go fishing. He never went fishing. I don't know why that's Mum's fault but I did blame her. At least partly." Paige lifted her shoulders in a shrug.

"Paige, that makes total sense."

"It does?"

"It's so much easier to blame someone else and release the pain and anger in someone else's direction, particularly someone you regularly argue with, than it is to process those feelings internally," Sophie said.

"Still."

"You can be nice to her from now on?" Sophie offered.

Paige met her eyes and made a face. "All the time?"

• • • • •• • • • • •

Roman sat in his car thinking about what he should do. More than half of the appeal of driving to Whangarei had been spending time with Sophie, so should he still go? Drive up now and see what he could find out? But now that Paige was back on deck maybe she should be included, or at least consulted. As he continued to mull over his next steps, his phone rang. When he looked at the display, he frowned. This could be interesting.

He answered the call.

36

Paige crumpled up her napkin and tossed it in the rubbish bin near the door. Their mostly finished Thai takeaway sat at one end of the table, case notes at the other.

"I have missed this so much," Paige said.

Sophie smiled. "It wasn't even remotely the same without you. This place, us, doesn't exist without Doctor Paige Garnet. Brilliant, tenacious, and," she paused to give Paige a cheeky grin, "tactless."

"Hey." Paige grinned. "My blunt interpersonal style has gotten us places we wouldn't have otherwise."

"Agreed."

"Okay, let's go over everything you and Roman learned once more."

"You're sure you're okay to do this?"

Paige nodded. "If it gets too much I'll let you know." She lifted her chin. "But it won't because I'm going to find out what happened to my dad. I'm going to send that bastard to jail."

"And I'm going to help you," Sophie said.

Once Sophie had summarised the progress they'd made with their investigation into the death of Terry Garnet, they both sat back.

"So we need to talk to Daniel Crane," Paige said.

"We do."

Sophie decided not to tell Paige that that's where they'd planned to go this very evening. It could wait until tomorrow.

"Is it worth asking your mum about this?" Sophie said.

Paige made a face. "Not sure. What would we ask?"

"I don't know, like, did anything weird happen that day?"

Paige tilted her head. "Okay, but it might work out better if you or Roman do that. Actually, Mum would probably respond very well to Roman's questions. Where is he, by the way?"

"He said something about following leads but didn't specify." Sophie got out her phone. "I'll message him right now."

"And Leo and Zelda are on their way, right?"

"I think so, although Leo didn't reply to me now that I think about it." Sophie glanced down at her phone display. "Oh, he's left a voicemail." She dialled into the message and listened to Leo explain that he and Zelda were on their way. She frowned. "Why didn't he just text?" She played the message again. "His voice sounds weird."

"Bad weird? Did Zelda do something to him?"

Sophie laughed. "No. It's almost like...." She played the message a third time. "It's like... before Leo begins talking, he laughs and says something to Zelda, obviously with him, and then his voice is like... it's almost as if he's mildly hysterical."

"Hysterical," Paige repeated.

"Wait." Sophie frowned. "Not hysterical. Elated? Euphoric." She nodded. "He sounds giddy."

"Oh!" Paige shouted. "He left a voicemail," she said.

"Uh, yes. I just listened to it three times."

"No. Not Leo. Dad." A strange combination of emotions flickered across Paige's face.

"You mean the one your mum listens to every day?" Sophie's eyes went wide. "Oh, yes, I see."

Paige started hurrying towards the door. "Call Leo back and tell him to meet me at Mum's. I think I might need him for this."

And so Sophie quickly messaged both Leo and Zelda, ultimately reaching Zelda because Leo was driving. Leo turned his car around and drove to the Garnet family home to meet Paige.

Nearly an hour later, the three of them returned to the S & S Investigations offices and joined Sophie in the conference room.

"Play it for them, Leo," Paige said, throwing her coat and bag on the table dramatically.

Leo set down his laptop. "Paige, just give me a second to isolate the bit we're interested in and see if I can enhance the sound."

"But—"

"Do you want us to play the whole message your Dad left over and over?"

Paige's shoulders dropped. "No, I guess I don't."

"Okay, then, just give me a minute." Leo set about his task.

"I'm pretty sure I know what this is all about but can you explain it just so we're all on the same page?" Sophie said to Paige, mostly to distract her.

"Right, sure. Mum told me that every night she listens to a voicemail Dad left her. It's the last time—" Her voice cracked.

Everyone waited for Paige to recover.

"It's from just before he left for the trip. I've heard it before, Mum played it for me ages ago, but I remember it clearly. He left the message right before he boarded the boat and I remember there being a lot of background noise, like distractions. He even breaks off to say something to someone else at one point. I thought there could be something there."

"Right, because according to DS Connolly, Terry was talking to someone on the dock right before they left," Sophie said.

"Maybe there's something in the message to tell us who."

"And is there?" Zelda asked.

"You can hear him talking to someone in the background," Paige said. "So maybe yeah, but it's hard to hear what he's saying. Hopefully Leo can make the sound clearer."

"Okay, here we go," Leo said.

They all listened as Terry Garnet broke off from the message he was leaving his wife, to say, "Oh, hey....[mumble] what are you.... [mumble]".

"He said a name, right?" Paige said.

"Yeah. And I think, "what are you doing here?" is the end of that sentence," Sophie said.

"Leo, is there anything else you can do to enhance the sound?"

"I'll try one more thing."

They waited while he did something on his computer.

"Okay, play it again."

They listened to the message. Again, and again.

"It's two syllables, right?

"Yeah, definitely."

"Barry?"

"Yori?"

"That's not even a name."

Paige's eyes went wide. "Oh my god." She lurched upright.

"What?" Sophie rose too.

"I know what name he said."

"And?"

"Laurie. He said Laurie."

"As in Laurie Jefferies? The lawyer who worked with your dad."

"Maybe. So what was he doing at the dock with Dad?"

"They worked together. Maybe it was about a case?" Sophie offered.

Paige sat down, pulled her laptop closer and started typing into a search engine.

"Is it just me or does Terry sound annoyed," Leo said, playing the message again.

"He does," Sophie said as Paige continued to type and scroll. "He's not happy that Laurie showed up. And it's unexpected. The way he breaks off. You can hear the surprise in his voice."

"It's not like, "Hey mate, you left your wallet in my car", or something," Zelda added.

"Roman spoke to Laurie a few times, right?" Leo said. "You should ask him."

Sophie grabbed her phone and called his number. It rang and rang without being answered. Sophie's face creased with worry. "Why isn't he picking up?"

She dialled again and left him a message to call her back, then texted the same thing.

"Paige, what are you searching?" Zelda asked.

"Laurie's name plus Dad's, their firm, and the year he died," she replied.

"I can work on that too," Leo said.

Sophie moved closer to Paige to look over her shoulder and Zelda did the same with Leo.

It took quite a bit of scrolling, and following leads down rabbit holes, but they eventually found the thing, or perhaps rumour was a better word, that linked the three of them.

A few weeks before Terry's fateful fishing trip there had been rumblings of a whistleblowing situation involving one of New Zealand's largest food-stuffs companies and some sort of regulations scandal. Some eager-beaver reporter had reached out to Terry, who had a reputation for being involved in such things. Terry hadn't confirmed it but it was a link, nonetheless.

"That company issued that product recall." Sophie nodded. "It was like, on the news for a whole week. I remember it."

"A whole lot of people got sick, right?" Zelda said.

"Yes. So how does that tie in...." Leo said.

"I don't know but their firm was involved with the foodstuffs company and Laurie was on the legal team," Paige said.

"Roman met with Laurie a few times," Sophie said, her voice shaky. "Laurie never said anything about seeing your dad just before he went on the fishing trip. Why would Laurie lie about that unless he was covering something up."

"Roman hasn't messaged you back yet?" Leo said. Sophie shook her head.

"Shit," Paige hissed. "When Laurie called me about my Dad's investigation, he was all like, so you're looking into your dad's fishing accident? I was like, no, why would you think that? He said something about Roman and then got all weird and said don't worry, must have been a misunderstanding. And I was just so shocked about the whole situation that the weirdness of the phone call didn't register."

Paige met Sophie's eyes, blinking rapidly with panic.

"He realised that it wasn't you driving the investigation," Sophie said. "He must have worked out it was Roman."

"If Laurie's covering up something, then he thinks the person he needs to silence is Roman," Zelda said.

"Who we now can't get hold of," Paige added.

"Leo?" Sophie turned to him. "Can you—"

"Trace Roman's phone?" He was typing furiously on his laptop, his eyes wild and his expression fierce. "Already on it."

37

Paige switched her headlights to full beam as they left the main road. The sun had long set and illumination from streetlights, houses, and buildings were starting to disappear as they voyaged into increasingly rural surrounds.

"Why is Roman in the Waitakeres?" Sophie asked, not for the first time.

Paige took her eyes off the road to glance at her best friend.

"It's going to be fine," she said, instead of providing the unnerving answer to Sophie's question: because the Waitakere ranges, a huge expanse of forest in west Auckland, was a very good place to make somebody disappear.

They didn't know for sure Laurie had taken Roman, or even that he was involved in Terry's death, but it was the explanation that made the most sense.

"Coverage isn't good out here," Leo said nervously from the back seat. He glanced at Zelda next to him. "Mobile phone tracking isn't going to be possible at some point, I'm pretty sure."

"Paige?" Sophie said.

"I know. Step on it."

The car surged forwards, jostling all four of them. For once, Sophie didn't say anything about Paige's driving.

"Take the next right," Leo said.

Paige barely slowed down to take the corner. Zelda was thrown against Leo in the backseat as Sophie gripped the armrest, bracing herself against the momentum. Paige leaned into the turn, her jaw set.

"We'll have to park here," Leo pointed at the carpark where you could enter the ranges with several hiking and walking routes available. "Go on foot from here."

"Look," Sophie said. "Is that Laurie's car?"

Leo read the license plate and grinned at Zelda. "Yeah."

Zelda had had the bright idea to look this up before they left, just in case they needed to be able to identify Laurie's car quickly and on the go.

"Where's Roman's car?" Sophie said.

"He probably met Laurie somewhere and they drove here together."

"God, I don't know whether to be relieved or worried," Sophie said. "They're probably here but what if...?"

"Come on." Paige leapt out of the car.

"Wait," Zelda said once everyone was outside. "What's the plan? Are we really going to just run into the bushes?"

After a moment, Paige nodded. "You're right, that's stupid. Zelda, you call the police and tell them we have a situation. Tell them we think DS Roman Leconte is in danger. Tell them where we are and that we've gone in after him."

Zelda lifted her phone to her ear. "On it."

"Leo, can you see where his phone is?"

He nodded and pointed to where a path led into the increasingly dense trees. "That way."

"Any idea what's in there?"

"From the map, it looks like there might be an open area, like for picnics or something? And maybe something like an information stand or a small hut?" Leo frowned. "But beyond that, nothing." He gestured at Zelda. "We can't all go in. I can't leave her here alone. What if Laurie comes out. Or we were wrong and...." Leo shrugged helplessly.

"Fine. Give me your phone so I can see where Roman is. At least, as long as we can track his phone. You take mine," Paige handed Leo hers. "Sophie and I are going in together and we're bringing Roman out. Right?"

"Right." Sophie's eyes flashed with resolve.

Leo looked from Zelda, to Paige, to Sophie, then nodded.

"Direct the police in after us as soon as they get here, okay?"

"Got it."

To Sophie, Paige said, "Let's go rescue your boyfriend."

· · · · ●· ●· · · ·

Paige and Sophie crept through the woods, their phone flashlights activated but kept low so as not to announce their presence before they were ready.

"What if he's gone really deep into the bush?" Sophie said quietly.

"Based on this," Paige held up Leo's phone, "they're not far," she whispered back, creeping forwards.

"But Roman could have dropped his phone, or Laurie could have made him turn it off or—"

"Stop," Paige hissed. "I heard something."

They both froze, straining their ears.

"That way." Paige pointed.

They moved quickly but cautiously towards the sound of a voice. After they'd gone a few metres, Sophie gripped Paige's arm. Her eyes wild, she pointed to two figures in a small clearing. Concealed behind a clump of bushes, Sophie and Paige watched the scene in front of them, trying to make sense of what they were looking at. Laurie and Roman sat in camping chairs facing each other but about three metres apart. Laurie was holding a beer in his left hand, taking the occasional swig as he talked, and his right hand was obscured by his body. Paige frowned as her eyes moved to Roman. Like Laurie, one hand wasn't visible, but his other held a beer.

"Are they just, like, hanging out?" Paige whispered. "Did we get this all wrong?"

"No." Sophie said, her voice low and her face pale. "They're not and we didn't." She motioned for Paige to follow her back the way they'd come.

Once they were far enough away so they could talk properly, Sophie said, "Laurie has him hostage. I'm pretty sure Roman's hand is handcuffed to the chair, and," she paused, her expression serious, "I think I saw a gun in Laurie's hand."

Paige's eyes widened. "That would explain why Roman is just sitting there not doing anything."

Sophie nodded.

"We have to act fast."

"What are we going to do?"

Paige thought for a moment. "What we do best. Distract And Ambush." She looked around, then darted forwards to grab something off the ground. She then stepped up to Sophie and smeared the dirt she'd just picked up on Sophie's cheeks.

"Hey!"

Paige dropped the rest of the dirt and wiped her hands on Sophie's jeans, then yanked Sophie's hair out of her ponytail.

"Ow."

"Sorry," Paige said, not convincingly. She mussed Sophie's hair so she looked as if she'd just stumbled out of bed.

Sophie opened her mouth to protest again, then nodded. "I get it." She pushed away Paige's fussing hands. "I get what we're doing." Sophie took off her coat and pulled at the neck of her t-shirt until it ripped.

Paige studied her then nodded. "Good. You make a perfect Damsel in Distress."

"Yay. Lifelong dream achieved," Sophie said wryly, but then brought nervous eyes back to Paige. "So what's the precise plan?"

38

"You distract Laurie, I sneak up and grab the gun," Paige said.

They stared at each other for a moment.

"Are we really going to just go in there? Gun and everything?"

"Yes."

"Is it going to work?"

"Yes." Paige lifted her chin. "Because if I can't get the gun off him, then at least Roman can spring into action. He's only tied to a camping chair and it's only one hand. The way I see it, the only reason he's not rushing at Laurie is because the gun is trained on him, right?"

"Right."

"So while you distract Laurie then either Roman or I or both of us can get the gun."

"Maybe the police will get here before anything happens," Sophie said hopefully.

"Well they'd better hurry up," Paige said.

They both fell silent, wide eyes searching each other's.

Sophie swallowed the hard lump in her throat. "Not going to lie, I'm kind of terrified. But there's no way I'm waiting here while Laurie does something to Roman." She took a shaky breath. "Let's do this."

They crept back to the clearing. Laurie was nearly done with his beer, but far from finished talking, it seemed.

"I remember it," Roman was saying. "Nearly two thousand people got food poisoning."

"You're forgetting the star athlete who died."

"Right."

"An Olympic hopeful. But that wasn't the problem. As it turns out, that was just the tip of the iceberg. Negligent management had created a toxic work environment and very substandard health and safety regulations. They may have been a leading brand, but they didn't have the operational processes to back it up. Or at least, not anymore. A bunch of deaths and accidents in the factory in the three years prior had all been covered up. It looked as if the same would happen for the most recent food hygiene issue but a whistle-blower brought the case to Terry."

Roman sighed heavily. "And Terry was going to shine a light on the operation."

"I tried to warn him but he wouldn't listen. He didn't realise how dangerous these people are. I told him not to go. Not to get on that boat."

Roman sucked in a shocked breath. "You knew?"

"I tried to warn him."

"You knew that if he got on that fishing boat he wouldn't get off again and you didn't stop him?'

"You're not listening. I tried to warn him off."

"Bastard," Roman said between gritted teeth.

"It was a shame."

Laurie took a sip of beer, then lifted his other hand to place it on the armrest. The gun was now clearly visible, loosely pointed at Roman.

"Who did the dirty?" Roman asked. "Who pushed him off the boat?"

Laurie shrugged. "They hired someone. He snuck on board and took care of it."

Sophie turned to Paige who'd gone still. Tears streamed down her face, glinting in the moonlight above the trees. Sophie squeezed her arm. Paige kept staring straight ahead for a moment, then turned to meet her gaze.

Paige's expression was a twisted, anguished combination of rage, fear and grief.

"*Are you okay*?" Sophie mouthed.

Paige dropped her chin to nod once.

"What are we doing here, Laurie. What's your plan?" Roman said. "What do you want from me?"

"They said to take care of it. So here I am, taking care of it." Laurie let out a strangled laugh.

Sophie shot wide eyes to Paige. They both nodded. It was time. As Sophie walked—stumbled—directly into Laurie's line of vision, Paige moved in the opposite direction.

"Please," Sophie said as she staggered into the clearing, her voice shaky.

Roman turned shocked eyes to hers.

"Who are you?" Laurie lurched upright but kept his body side-on so that the hand that held the gun was concealed.

As Sophie got closer, reaching out to Laurie, Roman's eyes found Paige, sneaking around the other side, behind Laurie. His mouth dropped open, his expression stunned.

"I'm lost," Sophie took a shaky breath and made her eyes wide as possible. "I've been lost for a whole day." She added a small pout and raised the pitch of her voice. "I'm sorry to interrupt, but I'm so thirsty." She tottered forwards. "Please, I need your help."

As Laurie took an uncertain step towards Sophie, he dropped the hand that held the gun to the side of his body, as if it was more important that he hide the gun from her than use it to control the situation. At this moment, Roman lurched upright, but Paige was faster. Before Laurie even knew she was there she'd crept up behind him and yanked the gun out of his hand.

He whirled around and lunged at her but she darted back and held up the gun. "Don't move, dum-dum."

"Give me that," Laurie growled.

Paige brought her other hand up to grasp the gun with both.

"You won't do it." Laurie sneered and took a menacing step towards her. "You don't have the—"

"Don't I? Wont I?" Paige hissed. "I would *love* to shoot you. Even if it's just in the leg. I'm not much of a crack shot, though. Maybe it'll end up in the groin."

She tightened her grip and lowered her aim a little. "After what you did to my father, I'd welcome the opportunity to shoot you."

Laurie recoiled, clearly only now realising who she was. "Paige?"

"Take another step, lunge at me, do your best. *Come on.*" Paige's voice was cold but her eyes were ablaze, and in that moment she looked entirely capable of anything.

Laurie raised his hands in defeat and stepped back. In the distance, sirens became audible. Roman's shoulders sagged with relief. Sophie ran over to where he was in the camping chair with one hand still tied, and wrapped her arms around his shoulders, pressing herself against his back and burying her face into his neck.

"Oh, thank god," she said, her voice muffled.

"No, thank *you*," Roman said, letting out a sigh, leaning into Sophie.

The wail of sirens got louder.

"The police are here," Paige said unnecessarily. She turned to focus a death stare on Laurie.

"And you're going down for the murder of my father."

39

Outside the door to the hypnotherapist studio, Sophie stopped Paige before she rang the buzzer. "Are you sure about this?"

"That depends. How sure are you?"

Sophie made a face. "Pretty sure."

After thinking about the two sessions she'd attended with Cassie, the not-at-all-subtle suggestion that she should trust tall blond men, and then the even less subtle appearance at their office with her brother in tow, a tall blond man, Sophie had a pretty good idea of what was going on.

"It could be an actual crime to try to implant ideas into people's brains for personal gain," Paige said. "At the very least she's getting a piece of my mind and you're getting your money back. You went to them because you needed help and look what she did!" She pressed the buzzer angrily, her mouth set in a line. After a moment they were buzzed upstairs.

Behind the reception desk was a middle-aged woman Sophie had never seen before. "Hello, can I help you?" she said pleasantly.

"We're here to talk to Cassie," Paige said.

"I'm sorry, Who?"

"Doctor Meadows?" Sophie added, starting to feel a little unsure.

"She's writing up clinical reports at the moment. What's this about?"

"The crime of improper use of hypnosis, that's what," Paige said haughtily. "Implanting suggestions for personal gain."

The woman drew back. "Excuse me?"

"And she wants her money back," Paige added, thumbing at Sophie.

Just then, a woman emerged from the clinical room, frowning as she took in the scene in front of her. "What's the problem here?"

"They're accusing you of improper conduct," the receptionist said.

"They are? Who are you?" the woman asked, looking from Paige to Sophie.

"Oh, um, I'm Sophie Swanephol. I came in a couple of weeks ago, but...."

The woman frowned. "But what?"

"Who are you?" Paige said to the woman.

"Doctor Meadows."

"That's who I was supposed to see," Sophie said quietly. "But I saw someone called Cassie. I thought she was you. Doctor Cassie Meadows."

"Do you have another hypnotherapist working here?" Paige asked.

"No. Just me." Suddenly her face changed. "Oh, Cassie. The temp we hired. She's gone. Did you need her for something?"

"Cassie was a temp?" Sophie said. "A temporary hypnotherapist?"

"No, a temporary receptionist. Both myself and Miranda here got a terrible flu at the same time and it came on rather suddenly so we hired a temp for a few hours each day to deal with all the cancellations and rescheduling etc. We were out for nearly two weeks. I don't understand what's happening."

"So just to be clear, Cassie has no hypnotherapy qualifications at all?" Sophie said.

Dr Meadows shook her head.

Paige turned to Sophie. "Oh my god, you were hypno-catfished by the temp."

• • • • • • • • • •

Leo and Zelda sat side by side on Leo's couch in his small studio apartment. Leo cleared his throat, feeling weird. Why was the atmosphere so tense all of a sudden? When he shifted his eyes to Zelda, she was looking straight at him.

Zelda tilted her head. "You've got a funny expression on your face."

"I do?" He coughed. "Um...."

Emmitt suddenly meowed loudly.

They both looked over to see Emmitt, previously prowling around the garden looking for excitement or perhaps just conducting a perimeter inspection of his territory, nosing his way through the cat flap. He strolled into the living room and stopped right in front of them. He tucked his bottom down and curled his tail over his front paws, then proceeded to regard Leo and Zelda as they sat there.

"Dude, what's up?" Leo said. "It's not even close to dinner time."

Emmitt continued to look from Leo to Zelda, then leapt up onto the couch and began the elaborate process of inserting himself into the less than six-inch space between them. Zelda scratched the top of his head and Emmitt let out a happy purr in reply.

"What are you thinking about?" Zelda said, continuing to stroke Emmitt's head.

"Odds are pretty good he's thinking about his dinner," Leo said.

"Ha-ha. I meant you," Zelda replied.

"Oh, just that...." He took a breath. "It's cool that Emmitt likes you."

"He doesn't like other people?"

Leo thought for a moment. "I guess I haven't really tested that out." His cheeks felt warm.

"Huh." Zelda said. "I guess he's picking up on my vibes."

Leo swallowed. "Your vibes?"

"Yeah. Pets can tell when people like their owners, right?"

His face suddenly felt very hot. "Like, as in...."

Zelda looked up to smile at him. "You don't know?"

For a moment they held each other's gaze.

No immediate head-over-heels for this one. No rushing in headlong. He would take it slow and give it a chance to be a proper relationship. He would let things unfold at their own pace.

A smile crept onto Leo's face. "I guess maybe I do."

· · · · ·· · · · ·

Sophie put down her wine and leaned into Roman. They were snuggled up on his couch but it was okay because he'd recently replaced several items of furniture, getting rid of the more intimate pieces that he'd shared with Anya.

"You know I always wondered how S and S Investigations solved their cases so quickly and easily," Roman said into the silence. "I know most of it is down to two brilliant psychological minds, but now one more piece of the puzzle has officially slotted into place."

"Leo and his not-totally-legal hacking skills?" Sophie, making an uncertain face. "Can you pretend you don't know that bit?"

"I'm going to have to, I think. It saved my life, right?"

"It did."

"Along with you and Paige, of course. Employing the classic S and S move."

"Distract And Ambush," Sophie finished, smiling as she nestled into the crook of his shoulder, enjoying the easy warmth and his closeness. "So what's next for Laurie?" she asked.

"He's currently at the station singing like a bird," Roman said with a chuckle. "He's spilling the beans on everyone."

"Thank god for that. I would have hated for there to be a long and protracted court case or something. For Paige and her mum to have to go through that."

"I mean, there still could be a few hiccups. A major foodstuffs brand like that is going to lawyer up and throw the best legal team in the country at this problem. I suspect the way it's going to go down is the actual guy who, ah, took care of Terry, will be offered like a sacrificial lamb. He will take the fall and Laurie will also go down for covering it up."

"And the big bad behind it all will get away."

"Unfortunately, that's the way life works, right? We just have to fight the battles we can win."

"And find some happiness along the way," Sophie added before reaching up to kiss Roman on the cheek.

He smiled down at her then raised one hand to gently stroke the side of her face. "I'm so glad we found our way to each other, Sophie Swanephol. I don't even know how to find the words to explain it."

"You don't need to," Sophie murmured in reply. "I already know."

· · · · ·· · · · ·

Paige raised her hand to knock on the door, but then dropped it. This was so weird. this was her house. Her home. It had been for years now. So why did she feel so uncertain about going inside? About whether she belonged here anymore?

The door swung open. "Paige?" Tim gave her a shaky smile. "What are you doing standing out here?"

"I, uh, wasn't sure...."

Paige had never, ever, found it this hard to find the right words.

Tim opened the door wider, half-smiling and half-frowning as she stepped inside.

They walked awkwardly down the hall towards the living room.

"Do you want a drink? Tea, coffee, wine?"

Paige swallowed. Tim was treating her like a guest.

"Sorry, I... you obviously can make a drink or whatever. You know where everything is and...."

Silence fell.

"Let's just go into the lounge and talk," Paige said, the words coming out in a rush.

"How have you been?" Tim asked as they sat about a metre apart on the three-seater couch.

"Uh, you know...."

But he didn't know and they were both excruciatingly aware of that, it seemed.

Part of her was desperate to tell Tim all about the recent cases; to chat about work and the mystery they'd solved like it was a normal day. A bigger part yearned to tell him what they'd discovered about her father. But before any of that, there was something else to discuss. And it couldn't wait any longer.

"I'm scared," she said suddenly, her voice cracking.

Tim's eyes went wide and he moved closer to her but Paige held up a hand. "I just need to get this out or I'll never say it."

Tim sat back and nodded.

"I know I'm not very good with people. I know I'm rude, tactless, thoughtless sometimes. I say the wrong thing. I do the wrong thing. I get caught up in myself and what I want, or completely absorbed in the case and the mystery and I forget everything else. I don't know how to be a mother, Tim. The idea is terrifying to me. I'd screw the kid up. How could I not?"

"But—"

"Please. Let me finish?"

"Okay."

"When I'm honest with myself, that's not even the biggest problem." She looked down and took a deep breath. "What if something goes wrong? What if something happens to them. To you? I can't do it again. I can't go through that. I can't even imagine what it would be like to lose a *child*."

Suddenly tears were streaming down her face. She sniffed them back and wiped them away but still they came, flooding down her cheeks and eventually she just let Tim take her in his arms and rock her gently until she was done.

"I get it. At least, I understand. But that can't be the reason, Paige. It just can't. We can't live like that. In fear of something that might never happen. It's not living at all."

I know," Paige said sniffling into Tim's shoulder. "But it's hard to get past." She took a big shuddering breath and looked into his eyes.

"What if I turn out like my mother?"

Tim suppressed a smile and stroked her hair. "Come on, she's not nearly as bad as you make out. You two argue because you're too similar. And you're both stubborn," he added under his breath.

Paige made a small noise.

"And what about me?" Tim said into the silence.

She pulled out of his embrace. "What do you mean?"

"We'd both be parents. You and me. I'd be at least half of the equation. Because once the first baby breast-feeding stuff—"

"You can't assume that I'm going to—"

"I can be the primary caregiver. In fact, I'd love it. I mean I can't have the baby, obviously, but after that I can take more of the responsibility if your business is still doing well and it pays the bills."

Paige stared at him. "Yeah?"

"Yes. House Husband. I love the idea."

They shared a smile.

"I found out something about Dad recently," Paige said after a while.

"Yeah?" Tim reached out and squeezed Paige's hand.

"There's so much stuff I have to tell you, actually, but the bit that is relevant now is... I think I've gotten some closure. I didn't know I needed it, but I think that's what happened. It feels as if I had been holding onto something, but not in a good way. Not in a helpful way. I've released something. And for some weird reason, now I feel like I can start a new journey.

"You can?" Tim's face lit up. "A new journey like starting a family?"

"Yeah." Paige gave him a small smile but then frowned.

"But not right now. Obviously."

Tim smiled. "Obviously."

40

At about six o'clock, Leo and Zelda walked into the second office to join Paige and Sophie at the conference table.

"We're here," Leo announced unnecessarily, as he liked to do.

"Finally," Paige said, as if they'd been waiting for hours when in actuality Leo and Zelda were right on time.

"Leo said something about you being involved in a catfishing situation," Zelda said to Sophie as she and Leo took seats.

"Yeah," Paige said before Sophie could reply. "It's kind of hilarious."

"Except for me going through two whole sessions with a fake hypnotherapist." Sophie rolled her eyes.

Zelda looked from Paige to Sophie. "Seriously?"

Paige nodded. "Seriously. The woman Sophie saw was just a temp who'd always wanted to try being a hypnotherapist and then when she met Sophie she decided she'd be perfect for her brother, so she tried to implant the idea of them falling in love."

"Bonkers, right?" Sophie said.

"Totally. Are you going to try the real hypnotherapist?" Leo asked.

"It's all paid for and I'm pretty keen to try it as a therapeutic option, so yes."

Loud footsteps clattered up the stairwell into the office.

"Who is that going to be?" Paige said.

"A new client?" Leo offered.

Four pairs of eyes turned towards the door as Richard Thinton stepped inside.

"Oh. It's just a dick," Paige said, scowling.

Richard's eyes widened, then narrowed, fixating on Paige. "You'll regret you said that."

"Your name is Richard," Paige explained patiently, "which is also Dick."

"Not really," Richard huffed. "Not in New Zealand."

"Why are you here?" Paige said.

"Just to let you know you can expect a call from the Ministry of Justice," he said, his eyes glinting with malice. "And when they come to do an inspection, to audit you, to shut you down for operating without a P.I. license, you can thank *me*." He smiled widely.

"Oh, an inspection?" Paige said. "Fun. We can show them the paperwork associated with our application for a Private Investigator License and give them a tour of our second-to-none, one hundred per cent success rate agency." She turned to grin at Sophie.

Richard visibly recoiled. "What?" His cheeks turned red.

"You heard me. You think we didn't know about the new licensing requirements?" She smiled sweetly.

"Hi Richard," Zelda said, standing up from where she'd been sitting, mostly blocked from sight by Leo. "Thanks for all the information you gave me, but I think I'd like to work with someone else. A different team. One that's not run by a bullying tyrant."

Richard started spluttering.

"Good job with the SOS Agency, by the way," Paige added. "What a crack team they turned out to be. Nice to get a new client though. He's already paid his invoice. I suppose we have you to thank for that too."

Richard took in Paige's ear-to-ear grin and Sophie's smile and puffed out his chest. "Now look—"

"Oh, give it up, Richard," Paige said. "You've got nothing on us. You keep trying to take us down and you keep failing. Face it. We're better than you, and every time you try, you get a little bit more pathetic."

"I, I—"

"Tell you what, Richie boy," Paige said. "If you stop hassling us now, we won't go on the offensive. You've already had a taste of what we can do. Remember Victoria and the blackmail? That could be just the beginning. Or you could walk away and we could both get on with our lives completely independently of each other and never have to see the other again."

Richard opened his mouth one more time, then closed it, turned on his heel, and left the office. He slammed the door behind him, a final display of childish temper, but it only served to illustrate that he'd been beaten.

They'd won.

In a move that surprised everyone, Paige included, she suddenly pulled Zelda into a hug.

"Uh, I'm not really a hugging person," Zelda said, her voice muffled.

"Neither am I."

"Well, let's stop then."

They broke apart. Paige cleared her throat. "Thank you."

"Oh, uh." Zelda seemed surprised. "You're welcome."

"Overall you've done a really good job." Paige smiled uncertainly. "But giving us the heads-up about the P.I. license situation so we could throw it back in Richard's face was *so* satisfying."

"I have to be honest with you," Zelda said. "I was at first genuinely interested in talking to Richard about postgrad programs. But the more I learned about him the angrier I got. So when I went to see him the other day I wanted to find something to mess with him." She shrugged. "I did what I could."

"Glad you're on our side. Part of *our* team," Sophie said, looking pointedly at Paige.

"Me too," Paige agreed. "I really am."

Leo let the moment hang for a moment so Zelda could absorb her compliments, then cleared his throat. "Okay, our table booking is for six-thirty, we'd better head out."

"You two go ahead, we'll close up," Paige said.

"See you at the restaurant."

Once they'd gone, Paige turned to Sophie.

"It's been quite the week, right?" Sophie said.

Paige shook her head. "Has it ever."

"But we pulled through."

"We always do."

"Squirrel and Swan," Sophie said.

"A detective duo like no other," Paige finished.

For a moment they held each other's gaze, grinning and basking in the glow of their accomplishments.

"Okay, we'd better go," Sophie said. They gathered up their belongings and walked to the outer door. "But we're more than a duo now. We're a team," Sophie said. "We'll have to come up with a new tagline."

"Ooh," Paige said as they switched off the lights. "Can we steal the SOS Agency one?"

"I don't see why not," Sophie said with a grin. "It's not as if they're using it anymore."

The End

Dear Reader

This was the last in the S & S Investigations series, I hope you enjoyed the journey!

I love these books and I absolutely adore the characters but for the moment, no further books are planned. For now, at least, Paige, Sophie, and everyone else in the Squirrel & Swan universe bids you farewell. To grizzle at me about this or for more information, you can email: mdaauthor@gmail.com But there is a Christmas Novella. Experience a southern hemisphere style Christmas in Death At A Barbecue.

(P.S. If you 're reading this then you're a true fan and I'll love you forever.

Thank you!)

Margot.

Acknowledgements

Thank you to everyone who helped me with this book. Julie, Lisa, Horst, and Barbara, as always. (PS, thanks for the cover-up idea, Julie!)
At the time I was doing my final review of this manuscript, I learned of Angela Lansbury's passing. AKA Jessica Fletcher of Murder She Wrote (of which I'm a big fan, you may have noticed). RIP Angela/Jessica. Thanks for all the mysteries.

Cases Solved

#1 The Disappearance of Polly Dixon
#2 The Persistent Petnapper
#3 The Strange Behaviour of Hazel Berryman
#4 The Corporate Gig
#5 The Murder at the Reunion
#6 The Hidden Inheritance
#7 The Locked Room Mystery
#8 The Woman Without A Past
#9 The Death of Estelle Royce
#10 The Terrible Troll
#11 The Two Michaels
#12 The Black Widow
And The Death of Terry Garnet